Also by Michael Wallace

Quill Gordon Mysteries

I0553814

1. *The McHenry Inheritance*
2. *Wash Her Guilt Away*
3. *Not Death, But Love*
4. *The Daughters of Alta Mira*
5. *I Scarce Can Die*
6. *The Slaves of Thrift*
7. *The Man in the Red Convertible*

Nonfiction

The Borina Family of Watsonville (California history)

True to You
In My Way

A Quill Gordon Mystery

Michael Wallace

True to You in My Way
Copyright © 2020, Michael Wallace
All Rights Reserved

ISBN: 978-0-9903871-6-9

Cover Design: Deborah Karas, Karas Technical Services

**In the spirit of
Ross Macdonald**

*For John and Kathy,
Who were married on a cruise*

"If you want a happy ending, that depends, of course, on where you stop your story."

—Orson Welles

Long Beach, California
May 15, 1995

DETECTIVE LINDSAY JUDD came out the front door of the house. It was a white stucco bungalow, built in the 1930s, a thousand square feet, two bedrooms and a bath, situated in a modest neighborhood of mostly well-maintained homes. It was the kind of house a single professional woman — approaching 40 with no prospect of marriage — would have bought for herself six years ago, after being promoted at work and coming into a modest inheritance. In a few minutes that woman would be leaving it for the last time, in a body bag.

Judd walked across the small front lawn, mowed in the past week, crossed the street and stopped at the car, where her partner, Tony Morales, was on his cell phone and smoking a cigarette. Morales cut the conversation short when he saw Judd approaching and removing her latex gloves.

"Well?" Morales said.

"It's her, all right. Francine Hawes. Even with the electrical cord around her neck, I could remember seeing her at City Hall. And her wallet and driver's license were still in her purse. No money, though."

"Robbery?"

"Could be. What did you find out?"

"Pretty much what the original call said. She didn't come to work this morning and didn't call. That wasn't like her, but they thought maybe she had a dental appointment or something and forgot to say. So they waited a couple of hours and finally asked for a patrol car to check her place. The back door was unlocked, and she went in ..."

"She?"

"Officer O'Hara. And she found what she found and called for us. It was her first one. She's pretty shook up."

"The first one's the hardest."

"Any idea how long she's been dead?"

"Doc says at least two days, maybe three. So figure most of the weekend. They'll know more after the autopsy. Anything else at City Hall?"

1

"She worked at the city clerk's office for 15 years. Reasonably well liked but didn't make any close friends in the office. Very competent. Promoted to deputy city clerk a few years back, and everybody figured she'd get the top job when Lorraine Wilson retires."

"Lorraine Wilson is never going to retire," Judd said. "The job is her life. She'd be dead in six weeks if she quit."

"I'm just telling you what they said."

"How about the neighborhood canvass?"

"Do you want the good news or the bad news first?"

"How about the good news for a change."

"Not many people around in the middle of the day Monday. But just about everybody we talked to remembered seeing the guy, though not in the last few days."

"That's it? That's the good news?"

"The bad news is nobody can describe him. The best they can come up with is a middle-aged white dude, average looking. Average height, average hair, nothing distinctive about him."

"In other words, a description that could fit a million men, just in Los Angeles County."

"Don't be so negative, Lindsay. Probably just half a million."

Judd drummed her fingers on the roof of the Crown Vic.

"Can I bum a coffin nail off you?" she said.

"I thought you were trying to quit."

"I am. And I'll try again tomorrow."

Morales extended a pack of Winstons and Judd took one. It wasn't her brand, but she needed tobacco. She took an engraved, gold-plated lighter from her coat pocket. It was a seventh anniversary present her ex-husband had given her before they broke up two years later. She lit the cigarette and took a deep drag.

"So, to summarize," Judd said, "our perp has a two- or three-day head start on us and nobody who saw him can give a description that's worth a rat's ass."

"That's about the size of it."

"Well, we can keep up the canvass as people start coming home from work. Maybe somebody saw something that could actually help us."

"You really believe that?"

"We can hope." She sucked on the cigarette again and threw it against the curb, half-smoked.

"You know something, Tony? There are some days when I really hate this job. And this is starting to look like one of those days."

Bodega Bay, California
May 15, 2000

TWO WEEKS EARLIER, Quill Gordon had been sitting at the desk in his home office, feeling bored, when the phone rang. The caller was a woman named Olema Marsh, who lived in the town of Barnstaple in the eastern Sierra. She said several people in that town had died recently in accidents she didn't think were really accidents, the sheriff was a nitwit who couldn't see the obvious pattern, and she'd heard that Gordon had been known to look into matters like this. By the end of the call, Gordon was no longer bored and had made an appointment to have lunch with her.

At the time of the call, Mrs. Marsh had been planning to visit her daughter and grandchildren in Bodega Bay, a coastal fishing village north of San Francisco and a location in Alfred Hitchcock's *The Birds*. The drive was about an hour and a half from his San Francisco apartment, but Gordon had allowed himself more time. It had been a wet winter with a late rain a week earlier, and he wanted to enjoy the spring green of the Northern California countryside.

It was a cool, overcast morning as he drove over the Golden Gate Bridge, and the weather report called for a chance of showers. He got off U.S. 101 at Sir Francis Drake Boulevard and followed that road through Greenbrae, Kentfield, Ross, San Anselmo and Fairfax. After Fairfax he drove over a rise and descended into San Geronimo Valley. It was country now, and it looked as if every seed of grass in the ground had taken nourishment from the rich, damp soil and sprouted. San Geronimo Creek and Lagunitas Creek were running high and fast for this time of year. The wet winter would probably mean good stream flows in the Sierra through the summer, but early season fishing would be problematic, owing to heavy spring runoff.

Eventually he reached State Highway 1 and turned north. He drove through the thriving town of Point Reyes Station — all three blocks of it — and continued north on the highway along the eastern shore of Tomales Bay, choppy with whitecaps. Past the town of Tomales, the highway turned west toward Bodega Bay, rolling through more deep-green hills dotted with dairy cattle. He came to a brush-lined canyon that descended to Bodega Bay and reached the outskirts of town at ten minutes to noon. He turned left into Joe's Wharf House three minutes later, parked and walked through the front door.

A woman in her mid-sixties, with glasses, gray shoulder-length hair and an air of authority rose from one of the waiting benches as he came in.

"Mr. Gordon?"

"Mrs. Marsh."

"I must say you look every inch the basketball player." She looked at her watch. "And you're five minutes early. Being on time is good, but being early is a sign of character."

He nodded, with a sheepish smile.

"I've picked out a window table for us," she continued. "Just to be clear, lunch is on me, and I insist you join me in a glass of wine. I have a lot of talking to do, and I'm going to get thirsty."

"By all means."

The hostess led them to the table. It was perched over the water, with a sweeping view of the bay and the fishing fleet across the way. As they sat down, a squall swept in, with gusts of wind blowing large drops of rain against the windows.

AFTER THEIR ORDERS had been taken and they each had a glass of house chardonnay in front of them, Olema Marsh leaned forward conspiratorially.

"Let me begin by saying, Mr. Gordon, that in a town the size of Barnstaple one accidental death is quite newsworthy. But three in seven weeks? That's an absurdity."

"I'd agree that it raises eyebrows," Gordon said, "but things like that happen in clusters sometimes."

"Hear me out, and you'll see why I don't think so. As much as anything else, it's the way these so-called accidents happened. Let me begin at the beginning."

She took a sip of wine, and Gordon took a note pad and pen from his messenger bag.

"Luther Whitman was the first. A very nice man. He came to Barnstaple over five years ago from Flagstaff, Arizona, after his wife died. His daughter and her husband have a one-bedroom apartment above the barn, and he lived there. After a few months he decided he needed something to do and applied for a part-time job as a general helper at the community church. He got to know people, and the pastor was very pleased with his work."

"How old was he?" Gordon asked.

"Seventy-two, but don't make too much of it. You're only as old as you feel, and he certainly didn't feel old. Anyway, our church has a lovely bell tower. It's a hundred feet high — the tallest structure in Barnstaple. It's the first thing you see as you approach town. One of Luther's duties was to go up to the top of the tower Saturday evening and make sure the bell and the rope were in good shape for next morning's service. He'd been doing that every week for two years and never as much as stubbed a toe. Until the night of February 26th."

She took another sip of chardonnay. The waitress brought a basket of bread, which neither of them touched.

"He was expected home at 7:30, and when he was half an hour late, his daughter called Pastor Moody, who went to look and found him lying on the gravel pathway directly below the bell tower. The coroner said he was dead as soon as he hit the ground, but I wonder if he was saying that for the family. Do coroners do things like that?"

"It probably depends on the coroner. And no one saw anything?"

"No, which isn't surprising. The church is a block off Main Street, and at that time of year almost no one would be out and about then. And it would have been dark or nearly so, depending on exactly when it happened."

Gordon nodded.

"I know what you're going to say," she continued. "That he was old and probably lost his balance. That's what the sheriff and coroner said. I blame myself for not being more suspicious at the time, but I was in shock. The more I think about it, the less sense it makes.

"Two weeks earlier there was a Valentine's dance at the Odd Fellows Hall. Luther Whitman wore out all the single women there, including yours truly. He's an absolutely fabulous dancer. Was. And he had the balance of a mountain goat. It defies all reason to think that such a healthy man, who moves so well, could lose his balance and stumble over a three-foot barrier to his death. He had to be pushed or tripped in some way."

IT HAD STOPPED RAINING, but a large, ominous cloud offshore suggested that the break in the weather was only temporary. Gordon took a sip of his chardonnay and looked back at Mrs. Marsh.

"You said there were three of these so-called accidents," he said. "What was the next one?"

"The next one was David Rowan. He owns Rowan's Rod and Gun, the sporting goods store. It happened just three weeks after Luther was found, the morning of March 20th. Dave lives in Pine Cone Heights, a little subdivision on a ridge about five miles out of town. Don't look at me like that, Mr. Gordon. I'm not rambling. Where he lives is critical to what happened.

"That subdivision is about 300 feet above the county road that leads to Gemini Lakes. It has a private road leading up to where the houses are, and for a fair part of the way, there's a pretty steep drop-off on one side of it."

"Guardrails?"

"No. It must have cost the earth to build that road, so they left the guardrails off. Anyway, on the morning of the 20th — that was a Monday — Dave started off to work. He ran off that road and went down a hundred feet. A passing car on the county road saw it in flames, and by then it was too late to do anything for Dave."

"Can I ask a couple of questions?"

"Please do."

"What was the weather like that morning?"

"Clear and sunny. The overnight low was 23 in town."

"So, to play the devil's advocate, there could have been some ice on the road?"

"I'm sure there was, but it wouldn't have been much. It had been clear for several days, and the road had been plowed. Dave's come down that road hundreds of times when it was a lot worse."

"What was he driving?"

"A two-year-old pickup with all-wheel drive and snow tires."

"I assume there was an investigation."

"Oh, the Highway Patrol looked into it. The truck was so badly burned it was hard to tell much from it, or so they say. So lacking evidence to the contrary, they called it an accident."

"Unless somebody saw something, it would be pretty hard to prove it wasn't," Gordon said.

"Nobody saw anything. But I can tell you this much. Diana Rowan told me last week that she doesn't believe it and neither do I. You want to know why?"

Gordon nodded.

"It's suspicious enough when a man with a good truck runs off a road he drives every day. But the clincher is this. A year and a half ago, I sprained an ankle and couldn't drive for a week. Several people offered to give me rides, and Dave Rowan was one of them. I only took him up on it once. Dave was without a doubt the pokiest, most cautious driver I've ever seen in my life. Riding with him would drive anyone nuts."

LUNCH ARRIVED, and they ate for a few minutes before Gordon asked:

"And the third so-called accident?"

Mrs. Marsh took a sip of her wine, and Gordon could see that her hand was trembling slightly.

"The third one was Lucy Starr, and that one hit me really hard. It drove me to the sheriff to see what he was doing about it, which was a big fat nothing. And that in turn led me to look for someone else who could help, and eventually to you."

Gordon nodded and let her keep talking.

"Lucy was a dear friend of mine. For more than thirty years. I still can't believe she's gone. Just two nights before it happened, we were at our monthly bridge party at Kathryn Livingston's house — actually, she's Kathryn Henry now that she married again. Anyway, as we were getting ready to go home, Lucy and I were talking about how now that the weather was getting nice again, we should take a shopping trip to Reno. And she said, 'Great idea. I'll call you next week.' And of course she never called because she was gone by then and I still haven't gotten to Reno."

She paused to take a bite of her lunch, and Gordon pounced.

"So what happened to Lucy?"

"It was Wednesday April 12th. I remember because the bridge game is always the second Monday of the month. We were having our first warm spell of the spring, and with all the snow we had, a lot of it was melting. The river was running high and fast that day, almost as if it was coming out of a fire hose. Lucy went for a walk after dinner and never came back. Her husband, Jim, was watching a ball game on TV and didn't notice she hadn't come back until it was after dark. The sheriff did a neighborhood search but there was no sign of her anywhere."

She stopped for another swallow of wine. The glass was nearly empty.

"They found her body several days later when it floated to the surface in the reservoir."

"The reservoir?"

"She liked to do a walk around town and often went through the city park. The sheriff thinks she was walking through the park near the East Gemini River and fell in. The way the river was running that day, anyone who fell in wouldn't have had a chance and could easily have been washed downstream into the reservoir."

"And you don't buy that?"

"I buy that she went into the river and was swept downstream all right. But she had to have been pushed."

Gordon looked at her.

"And no, I don't have any evidence, but I *know*. You see, Lucy was afraid of water and couldn't swim. The path along the river in the park is several feet away from and above the water, even at the height of spring runoff. And after that warm day it would have been perfectly dry. No way she could have fallen in from there."

10

"Did you bring this up with the sheriff?"

"He said she may have gone closer to the water to look at something and lost her balance. Uh-uh. She would have feared and respected the water's power. He said she might have lost her balance on the bridge going over the river. Baloney again. The railings on that bridge are three-and-a-half feet high, and Lucy was five-four."

"This is kind of sensitive," Gordon said, "but could they tell anything from the body?"

She shook her head. "She'd been dead five days when they found her, and the body was so badly beaten up from bouncing downriver that it was — well, let's say they had to do a closed casket."

She finished the last of her wine.

"That was the worst of it, Mr. Gordon. I never got to see her again and properly say goodbye. Maybe that's why I couldn't let it go and came to you."

THE SUN BROKE THROUGH the clouds as they finished lunch. They ordered coffee but skipped dessert.

"So what I'm hearing," Gordon said after his first sip, "is that three people died of accidents that would have been out of character."

"Exactly."

"A man with great agility and balance falls from a place he's in every week. A slow and cautious driver runs off a road he drives every day. And a woman who can't swim and is afraid of water somehow tumbles into a raging river."

"Does that sound to you like too many coincidences?"

"It sounds suspicious but not conclusive."

"You'll look into it, then?"

Gordon hesitated. It would mean canceling a trip that was already planned and going to Barnstaple instead.

"I'm intrigued," he said. "Did you bring the newspapers I asked for?"

"They're in a grocery bag in my car."

"And do you have any idea what might be going on? You live there, after all."

"That's just it. I have no idea — none at all. I think the people who live there — and that includes the sheriff and me — are too close to it to see a pattern. And there has to be a pattern."

"If those deaths weren't accidents, I'd have to agree with you. But it's hard to imagine what. Can you think of anything the three people had in common?"

"Aside from living in the same town and knowing each other, no. And just about everybody in Barnstaple knows everyone else. That's why we need someone with a fresh eye. Someone like you."

"All right," he finally said. "I have a trip coming up in three weeks. Let me see if I can cancel our reservations and get something near Barnstaple."

She smiled.

"Where I can reach you to let you know?" he said.

"I'll be at my daughter's until Thursday, and then I'm driving back on Friday."

"I'll know in a day or two. Now a few more things. First, can you prepare a list of people I should talk to, with their phone numbers and what they might know?"

"I'll get started on that right away. Would you like me to let them know you're going to be calling them?"

"Actually, I'd rather you didn't." He saw that she was surprised.

"You see," he continued, "if you're right about these so-called accidents, the fewer people who know you've talked to me the better. And for your own safety, the fewer people who know about your suspicions, the better."

"Don't worry about that, Mr. Gordon. It's better if they know you'll be calling, and they're all people I've known for ages. Besides, I can take care of myself."

Gordon finished the last of his coffee, put the cup in the saucer, leaned across the table and said in a loud whisper:

"I'm sure that's what Luther Whitman, Dave Rowan and Lucy Starr thought."

Monday June 5, 2000

THE FIRST LANDMARK Gordon and Peter Delaney spotted as they drew closer to Barnstaple Sunday afternoon was the church tower from which Luther Whitman had plunged to his death three months earlier. At the edge of town they drove over a bridge that spanned the East Gemini River. It was running high and fast, but probably not so high and fast as that April day when Lucy Starr had fallen (or been assisted) into its waters and swept to her death. Gordon and Peter spent no time checking the tower or the river. They had been on the road from San Francisco most of the day. After buying gas at the Chevron station, groceries from DeLuxe Supermarket, and ice cream cones from Happy Scoop on Main Street, they set out for Broderick's Gemini Lakes Resort.

The road to Broderick's ran 11 miles from town through a canyon carved by the East Gemini River and climbed nearly 900 feet in elevation. Four-and-a-half miles from town they passed the road leading to Pine Cone Heights — the road David Rowan's car had swerved from fatally. Gordon pointed it out to Peter.

"Feels like we're driving through the valley of death," Peter said.

Gordon grunted.

At the end of the road, past a Forest Service campground, an RV park, a marina, and a number of summer homes, they reached Broderick's, where Gordon and Peter had booked the last two available cabins. The entrance ran under an archway constructed entirely of deer antlers. Broderick's occupied most of the north shore of Upper Gemini Lake. It had 77 cabins for rent, 46 spaces for trailers and RVs, a well-stocked general store, an amphitheater wrapped around a fire pit, a restaurant serving three meals a day, a marina and boat launch area, and a large lawn by the lake, big enough to hold a volleyball net and croquet patch.

Now, on Monday morning, Gordon was in his cabin sipping a cup of coffee and assembling the fixings for a breakfast of bacon, eggs and toast. He had just finished filling the largest skillet with bacon strips when Peter walked in, pointed at the coffee pot and sat down at the kitchen table.

Gordon poured a cup, black, and handed it over. Peter took two swallows and began to sit up straighter. He looked around the room.

"Nice place you got us," he said.

"It came well recommended."

"So what time are we meeting the nosy old lady?"

"Her name is Mrs. Marsh. Olema Marsh. And we're due at her house at 10:30."

Peter took a sip of coffee and nodded.

"I thought," Gordon continued, "that we could take a brief detour on the way over and check out the city park where Lucy Starr was supposedly walking before she fell in the river. There was a sign pointing to it on the other side of the bridge when we came into town yesterday."

"Works for me," Peter said.

Gordon put the skillet with the bacon on the stove and turned on the heat.

"How do you like your eggs?"

"What are you having?" Peter said.

"I'm partial to scrambled."

"Then I'll have the same. No sense cooking two sets of eggs."

Gordon cracked six eggs into a bowl, then after a moment's hesitation added a seventh. The bacon was beginning to sizzle and scent the cabin. Ten minutes later they were sitting down to their meal.

"And what are we expecting to get from Mrs. Marsh?" Peter asked, after they had taken a few bites.

"She was going to have a list of people for me to talk to. Along with some backup materials."

"Help you hit the ground running?"

"That's the idea."

"Well, fair enough. But listen, Gordon. I'm hoping we can get in some fishing the next couple of days before the women get here. If you know what I mean."

Gordon nodded. "We're on the same page. What I was thinking was that we could meet with her, then I can make some phone calls to set up meetings over the next couple of days. That should leave us this afternoon and evening for fishing."

"Now you're talking," Peter said.

IT WAS A CLEAR, sunny morning as they drove toward Barnstaple. The broad mountain valley where the town was located was a carpet of lush, bright-green grass with countless little rivulets of water running through it, thanks to the snowmelt. In many places the water level had risen above the surface, forming miniature ponds where there was a slight depression in the ground. Well-fed cattle on the other side of barbed-wire fences grazed on the grass and sipped from the ponds.

Gemini Lakes Road met the highway three-quarters of a mile outside of town, and soon they were crossing the river at Barnstaple's edge. On the other side of the bridge, Gordon turned right onto Lincoln Street. On the first block was the post office and a repair garage that had seen better days, with several cars that had seen better days parked in front. The second block held a half-dozen houses with small front yards. Lincoln Street dead-ended at a fence with cattle grazing in the meadow behind it. On the right side of the street was a driveway leading to a gravel parking lot, with a sign reading "Amos Highsmith Park, City of Barnstaple." They pulled in and parked. Gordon's Cherokee was the only vehicle in the lot.

When they got out, they could hear the river rushing below them. The parking lot stood at the edge of a grassy benchland several feet above the river and several feet below Lincoln Street. There were a half-dozen picnic tables scattered on the grass, a children's play area about 50 yards from the parking lot and a covered group picnic area on the side of the parking lot farthest from town. A paved path six feet wide ran along the edge of the benchland closest to the river.

Gordon and Peter began walking down the path in the direction of the bridge. Halfway to the play area they stopped, and Gordon looked around.

"Pretty lonely place," he said. "No one but the cattle on the other side of the river, and we're down just far enough that we can't see the houses above. Which means they can't see us."

Peter pointed downstream. "It's visible from the bridge."

"A long ways away and probably only if you stopped. No, this would be a place where you could attack someone without unreasonable risk. Although your car could be seen entering and leaving the lot."

"Not if you parked a block or two away," Peter said. "I agree. It's feasible she could have been attacked here."

Gordon looked at his watch.

"Worth the journey to check it out. But Mrs. Marsh is expecting us."

OLEMA MARSH'S HOUSE at 332 Third Street was across the state highway and on the far side of town from the city park. It took Gordon and Peter three minutes to get there. The highway was Barnstaple's main street, and Third Street ran parallel to it. Her house was on the last block before the street stopped at the edge of town. It was a white frame house with dark-green accents, one story except for a room above the garage. There were only two other houses on the block and none on the opposite side of the street, so her home had a sweeping view of the valley, grazing cattle, Barnstaple Reservoir and the snow-covered mountains. A dark-green Subaru was parked in the driveway.

The Subaru gave Gordon a moment's pause. Gordon's wife, Elizabeth, drove an older model of that car, and Olema Marsh had been driving a white Ford when they met in Bodega Bay. He and Peter rang the bell at the front door and waited to see what happened.

A woman in her forties, bearing a vague resemblance to Mrs. Marsh, answered the door. She looked at Gordon and Peter expectantly.

"Yes?"

"I'm Quill Gordon and this is Dr. Peter Delaney. I had an appointment to see Mrs. Marsh at 10:30, but if this is a bad time, I can come back later."

She stared at him for several seconds.

"Oh my God," she finally said.

"I'm sorry. We can come back later."

"Oh my God," she said again. "You don't know?"

Gordon and Peter looked at each other.

"I thought everyone in town knew by now," the woman said. "Mother died on Friday morning. It was quite unexpected."

"I'm sorry," Gordon said quickly. "We're from out of town and just arrived yesterday. Perhaps we should go now."

"No, no. Please come in. I'm sorry. My manners seem to have gone south." She stepped aside to let them through the front door, from which she motioned them left into an immaculate and comfortable living room. "I'm Marilyn Rossi, by the way. Could I get you some coffee?"

They smelled it brewing and said yes. She got them seated on the couch and left for the kitchen. A minute later she was back with a tray and three cups.

"It just occurred to me," Marilyn said, handing them each a cup, "that you must have been Mom's 10:30 appointment. She had 10:30 written on the calendar for today, but no name next to it."

"That would have been us," Gordon said. "Are you the daughter from Bodega Bay?"

Marilyn nodded.

"I saw your mother just three weeks ago there."

"Of course. I remember her saying she had a lunch appointment."

"She looked fine then," Gordon continued. "This must have been quite a shock."

She didn't take the hint.

"I drove up here on Saturday," she said. "I'm still in shock. And I'm afraid I can't help you with whatever you came to see her about."

"I wouldn't expect that."

"Wait a minute. Gordon. Gordon. I've seen your name somewhere. It'll come to me in a minute."

"It's not important," Gordon lied. "You have enough on your mind as it is."

"I just got a call before you came," Marilyn said. "The medical examiner released the body. That means we can hold the funeral Wednesday afternoon. You're welcome to come."

17

"Thank you. I think I will."

"Wait. I've got it. Quill Gordon, right?"

Gordon nodded.

"There was something upstairs in her office with your name on it. Let me go get it."

She scuttled out of the room, and as soon as she seemed out of earshot Peter turned to Gordon and whispered:

"So is she going to tell us what happened, or do we have to read it in the newspaper?"

"Patience, Peter."

Marilyn Rossi returned in a minute with a 9-by-12 manila envelope and several newspapers.

"I remembered your name from the envelope on her desk. These newspapers were on top of it. I wasn't sure if they were for you or not." She handed everything over.

"Probably so," Gordon said, looking at the papers, then up at her. "She was doing a little research for me. I'd been hoping to discuss it with her today, but ..."

"She loved researching things," Marilyn said. "She was a born librarian. It may be that everything you need is in that envelope."

"I've no doubt it will be quite thorough," Gordon said.

"The funeral will be Wednesday afternoon. Did I say that already? Three o'clock at the community church. The one with the tall bell tower. You can't miss it."

"I'll be there."

"And the medical examiner said everything was in line with what it appeared to be."

Peter couldn't take it any longer. He leaned forward and in his softest, break-it-to-the-family voice, said:

"As a medical man myself, I appreciate how stressful this must be for you. And I wouldn't want to add to that in any way. But would you mind telling us what happened to your mother? We'd hate to say something at the funeral that would upset anyone in the family just because we didn't know."

"That's very thoughtful of you. And it's not like everyone else doesn't know. She apparently fell in the bathtub, hit her head on the side of it, was knocked out and drowned. It was a horrible accident."

"An accident," Gordon repeated.

"And the thing about it is, she almost never took a bath. She preferred showers. And it was a bath that killed her."

She was breathing with difficulty, as if her whole torso was somehow constricted. Several seconds later she began sobbing violently. Peter got her a box of tissues.

"DON'T GIVE ME the old stink-eye, Gordon. If I'd waited for you to ask the questions, we'd still be there."

"Really, Peter. She was terribly upset. I was trying to bring her along gently."

"All the more reason to get to the point. Holding things back isn't good for people. Anyway, now that we know what happened, where does it leave us?"

They were sitting at a table in the corner of the Pot Belly Deli, where they had repaired for soup. Gordon stirred his bowl of chicken and rice with a big spoon and took a taste.

"Really good," he said. "What I make of it is that unless this is the world's most accident-prone town, something or someone very bad is on the loose here."

Peter nodded and took a spoonful of his split pea.

"Four people are dead of accidents in three-and-a-half months," Gordon continued. "In a town of twelve hundred people, plus maybe another thousand in the immediate outlying areas, that's hard to accept as random chance."

"Does anything strike you about these so-called accidents?"

"You mean aside from the fact that every accident was out of character? A woman who doesn't take baths drowns in her bathtub after three other people die doing things they either don't normally do or did safely all the time."

Peter nodded. "What does that suggest?"

"That somebody's behind all this."

"And what else?"

"That there's one killer behind all this."

"We can agree on that. In a town this size, two killers would be even more improbable than four accidents. But what else?"

"It sounds like you have something in mind. I don't. You want to tell me?"

"Since you ask, all right. From my layman's knowledge, serial killers typically want the body to be found, or they hide it so there's a missing person. Either way, they don't care if foul play's suspected. In fact they might want it."

"But here," Gordon said, "we have four murders, if that's what they in fact are, that were carefully and deliberately made to look like accidents."

"Exactly. And what would be the reason for that?"

"Thrill of the game, maybe," Gordon said. "The killer wants to see if he (or, I suppose, she) can fool the investigators."

"That's one explanation. But I think there's a better one."

Gordon shook his head and Peter continued.

"Let me put it this way. If Olema Marsh was murdered, just before you got here, what would the motive be?"

"Somebody was afraid she knew or suspected something."

"Bingo."

"But that's the thing, Peter. She just thought there was something wrong about those other three accidents, but she didn't know what. That's why she came to me."

"Maybe she knew more than she realized. Maybe the other three people did too."

"That's a lot of maybes."

"Maybe. But it's a starting point. Do you know what's in the envelope she left for you?"

"It's supposed to be names and contact information of people she wanted me to talk to."

"Then that's a dangerous list."

"I don't follow you."

"The altitude must be affecting your thought process, Gordon. If she was killed because she knew too much, who'd know she knew too much? Probably one of the people she wanted you to talk to. What you have here," he tapped the envelope on the table, "is a list of suspects in the murder of Olema Marsh."

BEFORE HEADING OVER to the courthouse, Gordon wrote five words on a piece of note paper and folded it into an envelope that fit into his shirt pocket. After a brief discussion with Peter, they decided that Gordon would go alone.

Barnstaple was the seat of Boundary County, so named because its eastern border, more than 100 miles long, was the California-Nevada state line. The courthouse, a block off the highway, was an old, two-story wooden structure, painted white, with a large, shaded front lawn. When Gordon saw it, he thought two things. The first was that he had seen it in several western movies. The second was that it wasn't much bigger than some of the mansions being built in Silicon Valley and the tonier suburbs of San Francisco.

It was 12:45 when Gordon walked into the sheriff's office on the first floor. Most of the staff was out to lunch, and a couple of overhead fans were moving the air around without appreciably reducing the warmth inside the building. The sheriff's name was Rod Kanehl (pronounced Kuh-NEEL), and Gordon pronounced it perfectly as he asked to see him. The secretary, who had been putting away files when Gordon came in, was not impressed.

"What's it about?" she asked suspiciously.

"I have information about a crime," he said. "I need to speak with the head man about it."

"Just a minute." She trudged to an office at the back, conveying the impression that she was doing Gordon a huge favor by making the effort. She was back within a minute.

"He's busy," she said. "If you can wait a few minutes, Detective Paxton should be back from lunch."

"I expected him to be busy," Gordon said. "But it's Sheriff Kanehl I need to talk to. It's very confidential."

He took the envelope from his shirt pocket and handed it to her.

"This is what it's about," he said. "Could you please ask him to look at it and see if he could make a bit of time?"

She took it in and was back shortly.

"He can give you five minutes," she said, unlatching the swinging door that led behind the counter. Gordon followed her to the sheriff's lair. It was sparsely furnished, with a clean desk and several standard-issue office chairs facing it. Kanehl was six feet tall, lean but with the beginnings of a gut, and had dense, closely cropped black and gray hair. He looked like a lawman, and the sharp look in his eyes suggested he was no buffoon. He had turned his chair to the side so he wasn't facing Gordon.

"All right, Mr. Gordon. I have a lunch appointment in ten minutes, but I'll give you a hearing. Be concise. What makes you think there was foul play in the death of Olema Marsh when the officers at the scene and the medical examiner found nothing to suggest it was anything but a tragic accident?"

"If I didn't know better, I'd say that was a hostile question. And you strike me as a sharp man, Sheriff. There've been a lot of fatal accidents for a town the size of Barnstaple this year. That was bothering Olema Marsh, it's bothering me, and I suspect it's bothering you, though you won't admit it."

"She's talked to you about it, then?"

"We had lunch in Bodega Bay three weeks ago today. She told me about the string of accidents, and I was intrigued enough to agree to come up and look around."

Kanehl swung around in his chair, looking at Gordon.

"You didn't say you were a private investigator."

Gordon held up his hand. "I'm not. I'm a private citizen who's made enough money that I don't have to go to the office every day. So from time to time, at no charge, I look into things that interest me. This is one of those things that interests me."

"An amateur," Kanehl said. "God preserve me."

"I can give you some law-enforcement references if you'd like."

"Not necessary. Look, I don't have much time now, but let me just make a couple of points here. First of all, of course I'm suspicious about those accidents. Who wouldn't be? But you need to know that we run a thorough, professional office here."

"I never suggested otherwise."

Kanehl waved him off. "Every one of those accidents was carefully looked into. The county medical examiner works out of Sierra Pines, where the nearest hospital is. With the ski resort there, they know a lot about trauma. There's no evidence to show there was anything in the way of foul play in any of those deaths. If there had been, we'd have followed every lead. Sometimes there's just a run of bad stuff for no particular reason. Do you know what a hundred-year flood is?"

"Sure, it's a flood so severe that statistically it would only happen once in a hundred years."

"Right. Well my brother works for the San Luis Obispo County sheriff's department. Back in the '80s they had one of those. And then five weeks later they had another one. Two in two months. What are the odds of that? Well, from all the available evidence, our string of accidents is no more than the same sort of freak occurrence."

"Are you open to considering new evidence?"

"Always. This is unusual enough that I'd follow any fresh lead. But I don't think you'll find anything the professionals missed."

"Fair enough. Can I ask you one question about Mrs. Marsh?"

Kanehl looked at his watch. "One question. And I don't promise I can answer it."

"Would it have been possible for someone to come to Mrs. Marsh's home unobserved the day she was killed? It's a small cul-de-sac, after all."

"It's possible, but there's no evidence anyone did. No indication anyone else had been in the house for a couple of days, and no indication from the body that there'd been a struggle or violence done to her."

"Did the neighbors see anything?"

"The Baileys live next door, and they were working all day. It was Sharon Bailey who found the body after she came home and noticed Mrs. Marsh's front door was slightly open."

"How about the other neighbors?"

"The Gristhorpes. They're retired. They were out of town visiting their daughter in Colorado. We called and checked. Think about this, Mr. Gordon. How would someone know the street would be empty that day, or that the Gristhorpes would be out of town? You said the street is a lonely cul-de-sac, but that means any stranger going on to it would be taking a hell of a risk."

He stood up.

"I really have to be going now, Mr. Gordon. I have your number," he held up the card Gordon had given him. "I assume that's your cell phone." Gordon nodded. "And you know how to reach me. If you find anything that looks like new evidence, come straight to me and don't try to handle it yourself. I promise you a thorough look at it. And while I can't prevent you or any other private citizen from talking to people, I *can* do something if you annoy or harass them. So if I hear any complaints about your behavior, you will be called in here for a frank and candid discussion. Do you understand me?"

"Understood," Gordon said.

GORDON AND PETER RECONNECTED at the Happy Scoop. It was a medium-sized shack with windows for ordering and picking up. The menu consisted of hamburgers, hot dogs, fried chicken tenders, french fries, fried onion rings, milkshakes and ice cream. The ice cream was of the frosty variety and came out of machines in two flavors — chocolate and vanilla. For an extra fifty cents, you could get your cone dipped in a chocolate syrup. There wasn't a real ice cream scoop — happy or otherwise — anywhere in the establishment.

They each got a cone and sat down at an umbrella-shaded table in a cement patio set back slightly from the road. The temperature was now in the high 70s and climbing.

"Any joy?" Peter asked.

"About what you'd expect. The sheriff seemed reasonably competent, but he didn't appreciate my floating alternative theories about the so-called accidents. Said they were all thoroughly investigated according to the most modern criminal and medical standards and that nothing was amiss."

"I wonder."

"What?"

"You mentioned modern medical standards. I don't recall seeing a big new hospital in this town. Where would they send their stiffs for a proper examination?"

"Sierra Pines. It's a ski town 25 miles to the south with a hospital."

"Probably a good trauma center, too. Anything else?"

"The sheriff made one point that impressed me. The street where Mrs. Marsh lived was a lonely little cul-de-sac, but if someone parked there to go into her house, anyone who turned onto that street would see the car and it would be over. One of the neighbors, the Gristhorpes, are retired and usually at home, but they happen to be out of town this week. How would our killer know that?"

"There's a way he or she could, actually," Peter said. "Of course it would take the genius and cunning of Professor Moriarty and Hannibal Lecter combined."

Peter picked up a newspaper he had bought while Gordon was talking to the sheriff. It was last Thursday's edition of *The Barnstaple Miner*, the local weekly. He opened it, folded it twice, and set the top half of page 3 in front of Gordon. He pointed to a feature called "Names in the News."

"About halfway down the first column," he said.

It took Gordon only a few seconds to find the paragraph, which read in full:

"Mr. and Mrs. Martin Gristhorpe left Monday on a two-week trip to visit their daughter and grandchildren in Fort Collins, Colorado."

"Must have been a slow news week," Gordon said.

"And it seems to me," Peter added, "that you and the sheriff missed another clue."

Gordon looked at Peter.

"The sheriff said the other neighbor came home after work and found Mrs. Marsh's front door slightly open, right?" Gordon nodded. "Now why would she have left the front door open while she was taking a bath?"

Gordon slapped himself on the forehead.

"You need a break, Gordon. Are we going fishing today?"

"Yes, but we have to stop somewhere first."

Peter cocked his head expectantly.

"After sampling the sheriff's hospitality, I opened the envelope Mrs. Marsh left for me. One of the names inside was Judy Beck, the daughter of Luther Whitman."

"Who fell from the church tower."

"That would be the one. It's right on the way to where we'll be fishing. I'll feel better about fishing if I get started on the interviews first, and she's expecting us at two o'clock."

APPROACHING BARNSTAPLE from the south, another state highway forks off just before town. It parallels Barnstaple Reservoir for a while, then, below the dam, follows the East Gemini River into the wild solitude of western Nevada. The Becks lived five miles out of town on five acres of land, built on a gentle slope on the east side of the highway, with a view of the reservoir and the mountains behind it.

Gordon and Peter drove under an arch at the front gate and several hundred yards further on a gravel road to the main house. It was a sprawling single-story ranch house, and a hundred feet to its right was a two-story barn-workshop. Several sheep were grazing in a fenced area beyond the barn.

Judy Beck had opened the front door before they reached it. She was in her late forties with short sandy-brown hair, blue eyes, and a mouth that looked as if it had smiled a lot. She led them through the house to a walled outdoor patio on the side, seated them at a round table shaded by a large umbrella, and plied them with iced tea and oatmeal cookies with chocolate chips.

When they were settled in, she said, "Mrs. Marsh said you wanted to talk about Dad. Oh my gosh. Isn't it awful what happened to her?"

"We just found out this morning," Gordon said.

"That must have been a shock."

"Quite a shock."

"Anyway, what did you want to know about Dad?"

"Do you mind if I ask first what she — Mrs. Marsh — told you about why I'd want to talk to you?"

"She said she wasn't sure the accidents we had earlier in the year were really accidents and that you were some sort of detective who was going to look into them a bit."

Gordon nodded.

"I said yes because, well I can't believe anyone would try to harm Dad. I mean, he was one of those rare people who really didn't have an enemy in the world. But at the same time ..."

She hesitated. Gordon said nothing, and eventually she continued:

"At the same time, something about the way he died just doesn't seem right. Maybe I'm in denial, but I'd like a little more reassurance that it's been looked at as well as it can be."

"I'm no miracle worker, but I'd like to do a little looking around, as Mrs. Marsh wanted. Why don't you start by telling us a little bit about your father and how he came to Barnstaple."

She nodded.

"We're from Arizona. I grew up there and went to the University of Arizona, where I met Scott."

"Is he from Arizona too?" Peter asked.

"No. From here. He was an out-of-state student. We lived in Flagstaff, and Dad had a locksmith business. He made a decent living and managed to put a bit aside. He was well-known, well-liked, and active in the community."

"In what ways?" Peter said.

"He was active in the church, very much involved with the Chamber of Commerce, and really big in Rotary. He was club president, and for years he was the chair of the committee that put together the club's annual barbecue and square dance. It was their big fund-raiser."

"No involvement in politics or controversial issues?" Gordon asked.

"That wasn't his thing. He was just an all-around good guy."

"How did he wind up coming to Barnstaple?"

"It was kind of sad. He had some bad luck financially. All his retirement money was in a savings and loan that went under in the '80s." She laughed bitterly. "He wouldn't invest in the stock market because he didn't want to take chances with his money. But it was all in one place, and federal insurance only covered half of it."

"Ouch," Peter said.

"I know. Then Mom came down with ovarian cancer. She was 63 and Medicare didn't cover it yet, and their insurance plan had some gaps. By the time she died the medical bills had eaten up most of what was left of the retirement money."

"Did he blame anyone for that?"

"Only himself. Dad wasn't one to get bitter or point fingers. Well, he sold his business for less than he hoped and owned his house free and clear, so he thought he'd still be all right. But the house needed a new roof and a new coat of paint, and before you knew it, the proceeds from the business were evaporating. We offered him the space above the barn. He didn't want to leave Arizona, but he couldn't afford to stay. So he sold the house and moved here."

"I gather from Mrs. Marsh that he fit in pretty well," Gordon said.

"He made an effort to get involved. He joined the church and became their part-time caretaker. He joined the Rotary Club and was supposed to be their president starting in July."

"That's pretty quick." Peter said.

"It's a small club," Judy Beck said. "If you belong and breathe, you're going to be president. But he was clearly well-liked."

Gordon nodded.

"And not just by the Rotary Club. If you want to know the truth, I think Olema Marsh was a little sweet on him. I was hoping that might turn into something. It would have been good for both of them." Her voice began to quiver. "But now they're both gone."

GORDON WAITED A MOMENT before moving on. "Do you mind going over the night of his accident?" he asked.

She shook her head. "I need to talk about it. It just doesn't make sense. I keep asking myself why? How? Dad had been working at the church for nearly two years. Checking the bell tower Saturday night was part of the job. He had to make sure the rope wasn't frayed, that no birds had set up in the bell, that there were no cracks. In short, that it was good to go for Sunday morning. He must have done it a hundred times and in some pretty bad weather. One night there was a blizzard with winds up to 40 miles an hour. He never had any problem at all, not so much as a splinter in his finger."

"Was there any indication or explanation of how it might have happened?" Peter asked.

"The only thing they could come up with — and the sheriff's men went over everything very thoroughly — was that there was a bit of an ice patch on the floor of the bell tower. They said maybe he slipped on that, lost his balance and went over the side."

"There must be an enclosure of some sort," Gordon said.

"There's a wall that's about waist high, then above that and below the bell it's open so you can hear when it rings. He'd never even had a close call before. He was very agile for a man his age."

"And no one across the street saw anything?"

She shook her head. "He came down on the First Street side. Across the street are the backs of commercial buildings on the highway. By that time Saturday night, they'd all be closed, except for Bart's Lounge, and at that time of year, their customers would mostly be parked on Main Street, not First."

"Was it dark?" Peter said.

"It should have been. He had a checklist of things to go through and usually he did the bell tower last. That would be around 6:30 to 7."

"Pretty dark that time of day in February," Gordon said. He hesitated before going on. "Mrs. Marsh apparently talked to you about seeing me. Are you satisfied with the explanation of your father's death?"

"If it wasn't an accident," Judy finally said, "the only other explanation is that he was pushed. And that doesn't make sense either. Who'd do such a thing? Dad was a nice guy. Everybody liked him. He didn't have an enemy in the world."

"Not even one?" Peter asked.

"Not even one."

IT WAS FISHING that had brought Gordon and Peter together after a professional contact seven years earlier. In need of a hernia repair, Gordon had been referred to Peter, who was considered one of San Francisco's best general surgeons. That had led to their taking a couple of fly-fishing trips together and developing an enduring friendship. Also, Peter's medical knowledge and previous experience as an emergency-room physician had helped Gordon out on a couple of his investigations.

From the Beck house, Gordon followed the highway past the dam that formed the reservoir to a turnout a half mile below the dam and 30 feet above a grassy bench next to the river.

"Grab your rod and let's check it out," he said.

They made their way down an embankment where the anglers who had gone before had blazed a trail and then to the edge of the river. It was running smooth and clear, and they could see lush weed beds on the bottom — generators of the insects trout feed on.

"What's that sign say?" Peter pointed downstream.

"Let's go read it." They walked 150 feet to the sign, which read: "WARNING: Water flows subject to sudden and dangerous changes. Enter at own risk."

"So," Peter said, "what does that mean in practical terms?"

"It means we fish from the bank," Gordon said.

Peter looked upstream. "I don't know about this, Gordon." He pointed toward the dam, which loomed above them. "I hate to think what would happen if that dam broke."

Gordon looked at the dam. "The good news, Peter, is that if that dam breaks, we won't have much time to think, and it'll be over so fast we'll hardly know it. But the dam's not going to break today, so let's start fishing."

They fished for three hours, and the dam held, as predicted. Working nymphs over the weeds, they each caught and released several trout in the 12- to 18-inch range, mostly Rainbows and a couple of Browns. At five o'clock a caddis fly hatch began, and each man caught three fish on a dry fly. The hatch ended abruptly a few minutes after six o'clock, and Gordon declared it time to go.

It took less than a quarter of an hour to get back to Barnstaple, and Gordon parked on the highway across from the Barnstaple Inn, a three-story bright-yellow wood building more than a century old. They crossed the deserted Main Street and went in.

A small office for guest check-in was on their left, and a steep flight of stairs leading to the second floor was directly in front of them. To the right was a door to the dining room and bar, with a stand for the host or hostess just inside. A redhead with a ponytail and a heart-shaped face led them to a table against the far wall, across from the bar and a few tables from the windows overlooking Main Street. The dining area was two-thirds full, with enough background noise that they would be able to talk without being overheard. The special was grilled trout with herbed potatoes and asparagus, and they both went for it.

"Well," Peter said after they ordered, "what are we to make of Saint Luther? I don't know about you, but whenever I hear that someone doesn't have an enemy in the world, I right away want to know the real story."

Gordon smiled. "There *are* nice guys in the world, Peter. And I could think of several things that might get a nice guy killed. Like knowing too much, or seeing something they weren't supposed to see."

"You think that's the explanation?"

"It makes sense, anyway. I think I'm going to drop in at the church tomorrow and see if the pastor will let me go up to the bell tower."

"I'll stand below and call the ambulance if you fall," Peter said. "I get nervous with heights."

"The question, though, is what Luther might have seen. Or known. I don't get the sense there are a lot of criminal enterprises around here."

"And if you're onto the answer," Peter said, "it would have to be something the other two 'accident' victims came across, too."

"Maybe."

"What do mean, maybe?"

"It's also possible that one or even two of those accidents was really an accident," Gordon said. "But I don't see how all of them could have been, especially Olema Marsh. When someone comes to a private inquiry agent — or whatever you want to call me — to say there have been too many accidents in her town, then she herself dies in a so-called accident ... well, that's too much coincidence to be coincidence."

"So you're sure she was murdered?"

"I can't prove it yet, but that's what I believe until proven otherwise. And if that's the case, at least one of those other three accidents was a murder, too, and the killer got wind that she was onto something."

Peter took a sip of his iced tea.

"Then we come back to that list of people she left for you. You'd better take a close look at it."

BY THE TIME they got back to Broderick's, the sun had not yet set but had gone behind the mountains. The resort and the near shore were in shade, but the far side of the lake was brightly lit. Gordon took his cell phone and Olema Marsh's envelope to a bench on a grassy knoll by the lake. The phone had two bars, and he had solitude as he called several people on her list, reaching a few and making appointments for Tuesday and Wednesday.

The opposite shore of the lake was nearly in shadow when he had gone through the list and decided to call Elizabeth. She picked up on the second ring.

"Gordon," she said, "your timing is perfect. I don't know how much longer I could have stayed awake."

"You got the grades turned in?" Elizabeth taught at City College of San Francisco.

"At 4:30. Half an hour before deadline."

"Better than some semesters."

"It gets better with practice. But I want to hear all about your suspicious old lady. Did she have any new leads for you?"

He paused, considering exactly what to say.

"Actually, it's looking more serious. We went to her house this morning — Peter and I — only to be greeted by her daughter, who told us her mother had died last Friday."

"Oh my God."

"Of an accident, no less. The official story is that she slipped in her bathtub, hit her head, was knocked out and drowned."

There was a long silence on the other end, before Elizabeth said:

"I take it you're not buying the official story."

"Not for a minute. I suppose it could turn out to be true, but one thing her daughter said made up my mind for me. She said her mother almost never took a bath — preferred showers."

"So she died out of character, so to speak."

"Just like the people in the other three accidents."

"But wouldn't the killer have been taking a huge risk, going into her house in a small town like that?"

"A risk, to be sure. But every crime involves some risk. Her house is on a cul-de-sac at the edge of town, with only two other houses. They were both empty the morning it happened."

"And the sheriff? Did you talk to him?"

"Briefly, before he gave me the bum's rush. He seems reasonably sharp, and he says all the accidents were thoroughly and properly investigated and there was no indication they were anything but what they seemed to be."

"But how hard was he looking for something else?"

"Just the point I was about to make. Probably not very hard."

"This is getting serious."

"I agree. I'm looking forward to having you here."

"In less than 48 hours, darling. Tomorrow I'm doing nothing but sleeping, packing and shopping."

"Get plenty of rest. The drive up here is longer than it seems."

"I will. And Gordon —"

"Yes?"

"Be careful. This fourth so-called accident is really bad. You could be dealing with someone who's not only dangerous but really smart."

"Noted."

"You're going to ignore the advice, aren't you?"

"Good night, Elizabeth. I love you. Sleep well."

AS NIGHT FELL, Gordon and Peter retreated to Gordon's cabin, where he made a pot of herbal tea and got out the envelope and newspapers Olema Marsh had left for him before she died. He placed them on the dining table.

"In Bodega Bay, she brought me copies of the local papers that had the news stories of the three accidents. Later, I asked her to get me the papers for the two weeks before. So we have nine issues of *The Barnstaple Miner* to go through — three for each accident."

He looked at his watch. "I think we have time to go through one accident apiece before turning in at a civilized hour. How about Luther Whitman and Lucy Starr?"

"I'm in. Which one do you want to take?"

"Why don't you take Luther," Gordon said, pushing a pile of papers toward Peter.

Peter nodded, and the two of them settled into sipping tea and reading newspapers. *The Barnstaple Miner* was a full-size paper, eight pages most weeks and 12 pages in one of Gordon's weeks. Slightly less than half of it was advertising, but it still took the better part of an hour to read (or skim) three editions.

It was a little before 10 o'clock when they finished, and the remaining tea had turned cold. The kids who had been playing outside when they started had gone into their vacation dwellings. Aside from an owl that hooted occasionally, it was still and quiet outside. Gordon stood and stretched.

"Well?" he said to Peter.

"You first."

Gordon sat down and shook his head. "Nothing jumped out at me," he said. "Of course, it would help if I knew what I was looking for. I'd suggest we hang onto these papers and look at them again in a couple of days — after we've talked to a few more people and have some background. How about you?"

"Well," Peter said, "I've learned more about the workings of the Barnstaple Community Water District than I ever thought I'd know. Or want to know. Problem is, I can't figure out whether the water board is a group of exceptionally dim bulbs or whether the people questioning them are a bunch of paranoid cranks."

"Probably both. Small-town politics can be contentious."

"Anyway, I didn't see anything in the news stories that seemed relevant, given what we know."

"So we both whiffed."

"Not so fast, Gordon. There was nothing in the news stories, but something I almost didn't read yielded a nugget."

"An ad?"

"Better than that. The weather report."

Gordon gave him a blank look. Peter continued:

"Luther Whitman fell from that tower on Saturday February 26th. According to the weather summary in the paper, the high temperature that day was 53. On Friday, the day before, it was 54. Thursday it was 50, and Wednesday it was 47. And according to the paper, there was no precipitation any of those four days."

"Is there a point to this, Peter?"

"I'm surprised you didn't see it yourself. The sheriff found a little patch of ice on the floor of the bell tower and surmised that Luther had slipped on it and gone over the edge. But if they were having a midwinter warm spell, and there hadn't been any rain or snow for four days, where would the ice have come from?"

AFTER PETER WENT BACK to his cabin, Gordon strolled to the lake again. The moon was waxing toward the first quarter, so he had to rely on his flashlight, and the chill in the air served as a reminder that it wasn't yet summer. He sat on a bench and looked out at the lake.

The reality of Olema Marsh's death was beginning to hit him. He realized he'd liked her and had been looking forward to picking her brain on the investigation. If her death was as fishy as it appeared to be, Elizabeth had a point. If a killer suspected she was getting onto something, Gordon stood to be in some danger once her killer realized she had talked to him about it.

And, come to think of it, he probably owed Elizabeth an apology for being flip when she expressed her concern. Vague concern irritated him, but he knew it was expressed because she cared for him — and, to be honest, she knew he had put himself in peril during several of his previous investigations. He concluded he owed her an apology and that he would offer one when they talked on the phone tomorrow.

He stood up and trudged back to the cabin, hoping his commitment to the apology would enable him to sleep better.

Tuesday June 6

THEY ARRIVED AT THE CHURCH at nine o'clock and followed a gravel path to a door at the side of the building that said "Church Office." It was unlocked, and they went in. A woman in her fifties sat at a desk near the entry door. She was on the phone but wrapped up the call in half a minute and asked what she could do for them.

"My name's Quill Gordon, and this is my friend, Dr. Peter Delaney. I've been going around the state looking at interesting features of old churches in small towns and taking photographs. I was wondering if it might be possible to go up in the tower of this one."

"Let me check with the pastor." She walked back into an office that was off to the right of the reception room. A minute later, a young man in his early thirties with dark hair and glasses came out.

"Matthew Moody," he said, extending a hand. Gordon and Peter both shook it. "What can I do for you?"

Gordon repeated the fiction he'd told the receptionist, and Pastor Moody nodded.

"I don't see any harm in it. It's a good thing, as far as I'm concerned, when people take an interest in older churches. In small towns like this, the church was often the building to which the most thought was given in terms of design. You know, in a lot of towns in New England, they don't allow any building to be taller than the church tower."

"I've heard that," Peter said.

"The only thing," the pastor continued, "is that we'd ask you to sign a liability release. Louise, do you know where we keep those forms?"

Louise opened the second drawer of her desk, took a piece of paper off the top, and handed it to the pastor, who glanced at it and handed it over to Gordon. It was a short, simple form, and seeing nothing in it that would allow the church to come after him legally, he quickly signed it.

"Will your friend be going up, too?" the pastor asked.

"No thanks," Peter said. "I'm just watching."

"All right, then. Be careful. You should be pretty safe up there, but we had a tragic accident earlier this year."

"Really?" Gordon said. "Do you mind if I ask?"

"It wouldn't matter if I minded. Anyone in town could tell you about it. The man who was our handyman-assistant was up there on Saturday night making sure the bell was in order for the next day's service and fell to his death."

"That's awful," Gordon said. "I'm sorry to hear it."

"We were all sorry. A very sweet man, Luther Whitman was. Everyone loved him." He paused. "I was the one who found him, too."

"That must have been hard on you," Gordon said.

"His family called when he hadn't come home as expected. I'd been planning to swing by the church — the pastor's house is only two blocks away — so I went over right after they called. He was lying on the gravel path just outside and quite beyond human help when I saw him. Obviously an accident of some sort, but we'll probably never know the whole story. Just take reasonable precautions and you should be all right, though." He plucked a key from a row of them on the wall. "I'll walk over with you."

The tower was entered through a door from the outside. Pastor Moody opened it with the key and tested the knob. "Just push it all the way shut when you leave, and it should lock on its own. I hope it lives up to your expectations."

When he was out of earshot, Gordon turned to Peter.

"Why don't you go stand on the gravel path about where it looks like someone would land if he fell or was pushed out of the tower."

"That's easy enough."

Gordon stepped inside. A spiral staircase, with the stairs about two feet wide, led up to the bell tower. Inside the climbing space it was dark and musty-smelling, and it felt close and confining. Gordon considered himself to be in good shape, but between the climb and the altitude, he was winded when he reached the trap door to get into the top area, where the bell was.

There was enough room in the tower to walk around the bell, and a sturdy wooden barrier three feet tall seemed an adequate safety measure against the open air above it and the ground a hundred feet below. Gordon put two hands against the barrier and leaned into it. Standing nearly six-five, he nevertheless felt fairly protected against a fall.

He looked around, taking in the larger view. On the side where Peter stood, Gordon could see over the tops of the commercial buildings to Main Street and the Barnstaple Inn beyond. To his right, he could see the highway running north out of town through the green valley. Turning around, he could see what there was of the settled town before it ended at a meadow two blocks away. Looking left down the last street, which would be Third Street, he took note of the roof of what must have been Olema Marsh's house at the end.

"Well?" Peter called up.

"Top of the world, Peter. Top of the world."

Gordon looked up. The roof of the bell tower sloped down to a point around the top of his head and a couple of feet from the outer wall. With a stiff wind, he thought, it would be possible for falling snow or rain to be blown into the bell tower, but given the size of the open area and the angles, it would take a real gale for that to amount to much.

He circled the bell again and noticed Pastor Moody walking across the lawn, getting into a car and driving off. Gordon immediately started down the stairs. Going down was more demanding than coming up — not because of the exertion, but because he could see how far down the bottom was, and it was far.

"Next?" Peter said, when Gordon came out.

"I have an idea," Gordon said, "but first I want to have a word with Louise."

Peter followed him into the office, where Gordon, acting innocent, asked if he could speak with the pastor.

"He just drove off," Louise said. "I'm surprised you didn't see him from the tower."

"I was looking in all directions. That's quite a view from up there."

Louise said nothing, and Gordon pretended to take it as encouragement.

"I just wanted to ask him a question," Gordon continued. "He was talking about the gentleman who fell from the tower a few months ago. I could sure see getting dizzy up there, but the walls around the perimeter of the tower seem pretty solid. I'd think they'd stop someone who stumbled into them. I couldn't help wondering what went wrong."

Louise looked up.

"I'm not sure anyone can answer that," she said. "It's still sort of a mystery. And if you ask me, there's one more thing about it that didn't make sense."

"Really?"

"When the pastor found poor Luther on the path out there, the door to the tower was open."

"But he'd have had to open it to go in, wouldn't he?" Peter said.

"He would. But he always closed it and locked it behind him. He was a very scrupulous man, Luther was. He worried that a small child might go inside and fall off or down the stairs. No one's really explained why that door was open when Luther fell from the tower."

KATHRYN HENRY, who had hosted the bridge party two nights before Lucy Starr was swept to her death in the East Gemini River, lived about a mile out of Barnstaple on the main highway. The house number was inconspicuous enough that Gordon passed it on the first try and had to come back. A steep but freshly paved driveway led up the side of the mountain from the highway to a flat area a hundred feet above the road, on which was built a sprawling ranch house with an adjacent tennis court. There was enough room in front of the house and garage for several cars to park, but when Gordon parked the Cherokee, careful to keep the path from the garage clear, his was the only vehicle there.

With Peter at his side, Gordon rang the doorbell, and half a minute later, it was opened by a man in his fifties, wearing jeans and a blue Brooks Brothers shirt with a white stripe. He was a couple of inches under six feet, with close-cropped salt and pepper hair, regular features and a military-style mustache on his upper lip. Gordon introduced himself and Peter.

"Ah, Olema's friend," the man said. "What a shock that was." He extended his hand. "Skip Henry. Pleased to meet you."

He shook hands with both of them, then stepped aside to let them in.

"Kathryn's expecting you," he said. "She's a bit shook up about Olema. I think we all are, and by all I mean just about everybody in Barnstaple." He lowered his voice. "Just be aware of that, and it should be fine. Your visit will probably do her some good."

He led them down a short hall to a family room at the back of the house. It had a large TV with a couch and two overstuffed armchairs facing it, and in one corner of the room was a small desk, where Kathryn was sitting. She stood to greet them. She was five-four and wearing white slacks with a print blouse, neither of which, Gordon suspected, had been purchased in Barnstaple. With an oval face and good bones, helped out by money and activity (Gordon guessed from her figure that the tennis court wasn't for show), she was the kind of woman who probably looked better at fifty than she did at twenty and would have been perfectly at home in the more affluent suburbs of San Francisco. After introductions and handshakes, she motioned Gordon and Peter to the couch.

"I need to get back to those reports for the board meeting," Skip said, "but before I go, could I offer you water or coffee? I just made a fresh pot."

They each accepted a cup, black, and sat down.

"I apologize for bothering you at a time like this," Gordon said. "I gather Mrs. Marsh was a good friend of yours."

Kathryn Henry nodded. "We've known each other for years. In a small town like this, the people who are active in the community are always being thrown together. Can I ask you a question?"

Gordon nodded.

"Did you have a chance to talk to Olema after you got here?"

"I'm afraid not," Gordon said. "We were supposed to meet with her yesterday morning, but her daughter answered the door and gave us the news. We had no idea."

"She was worried about something and hoping you could help."

"The accidents, you mean?"

She nodded. "She didn't think they were accidents, of course."

"What do *you* think, if you don't mind my asking?"

Skip returned with a tray holding three cups. He gave one to his wife and the other two to Gordon and Peter.

"I'll be in my office if you need me," he said on the way out.

She took a sip of coffee, holding the mug with both hands. Gordon tried to give her time and space to frame her answer.

"I don't know," she finally said. "On the one hand, all those accidents at once seem a bit suspicious, like Olema said. But Skip says that when he was in the Army, it seemed like accidents on a military base tended to come in bunches. And that makes sense, too."

"Did she ever suggest what might be happening?" Peter asked.

"Never. She was just suspicious as can be. That's why she asked for your help."

"And that's about as much as I got out of her in our one meeting," Gordon said. "Let me ask you something else. You and Mrs. Marsh were at the same gathering at this house, if I understand right, two nights before Lucy Starr died. Do you remember anything unusual, anything out of the ordinary from that night?"

"I don't think so. It was our monthly bridge party, and we rotate around to each other's houses. We've been doing it for 20 years, and no matter whose house it's in, they're pretty much the same. I don't recall anything out of the ordinary about this one. The hands were pretty average, no one got angry or said anything out of line. We all ate a bit too much, but that's par for the course."

She shook her head. "You might try Helen Overton. She was the fourth at the table."

"Thanks," Gordon said. "I'd been planning to talk to her." He took a sip of the coffee.

Peter stepped in. "This is kind of a strange question, but what happens to your bridge group with two of the four members gone?"

"I really don't know," she said. "Florence Robertson was the backup fourth if one of us was out of town, and she could probably become a regular. But that still leaves us with an empty chair at the table."

HELEN OVERTON began the conversation with Peter and Gordon by saying she doubted she could be of much help. She wasn't selling herself short.

"That bridge party was nearly two months ago," she said. "I can hardly remember what I had for lunch yesterday."

Mrs. Overton was a woman in her late fifties who had given up on the battle to appear still young and seemed happier for it. She lived in a modest green house on First Street, several blocks from Olema Marsh's home. Her husband, who she said still had two years to go before retirement, was off at work.

"I mean, we always have a good time," she continued, "but part of that is that we don't usually discuss serious matters. We're there to relax."

Gordon nodded, hoping she'd keep talking.

"Do you really think it's important?"

"I don't know," Gordon said. "Probably not. Did Mrs. Marsh talk to you about Lucy Starr's accident?"

"Did she ever! She didn't think it was an accident and kept telling me why."

"What about you?" Peter said. "What do you think?"

"Well, it *is* strange that we've had all these accidents, including Lema's now. But accidents do happen, and the sheriff seems pretty sure they were accidents. So that's probably what they were."

"It's the most likely explanation," Gordon said. "But Mrs. Marsh wanted me to talk to some people about it, and now that she's gone so suddenly, I feel an obligation to do what she asked the best I can."

Helen Overton nodded.

"So with Lucy Starr at that bridge party two nights before she died, I kind of feel I have to ask if she might have given any indication that something was amiss. Did she seem worried or agitated that night?"

"Not that I could tell."

"And she didn't say anything that might indicate something was bothering her?"

"Nope. She was pretty calm all night."

"How about the cards?" Peter asked.

"The cards?"

"I mean were there any unusual hands? Any memorable bids that you were all talking about?"

"I don't think so. Everything was pretty ordinary and conservative as I recall."

"And no one at the party — not just Lucy — said anything out of the ordinary?" Peter asked.

Helen shook her head. "I don't think so. The conversation was all pretty much in one ear and out the other. I don't even remember any good gossip."

"I don't suppose you had any chance of talking to Lucy after the bridge party?"

"No. It was the last time I saw her."

Gordon and Peter looked at each other. Gordon moved his head a fraction of an inch toward the front door, and Peter nodded.

"Well, thank you for your time, Mrs. Overton," Gordon said, rising. "As I said, there's probably nothing to this, and you're just helping confirm it."

"Are you going to the funeral tomorrow?" she said, getting up, too.

"I am. I expect you'll be there."

"Along with everybody else."

"Then we'll meet again tomorrow." He paused. She seemed to be deep in thought. "Is everything all right?"

"It is, but for some reason ..."

Gordon stood still.

"... I just had a thought that something kind of unusual was said that night, but I can't remember what it was."

44

Gordon took a card from his shirt pocket and handed it to her.

"It may not be anything, but if it comes to you, could you please give me a call?"

She looked at the card.

"All right. It's probably not important anyway."

"Probably not."

THEY PICKED UP SANDWICHES at the Pot Belly Deli and took them to the park by the river. No one else was there, and they took a shaded table overlooking the water.

"We don't seem to be getting anywhere," Peter said, after taking a bit of his roast beef and Swiss. "And we're taking a lot of time doing it."

"Agreed. It would help if we had some idea of what we're looking for. I'd been hoping for some direction from Mrs. Marsh." He took a bite of his turkey and Monterey Jack. "Maybe Lucy Starr's husband will tell us something interesting after lunch. Maybe Mrs. Overton will remember what she heard that night."

"Maybe. But I have a question. From what you tell me, Olema Marsh was quite the information hawk, right?"

"I'd say not much got past her."

"That being the case, wouldn't you think that if something noteworthy had been said at the bridge party, she would have picked up on it herself?"

"I expect she would have, but you never know. She wanted me to talk to Mrs. Henry and Mrs. Overton, so I suppose she thought they might have picked up on something she didn't."

"Or talked to Lucy after the party. We didn't ask Kathryn Henry about that. Are you all right, Gordon?"

Gordon was looking intently at the water.

"I thought I saw a fish rise against the far bank," he said.

THE MAN WAS HUNCHED over the computer, carefully reading every word, as he had been taught to do years ago. It was the third time he'd been through the text, and he was fairly well satisfied that there were no typographical errors and everything made sense.

He leaned back and smiled, not from happiness — he was rarely happy —but with satisfaction.

All those murders in all those places over all that period of time. And the police still had no clue. He was going to have to give them a prod, and he was sure they wouldn't like it. The thought gave him a perverse pleasure.

Could it be considered taunting?

Perhaps, but he felt the police deserved it. And after all, he was merely giving them the outline. There was no indication as to who the next victim would be or when and where it might happen. It would be up to the cops to figure that out, and good luck to them. They'd need it. A lot of it.

He leaned forward and looked at the computer screen again. No point in waiting any longer; he might as well pull the trigger now.

The man put his fingers above the keyboard like a piano virtuoso about to begin a sonata. He held them there for several seconds then banged out the commands without a missed stroke.

The website was live.

How long would it be, he wondered, before one of the detectives stumbled upon it? It could take a while, given that the police were not as smart as they liked to think they were and most likely not given to doing random internet searches. It could be days, weeks, maybe even months before the website was discovered, and he'd have the chance to gloat.

Actually, he was gloating already.

THE HOME OF JIM (and, formerly, Lucy) Starr was a plain gray house of 1960s vintage. It was a rectangle of 1,500 square feet, with three bedrooms, one and a half baths, a two-car garage, and a front lawn large enough to hold a beach towel or two fully laid out. It was on the other side of the highway from Olema Marsh's home, about three blocks from the city park where Lucy Starr was last seen before somehow winding up in the East Gemini River that unusually warm April night.

It was a little after 2 p.m. when Peter and Gordon arrived. The sun was beating down, the temperature was approaching 80, and the cumulus clouds forming in the sky didn't look as if they were bringing rain. Starr answered the door, offered them lemonade (which they accepted) and muted the volume on Fox News.

"So Lema said you wanted to talk about Lucy," Starr began. "Shame what happened to her."

Gordon guessed the pronoun referred to Mrs. Marsh but said, noncommittally, "Yes, it was."

"She seemed to think you might be able to get some answers about what happened to Lucy. Don't know how."

"Neither do I," Gordon said. "But I promised her I'd try."

"Then you have to do it. Well, tell me what you want to know, and I'll tell you what I can."

Starr leaned back in his chair. He was a man of medium height and more than medium weight, with thinning hair that could use a cut and a face of white stubble a day or two old. The house seemed to hang heavy around him.

"I realize it's probably painful to talk about," Gordon said, "but could you tell us in your own words what you remember about the night Lucy disappeared?"

Starr sat quietly in his chair, looking at a point a foot above the silent television for a full minute before answering.

"Shoot, I don't know what to tell you. Just like a lot of other nights, until she wasn't there. We ate dinner in front of the TV," he gestured at it with his head.

"Watching the news?" Peter said.

"Not the news. The A's were playing that night. They were in Baltimore. I'll always remember Baltimore. Lucy'd made macaroni and cheese with ham, which was one of my favorite meals. Haven't had it since. Well, except for the leftovers from that night. We ate and watched the game. Lucy didn't like baseball as much as I do, but she was all right with watching it during dinner when there was a game on. After that, she said it was a nice night and she was going to go for a walk."

"When was that?" Gordon asked.

"Top of the fourth inning."

"I meant what time?"

"We usually ate about 5:30, so probably a bit after six o'clock."

"And it was still light?" Peter said.

"Oh, yeah. Would be for another hour and a half or so. Anyway, I told her to have fun and settled in to watch the game. It was a good game, and it took me a while to realize Lucy hadn't come back."

"When was that?"

"Bottom of the seventh." He looked at Gordon. "Probably about 7:30. It was getting dark outside. The score was 4-4 and the Orioles were coming up to bat when I realized Lucy hadn't come back yet. Or I hadn't heard her, anyway. I called her name and checked the house, but she wasn't here."

"Were you worried?" Gordon said.

"Not too much just then. I figured she'd run into someone she knew and they'd started talking. Lucy loved to talk. So I watched the bottom of the seventh and top of the eighth. By then it was dark outside and she still wasn't back. That's when I started to worry. She wouldn't be talking to someone outside after dark, and if she'd gone to someone's house, she would have called. I decided to go looking for her. Got the car out and covered the whole town. No Lucy. That's when I really started to worry."

"Did you call the sheriff?"

"I did. And they weren't too excited. Said she probably stopped at a friend's house, got talking and lost all track of time, and that I should call back in the morning if she hadn't come home by then."

"So you called again in the morning?"

"Hell no, I didn't. When she hadn't got home by ten, I called again and raised a stink. The patrol car came by a bit later, and the deputies drove me around town, asking where she might have gone. I told them she usually swung by the park when she walked, so they got out flashlights and we looked there, but no sign of her."

"Was she carrying a purse?" Peter asked.

Starr shook his head. "When she went for a walk, she took her fanny pack with a wallet and keys and phone. She was still wearing it when they pulled her out of the reservoir.

"When she wasn't back the next morning, they stepped it up a bit, but they didn't find much. Sheriff Rod himself went door to door at the houses across the street from the park. Bernice Brown said she saw Lucy starting down the stairs into the park, but that was all."

"She didn't see Lucy coming back?" Gordon said.

"She only saw her going in because she was pulling the curtains on the front window. After she did that, the Browns didn't see anything else."

"And there were no other sightings, no more information or indication as to what happened?"

"Other than she went into the river — no. It's a mystery."

"Do you have a picture of Lucy?" Peter asked.

Starr nodded, and with some effort got up from the chair and went into the kitchen, returning a minute later with a framed photo.

"This is probably the best one I have. Lucy and her sister Viola. Lucy's on the left."

Gordon took the photograph and held it between himself and Peter, who was next to him on the couch. The two women both looked happy. Lucy had short, well-coiffed chestnut hair, bright brown eyes with a twinkle, and an intelligent, alert expression.

"It was when they went on the cruise," Starr said.

Gordon looked more closely at the picture.

"So that blue in the background is the ocean," he said. He looked up. "I seem to recall Mrs. Marsh telling me Lucy was afraid of the water."

"She was. But her sister won the cruise at a charity raffle and really wanted her to go. Said she could stick to the middle of the ship and not get too near the water, so she did. Enjoyed it more than she thought she would."

"I see."

"And Viola had just lost Bill, so Lucy felt she had to go with her. Lucy was big on standing by her family. Doubt she'd do it again just for herself." He paused. "Lema seemed to think that what happened to Lucy wasn't an accident. What do you think, Mr. Gordon?"

Gordon looked at Peter and handed the photo back to Starr.

"So far, I haven't seen any evidence to indicate it wasn't an accident. That's about all I can say at this point. Do you have any feelings about that?"

Starr looked at the photo of his wife and her sister for several seconds, then set it face down on the small table next to his chair.

"I don't know. I really don't. I can't imagine Lucy being careless near that river, especially when it was running like that. But I can't imagine who'd want to hurt her. She didn't have an enemy in the world. Right now," he swallowed, "what I really want is an answer about what happened. And if it was an accident, I'm probably never going to get an answer."

IT WAS MIDAFTERNOON when they wrapped up with Jim Starr and began discussing their fishing options.

"I'm thinking we should take advantage of being at Broderick's," Gordon said. "Fish have been rising before sunset the last couple of days, not far off the pier by their marina. And if the pier is full of kids, we can always fish from shore. There are a couple of good spots."

"I'd prefer stream fishing," Peter said, "but we're kind of running out of time to do much and get back for dinner."

"The restaurant at Broderick's opens at 4:30. We could have a light early dinner, get in three hours of fishing, and be walking distance from the cabin when we're done. I'd like us to both have a look at that last set of newspapers before we turn in."

"Let's do the lake at Broderick's tonight and hit the stream next time."

They returned to the resort, got their fishing gear rigged up and rested briefly in their cabins before heading to the restaurant. It was a rectangular building with pine-log sides and a corrugated metal roof. By virtue of being there early, they got a window table, overlooking the lake. Gordon stared out the window for several minutes after their orders were taken.

"It's a good thing I'm not charging a fee for this," he finally said. "I wouldn't have earned a dime of it today."

"I'm not so sure of that," Peter said, sipping his iced tea. "We got a lot of information today, it's just that we don't know the importance of it yet. And I think we're onto something here."

"How sure are you?"

"Look, Gordon, in a town this size, I could buy two accidents in two months as being coincidence. Three accidents in three months, it could still be coincidence, but the odds are leaning the other direction. But four accidents in four months? Sorry. At that point, coincidence is a 40-1 nag at Santa Anita."

"You're more open-minded than Olema Marsh. She thought three was too many."

"Considering what happened to her, she was probably right. But think about it. If these accident victims, or even three out of four, were bumped off by someone, what's the conclusion you'd draw from it?"

Gordon thought for a moment.

"I don't have a conclusion, but I have a question. These murders — if that's what, indeed, they are — were made to look like accidents. And at great risk in some instances. I mean, entering Mrs. Marsh's house in broad daylight? Pitching Lucy Starr into the river at a public park? Going one on one with Luther Whitman in the church tower? Why take chances like that to make it look like an accident?"

"Exactly. And there's a pretty obvious answer, don't you think?"

"If it's so obvious, tell me."

"I think those people knew something about someone in town. If they were obviously murdered, the investigation could reveal that something. But if it's an accident, nobody's going to look much deeper into their lives."

"No one but us. There's just one problem with your theory, Peter. If they knew something, why didn't it come out before?"

"I'm thinking," Peter said, "they didn't fully appreciate what they knew. And they had to be eliminated before it dawned on them."

FOR DINNER THEY SPLIT an order of crab cakes. Gordon had soup and Peter ordered the salad, which was heavy on iceberg lettuce but was redeemed by real chunks of blue cheese in the dressing. They were done eating and on the lake by 5:30.

The warmth of the day lingered well into the evening, even at 7,000 feet. Several kids were fishing from the end of the pier, so they went a hundred yards down the shore to a grassy point that extended into the lake. It formed the edge of a small cove, with a weedy bottom that sloped slowly to a depth of 12 feet. No fish were rising or visibly cruising the weeds, so they fished with nymphs (small flies representing insects just emerged from their larvae) below indicators on the surface. Nothing happened for half an hour, and Gordon was considering switching to a streamer, which would imitate a leech or minnow below the surface, when Peter called out, "Fish on!"

Gordon looked over to see Peter with his rod held high, bent by the pull of the trout he'd just hooked. Looking back at his own indicator, Gordon saw it duck underwater and set the hook.

"Same here," he shouted.

For the next hour, they couldn't have paid the fish to stay away. They got a bite on nearly every cast, and each man landed and released more than a dozen fish. Most were Rainbows, but there were a few Brook Trout in the mix, and Gordon landed a 17-inch Brown Trout. Then, as suddenly as it had started, the trout-feeding frenzy stopped. The sun had gone behind the mountains to the west, but the eastern part of the lake was still in sunlight.

"The kids are gone from the pier," Peter said. "Shall we move over?"

Gordon nodded. They walked to it and out to its end, where it formed a T. Peter moved to the right side and Gordon to the left. At that point, a trout rose to the surface to take a fly about 40 feet off the edge of the pier. Another fish rose a few seconds later and a few feet away from the first.

"Showtime," Gordon said. "Give the dry fly a look." He was carrying two rods, one with a nymph at the end of the leader and one with a #16 Adams, a gray dry fly that floated on the surface and vaguely resembled half the insects to be found in mountain waters. While Peter was changing the fly on his one rod, Gordon made a cast that elegantly dropped his fly in the water, halfway between where the two fish had risen a moment ago. One of them — or perhaps another trout altogether — smacked it within three seconds of its hitting the water. It was a healthy 14-inch Rainbow that swam off quickly when Gordon released it.

They had the pier and the fish to themselves for more than an hour, and the fish took their flies on nearly every cast. Finally, when it was getting too dark to see the flies on the water, they called it a night. They'd gone three hours without thinking at all about Barnstaple's unlucky accident victims.

THE STORE AT BRODERICK'S stayed open late from Memorial Day to Labor Day. Peter and Gordon went in on the way back to their cabins (leaning their fly rods on the wall near the front door) and bought ice cream bars, which they unwrapped at the picnic table in front of Gordon's cabin. Lights were on in most of the cabins, and the gleeful shrieks of children playing past their usual bedtime pierced the cool night air.

"Do you want to call Stella?" Gordon asked. Stella Savoy, an emergency-room nurse, had been in an on-again-off-again relationship with Peter for several years.

"Wouldn't matter if I did," Peter said, taking a small bite of his bar. "She's working swing shift tonight. I can get started on those newspapers while you're talking to Elizabeth."

Gordon said yes, and in a few minutes Peter finished his ice cream and went inside. Gordon sat alone with his thoughts for several minutes. The light from the cabins only slightly diminished the brilliance of the stars above, and an occasional sigh of wind rustled the tops of the trees, raining a few pine needles on the picnic table. When the other noises died down temporarily, he could hear a man's voice in the distance, droning on soothingly. It sounded familiar, and Gordon finally realized it was Vin Scully, calling a Dodgers game on the radio. He found himself wondering what combination of atmospheric conditions and topography enabled the signal to find its way to this spot in the mountains. Then he began thinking about Jim Starr, watching a ball game on TV as he had so many nights before, when his wife left at the top of the fourth inning for a walk from which she wouldn't return alive.

He took out his phone and called Elizabeth.

"Gordon? I was beginning to wonder if you'd call tonight."

"Before we go any further, I want to apologize for being abrupt when you told me to be careful last night."

"I'd forgotten all about it."

"I hope you weren't worrying tonight."

"Not really. I figured the fishing must have been pretty good somewhere."

"It was. Downright sensational, in fact. For three hours, I forgot all about the case."

"How's the case going?"

"I don't know how it's going, but I can tell you where it's going. Nowhere, at the moment."

"Are you sure?"

"Well, Peter seems to think we're picking up valuable information, but we just don't know what it is yet."

"Peter? Optimistic? That's a change."

"I think he's being more contrary than optimistic. We talked to three people and visited the scene of one of the accidents today. All I got out of it was a suspicion or two. I'm hoping you can spur my imagination when you get here."

"We'll have to work that around my painting. I've never seen that part of California, and I'm expecting it to inspire me."

"The light was good today."

Neither of them said anything for a minute, then Elizabeth broke the silence.

"Gordon, I'm not sure about this whole couples trip thing."

"Because of Peter?"

"Peter I'm used to. I'm more concerned about Stella. The few times we've been together, we just haven't clicked, and the prospect of having her next to me for a six-hour drive is, well, a bit daunting."

"Be an optimist. Look at it as your chance to really connect with her for the first time."

"I'll try. Really, I will. But what if we're two hours into the trip and it's going badly?"

"Well, Peter said Stella's working the swing shift tonight. She'll probably sleep for half the trip."

"Gordon, I'm not looking for advice. I'm looking for empathy."

"I feel your pain."

"That's not good enough. Say something to make me feel better if the second half of the trip is a disaster."

He thought about it for a minute and finally said:

"Your car has a tape deck, doesn't it?"

PETER HAD FINISHED reading the back issues of the papers surrounding David Rowan's fatal auto crash in March, and the stack sat neatly on the table in front of him.

"Well?" Gordon said.

"I'd rather not say until you've looked at them."

Gordon took the papers and went through them, turning the pages slowly. Twenty minutes later, he set the last issue on top of the others.

"Can't say I see anything there," he said. "How about you?"

"Me neither. Aside from the fact that the water board and its customers don't seem to be improving with the passage of time. Maybe we should put the papers aside and come back to them in a couple of days."

Gordon looked at his watch.

"It's only ten o'clock. How about I make some herbal tea and we each look at the papers the other guy read last night. Then we'll both have gone through all three sets."

"Sure. Why not?"

Peter was halfway through the papers leading up to and following Lucy Starr's death when Gordon returned with the teapot and two cups. Gordon poured out the tea and went through the issues before and after Luther

Whitman's fall from the church tower. Peter was ready to talk when Gordon finished the last page of the last paper.

"You first," Peter said.

"Well, nothing suggests anything new about Luther Whitman, but I think I saw another connection."

Peter raised his eyebrows. Gordon took a paper from the Rowan stack. It was the issue reporting Rowan's death, which was the top story on the front page. There was a picture of his burned, smashed-up pickup and a close-up photo, probably a studio portrait, of Rowan himself. Gordon then opened the paper from Thursday February 17, the issue that came out nine days before Luther Whitman's fall was a front-page story. On page 3 was a full page of photographs from the previous Saturday's Valentine's dance at the Odd Fellows Hall. Gordon set the two papers in front of Peter.

"If I'm not mistaken," he said, pointing to the close-up of Rowan, then to the other page, "that's him at the Valentine's dance."

"All right," Peter said.

"Luther Whitman didn't make the paper then, but he was at the dance, too. And dancing like a dervish, Mrs. Marsh said. That makes two of our accident victims who died within a few weeks of being at that dance. I don't know if that means anything, but it might."

"Maybe," Peter said. "But judging from the paper, most of Barnstaple was at that dance. That Luther Whitman and Dave Rowan were both there hardly qualifies as more than coincidence."

"The odds are in your favor, Peter. But I'm thinking about what you said at dinner. If we're right in thinking those accidents weren't accidents, then the people who died must have known or suspected something about somebody. That means there had to be a point at which they crossed paths with their killer and something came out. I wonder if that dance was the crossing point."

"Insufficient evidence at this stage, Gordon. In a town this size the crossing point could have been plenty of other times and places."

"Granted. But the timing of that dance and the fact so many people were there would have made it a good place for someone to see someone else and make a connection. Let's keep it in mind. And I'm calling Jim Starr tomorrow to see if he and Lucy were there."

"Fair enough."

"And on that note, I think it's time to turn in."

"Aren't you forgetting something, Gordon?"

Gordon gave him a quizzical look.

"You forgot to ask," Peter continued, "whether I picked up any clues in the papers surrounding Lucy Starr's demise."

"Sorry. I'm losing it. Did you?"

"No," Peter said. Gordon picked up the teapot and cups and began carrying them to the sink. "But I did have a thought about an avenue for further investigation."

Gordon put the dishes in the sink and came back to the table.

"Yes?"

"I was reading the story about the finding of Lucy's body," Peter said, "and there was a line in there to the effect that the medical examiner said the injuries to her body were consistent with her being bounced down that river. The language wasn't that blunt, but that was the gist of it. And it got me wondering."

"Wondering what?"

"What the medical examiner found in the autopsy on Olema Marsh."

"That's a damn good question, Peter. Are autopsy reports public records?"

"They are in California, but there's a hitch. The authorities are allowed considerable leeway in determining how fast they have to provide them and what sort of process you have to go through to ask for and get one. So it could take you or me a long time to get hold of that report."

"Hmm."

"On the other hand, a family member should have no difficulty requesting and getting that report."

"Hmm."

"Yeah. So I'm thinking. Tomorrow is Mrs. Marsh's funeral. Maybe you could go up to the family afterwards and ask them if they could request a copy of the report so I could have a look at it."

"Just like that?"

"Put your charm to work."

"Right. 'I'm sorry for your loss, oh, and by the way do you happen to have a copy of the autopsy report that I could borrow?' You're the doctor, Peter. If anybody has to ask, it would make more sense coming from you."

"Look, Gordon. I'm a first-rate surgeon — no false modesty there — but in all the time I've been practicing medicine, no one has ever suggested I have a good bedside manner. This is a job for you."

"Actually, it's more of a job for Elizabeth, but she'll still be on the road at the time of the funeral. And I don't want to take a chance on alienating Mrs. Marsh's family. I may need their help later on."

"I hear you. And this is just a fishing expedition on my part at this point. But if you see an opening ..."

"All right. I'll watch for an opening, but wish me luck. And you've sold me on one point. If there's any talking to be done, let me do it, Peter."

Wednesday June 7

"UNTIL THE LAST HOUR," Stella Savoy said, "it was a pretty quiet shift. Then Marty the Ferret came in and everything went to hell."

"De Fairatt," Elizabeth said. "That's an unusual last name."

"It's not his last name, honey. It's his handle. The. Ferret. As in the polecat-like creature that finds things out."

"I see." Elizabeth paused. "Did he look like a ferret?"

"Hard to say with all the blood on his face. It looked like somebody had been using it for carving practice."

Stella was riding shotgun in Elizabeth's Subaru as they drove over Altamont Pass, leaving the Bay Area behind and heading into California's Central Valley on their way to Barnstaple. The traffic was moving well in their direction, but going the other way — toward Oakland, San Francisco and San Jose — it was at a crawl.

"So he came in by ambulance? Marty?"

"No, no, no. I gather that the cause of his need for medical attention was close on his heels and he didn't want to call 911 and wait for the free ride. He hailed a passing taxi and had them drive him over. Probably bled all over the back seat."

"So it must have happened near the hospital."

Stella snorted. "That's not how it works. We have a reputation for trauma care. When the criminal classes are in need of such attention, they ask for us if they're conscious enough to speak."

"Really?"

"Really. Fact of the matter is, they're all Republicans when it comes to medical choice. Would you believe it — we actually had one guy come in a few years ago and ask if Dr. Delaney was working that night. Wanted to be treated by him if he was. He wasn't."

"Were you and Peter going together then?"

"Actually we weren't. But it made me realize I kind of missed the miserable son of a — sorry. So I called him the next morning, Peter that is, and we ended up getting back together for a little over a year. Life's a funny dog, isn't it?"

"We were talking about Marty the Ferret," Elizabeth said. "Was he seriously hurt?"

"The slice-and-dice somebody did on his face was serious enough. But it wasn't life-threatening. In fact, as soon as the doctors got the bleeding under control, Marty asked me to call his plastic surgeon. I guess he has a regular one."

"That's not a good thing."

"I didn't think so, either."

"Did you call the plastic surgeon for him?"

"Hell no. I told him I wasn't calling anyone for him until he sobered up. He reeked of alcohol."

"Oh. How did he take that?"

"He was pretty docile about it. He's probably heard that before."

Elizabeth murmured something indistinct.

"Then he started talking," Stella said. "The drunks always do, at least when they're conscious, and it can be hard to stop them sometimes. He said this is what happens when he drinks at the wrong bar."

"The wrong bar?"

"Yeah. I asked him how he knows which bar is the wrong one, and he said that's the problem. You don't know until it's too late."

In the back seat, 19-year-old Leah Drake stirred and leaned forward. She had just completed her freshman year at San Francisco State, knew Gordon and Elizabeth from an earlier case of theirs, and was joining them on this trip to assist Elizabeth with her painting. She had been transfixed by the conversation the two women in front had been having since San Francisco. Leah had grown up without a sister, and her mother never said anything interesting in her presence, so, like a sponge, she was soaking up how two successful and apparently grounded women dressed, behaved and spoke to each other in a running conversation. She could have been an anthropologist studying some remote tribe in the jungle, and she was loving every minute of it.

"I don't understand," Leah blurted out. "If he gets his face cut up when he goes into bars, why doesn't he just stop drinking? Or at least not drink in bars."

Stella turned around and looked at Leah, a hint of a smile on her face.

"An excellent question, kid, and one I asked him myself. Would you care to guess how he answered it?"

Leah shook her head.

"He said, are you ready, 'Oh, I couldn't do *that*. How would I have any fun?' "

SHORTLY AFTER 9:15, Gordon and Peter turned off Gemini Lakes Road onto Quail Run Lane. They had an appointment for 9:30 with Diana Rowan, who had been widowed in one of the accidents that made Olema Marsh suspicious. Gordon had wanted to be early in order to take a close look at the road David Rowan and his pickup had run off.

Quail Run Lane was cut into the side of a mountain and rose at a relatively steep grade until it had climbed more than 300 feet to a flat area that had been begun by nature and completed by construction crews to create space for a half-dozen houses. The road was paved, in reasonably good shape, wide enough for two cars to pass slowly, and had no barriers at the edge where it dropped off.

Halfway up, they came to a curve, and Gordon stopped in the middle of the road.

"The story in the paper said he ran off the road at a curve," Gordon said. "This looks like the only one."

On the right, the mountain rose steeply above them. A few scattered pine trees sprung up from the ground, but generally it was lacking in cover. To their left, the hillside fell off sharply, the slope peppered with low brush and boulders. They could see Gemini Lakes Road 150 feet or so below, and the town of Barnstaple in the distance. They were facing northeast as they looked toward the town. The sun was high enough not to be directly in their eyes.

"The sun would have been behind him if it was a clear morning," Peter said. "And I can't see anyone lying in wait here. It'd be a rough climb up that hillside, especially if there was snow or ice on it."

"And no place to park a car," Gordon said.

"That, too."

They continued to the top of the road. At the flat, it widened enough to accommodate cars parked on both sides. It ran by six houses, all with their front doors facing the road and their back sides overlooking the valley and the mountain ranges on all sides. It ended at a loop in front of the seventh house, which bore the number 179 — the Rowan home. It was built about ten feet above the road, with a wide driveway. Gordon parked against the curb on the loop, and they walked up the driveway to the front door. Peter was slightly winded by the time they got there.

Diana Rowan opened the door before they found the doorbell. She was a plump woman, about five-eight, with light-brown hair and brown eyes. Even when she was standing in place, parts of her were constantly in motion, as if an electrical current was running through her body. She invited them in and offered coffee and muffins. They accepted, and she brought the food and drink out with twice the normal amount of motion such a task would take. Gordon wondered if she had always been such a bundle of nervous energy and movement or if the unexpected death of her husband had increased that tendency.

Peter and Gordon were seated on a large couch in a living room near a picture window overlooking the valley. They sipped their coffee and nibbled on their muffins for a moment, while she watched them.

"This is an excellent blueberry muffin," Gordon finally said. "My compliments."

"Thank you."

He and Peter took another sip of coffee.

"Thank you for meeting with us," Gordon said.

"Olema asked me to. Wasn't it awful what happened to her? We've had so many tragedies in this town the last few months."

"She seemed to think so, too."

"Are you going to the funeral?"

"Yes we are."

"There should be a good turnout. She was really held in high regard."

Gordon nodded.

"There were a lot of people at all three funerals. The accident funerals."

"I can imagine."

"I hope this is the last one."

Gordon couldn't think of a response that wasn't inane, so he said nothing. There was a silence, then she continued.

"I don't know if I can help you."

"I don't know either, but I appreciate your willingness to try. This is awkward for us, too, and I'm at a bit of a disadvantage in not knowing what Mrs. Marsh told you when she asked if you could meet with me."

"She said she didn't believe the accidents were accidents and she was asking you to look into it."

Gordon nodded. Diana Rowan was tense and nervous, and he needed to get her more at ease before he raised the points he wanted to talk about.

"I really don't know where to start," he said. "And I'm still feeling my way around this town. Could I ask you to tell me a bit about your husband and the sporting goods store, and how you met?"

"What do you want to know?"

"Let's begin with the store. I've been coming up to the mountains since I was a kid, and Rowan's Rod and Gun has been here at least since then. When did it get started?"

"After the war," she said. "Dave's father, Bob, bought out the fellow who owned it before. In 1946." She seemed to unwind slightly as she talked about the past.

"Was he from around here?"

She shook her head. "Carson City. His father, Dave's grandpa, was a Nevada state senator. But Bob figured that after the war, people would be going back to work and taking vacations and that there was money to be made from that."

"A shrewd businessman," Peter said. "He was right."

"He married his high school sweetheart and bought the store when he got out of the Marines. Dave came along in 1948."

"Is Bob still alive?" Gordon asked.

"He died in '95. Cancer. He was a smoker. He was 74."

"And Dave took over the store?"

"He bought out his dad nine years before that. And now Michael, our son, will probably be taking it over."

"So it'll stay in the family," Peter said.

"We hope so."

"And how did you and Dave meet?" Gordon said.

"At college, when he got back from the Army."

"He was in the Army?" Gordon did the math in his head. David Rowan would have been 18 in 1966, just as the Vietnam War was escalating toward the highest American troop levels.

"He served in Vietnam. He was very proud of that — that he went. But he never talked about what he did."

"A lot of soldiers don't," Peter said.

"He was a door gunner in a Huey. That's all I can tell you."

"That speaks volumes about his courage."

"He didn't see it that way. He said he was just doing what he had to do. Like all the other soldiers."

Gordon sensed that it might be time to move to the matter at hand.

"This has been very helpful," Gordon said. "It establishes that you have deep roots in this town. Could we get back to Mrs. Marsh?"

She nodded, a bit less jerkily than before.

"Can I ask — and stop me if this is feeling uncomfortable — what you thought when Mrs. Marsh said she didn't believe the accidents were accidents?"

"I was surprised."

"So it had never occurred to you that there was something strange about all those accidents in that short a period of time?"

"I didn't say that. Of course I thought it was strange. But what could they be if they weren't accidents? The people it happened to didn't have an enemy in the world."

"Including Dave?" Peter asked.

"Especially Dave. If Barnstaple was a real city, he could have been the mayor. He wasn't just liked — he was respected."

"And he hadn't been worried about anything at the time?"

"Only how good business would be this summer. The store gets three-quarters of its sales between Memorial Day and Labor Day. But he worried about that every year."

"Could I ask a quick question?" Peter said. "The night before your husband's accident, was his car parked in the garage?"

She stared at him for several seconds, her mouth open.

"I'd forgotten about that. It was parked outside that night. Dave had a dresser he was refinishing that weekend in the garage. His car was parked outside Saturday and Sunday. I remember it was covered with ice in the morning. But surely you don't think ..."

"We don't think anything yet," Gordon said. "Just trying to ask questions."

"It can't be," she said. "Anyone who came up here would be really obvious."

Gordon felt the interview was getting out of hand and had mixed feelings about it. On the one hand, Peter had asked a question that Gordon hadn't thought of and elicited what could be a critically important fact. On the other hand, he wished it had happened at the end of the interview, when he didn't still have a critical question of his own to ask.

"You have a good point there," Gordon said. "People aren't just going to be driving through here, and a stranger would be obvious, as you say. Let's drop it for now and let me ask just one more question, then we'll leave you be."

He reached into his messenger bag and took out a copy of *The Barnstaple Miner*. He opened it to the page of photos of the Valentine's Day dance.

"I'm guessing from this picture of Dave that you and he were at the Valentine's Day affair at the Odd Fellows Hall."

She looked puzzled.

"Yes, but so was just about everybody else in town."

"And it's probably nothing, but I'm just looking at every loose end. Do you remember anything unusual happening there?"

"No, not really."

"No arguments? No unusual comments?"

"Nothing. People were having a really good time, that's all."

"And did Dave say anything to you about it afterward? Anything you can remember?"

She was staring straight ahead, utterly motionless.

"Mrs. Rowan," Peter said, in his best calm-doctor voice.

"No, no. I'm all right. It's just that I'd forgotten all about it until Mr. Gordon asked."

Gordon leaned forward and shot Peter a keep-quiet look.

"Dave seemed to be more quiet than usual on the way home, and when we got back, I asked him if anything was wrong. He said he'd had a conversation about Vietnam at the party and it had bothered him."

"Did he say 'bothered' or 'upset'?" Gordon asked.

"He said 'bothered,' but that could have meant 'upset,' too. Dave wasn't good at talking about his feelings."

"Did he say who the conversation was with?"

"He might have. I think he did, but I don't remember."

"You wouldn't know who it might be?"

"There were so many people there, and everyone was moving around. It could have been anyone. Why? Is it important?"

"I don't know," Gordon said. "We're in the early stages of collecting information, and it's hard to say what's important or not." He took a card from his shirt pocket and handed it to her. "But if you remember who he was talking to about Vietnam, I'd appreciate a call."

THEY DROVE BACK to Broderick's in silence and went into Gordon's cabin. Two cups of relatively hot coffee remained in the thermal carafe, and Gordon poured them at the table. They each took a couple of sips before he spoke.

"What do you think, Peter? Does this have something to do with Vietnam?"

"I don't know. What do you think?"

"I was hoping you'd go first. I think it might, but I was thinking about it all the way back and I can't see how."

"A lot of stuff happened in Vietnam that doesn't get talked about much. Do you think David Rowan did something that came back to get him?"

"He could have. Or he could know something about someone else and had to be silenced. But either way, how does that account for the other accidents?"

"There's another possibility, you know," Peter said.

"What's that?"

"What if these weren't all crimes, as we're thinking. What if one or two of the accidents were really accidents, and the others were murders? How would we tell which was which?"

"Just what we need," Gordon said. "Another complication. I'm starting to feel the problems with this case are piling up faster than the evidence."

"We can't think like that. We have to keep digging until we connect the dots."

"You're mixing metaphors."

"You know what I mean."

They drank more of the coffee.

"I'll tell you one thing, though," Peter said.

"What?"

"I've concluded if I want to live to a ripe old age, I should move to Barnstaple."

"Why?"

"Because the only people who seem to die here before their time are the ones who haven't got an enemy in the world. With my disagreeable personality, I could live forever."

ELIZABETH PULLED OFF THE HIGHWAY at a small town in the foothills near the beginning of the pass that would take them to Barnstaple. It was an old Gold Rush town that had been rejuvenated in recent years by an influx of retirees and people seeking to get away from the stress and crowds of urban life. They saw a delicatessen on Main Street and decided to stop for lunch. There were two empty diagonal parking spaces on the street in front of it, and Elizabeth pulled into one.

"A parking space right in front of the restaurant? We're not in San Francisco anymore," Stella said.

The deli was in an old brick building that might have been an office at one time. It had 14 tables inside and another seven out the side door in a former alley between the deli and the next building. Elizabeth ordered a tuna salad sandwich, Leah had a turkey and ham sandwich with a bowl of clam chowder, and Stella ordered a cup of vegetable soup and a side salad with oil and vinegar dressing. The cashier gave them a number that they took to one of the outside tables.

It was warming up in the foothills, but in the alley it was shady and pleasant. Stella had on a pair of oversize sunglasses, Elizabeth was wearing her regular glasses, which were tinted, and young Leah wore no glasses at all.

"So," Elizabeth said, "you think Peter's getting serious?"

"He does from time to time."

"And?"

"And, I'd have to be crazy to marry a man who's already had five failed marriages."

"He was drinking then. He's gone nearly four years without a drink now. He must be at least a little bit better."

"I knew him when he was still drinking, and trust me, he's better. But you have to consider what the baseline was." She turned to Leah. "What do you think of Peter? You can tell the truth."

Leah took a sip of her iced tea. "I don't know him as well as you do," she finally said, "and I know he can be irritable and cranky sometimes ..."

"Don't forget opinionated," Stella said.

"That, too. But I get the feeling he's a decent guy." Leah turned to Elizabeth. "I mean, he probably wouldn't be Gordon's friend if he wasn't, right?"

"I guess not," Elizabeth said. "Gordon tends to shy away from people who need reforming."

"It's probably a question of how much coal you're willing to cut through to get to the diamond underneath," Stella said. "And there's no escaping the fact that we keep breaking up with each other."

There was a pregnant silence, which Leah finally broke.

"But you keep getting back together, too. Maybe you should think about the reasons for that."

Stella let out a horse laugh. She shook her head.

"From the mouths of babes," she said.

The food arrived and they began eating. After a few minutes Stella turned to Leah again.

"Am I imagining things, or are you looking at my food?"

"Sorry," Leah said. "It's just that you don't seem to be eating very much."

"I can't afford to, kid. I'm 46 years old, so in less than four years I'll be 50. You know what they say about a woman over 50?"

Leah shook her head.

"A woman over 50 is like Greece. Rich in history, but with only a few antiquities left worth visiting."

Leah and Elizabeth both laughed, but Elizabeth caught herself right away.

"That's horrible," she said. "Did Peter say that?"

"Not Peter, honey. One of the other doctors. He thought he was being funny. I set him straight."

"Good for you."

"Unfortunately it's true. Maybe Peter's my best hope."

THE CHURCH WASN'T big enough to seat all the mourners at Olema Marsh's funeral, and Gordon and Peter found themselves standing against the back wall. Jim Starr was in a pew a few rows ahead of them; Kathryn and Skip Henry were closer to the front; Judy Beck and a man Gordon assumed to be her husband, Scott, were seated near the center aisle; Diana Rowan sat in the back. Sheriff Kanehl stood at the side of the church, opposite Gordon and Peter, arms folded, looking at the crowd. Gordon wondered if the sheriff was on duty or paying respects, then his mind wandered to the ghosts of those who couldn't be there: Lucy Starr, David Rowan and Luther Whitman.

The service started 15 minutes late to allow everyone in and some time to come up with folding chairs for the more elderly standees. Gordon found himself absent-mindedly singing along with the hymns and half-listening to the prayers. He wanted to hear what people would say about Olema Marsh.

In addition to Pastor Moody, who moved things along and lent the proceedings an appropriate tone, three people spoke about Mrs. Marsh.

Her daughter Marilyn talked about what a good mother Olema Marsh had been, raising her children to be kind to others, work hard, and never look the other way if they thought something was wrong. Gordon couldn't help thinking that Mrs. Marsh had certainly possessed the latter quality herself, and that it may have led to her premature death.

Maxwell Rutherford, the editor of *The Barnstaple Miner*, who had known Olema Marsh for years, talked about how whenever there was a community activity or fund-raiser she was actively involved. He told a couple of humorous stories about her insisting something be done differently or better and drew a few chuckles from the audience.

Throughout the proceedings, Gordon was keeping an eye on the other mourners. Diana Rowan was sitting stoically through the proceedings, as if in a state of shock. Jim Starr was focusing relentlessly on what the speakers were saying, as if to crowd his own sorrow out of his mind. Kathryn Henry was fighting back tears, dabbing at her eyes with a tissue in her left hand while her husband held her right hand in both of his. Judy Beck looked agitated and emotional, and her husband looked uncomfortable.

The final speaker, to Gordon's surprise, was Sheriff Rod Kanehl, who turned out to have a gift for public speaking. He praised the work she had done on Sheriff's Posse fund-raisers, the youth programs she had developed while working at the library, and the high regard in which she was held by the community. He concluded by saying:

"And last, but not least, Olema was the most honest person I've ever met. You always knew where you stood with her, and she was one of the few people in the community who would tell me to my face when she didn't think I was doing my job right." Gordon suppressed a smile, wondering how many people in the church picked up the full meaning of his remarks. The sheriff continued, "Olema Marsh's life was a gift to the town of Barnstaple, and we are all going to miss her more than we realize."

There was a reception afterward in the parish hall. A groaning buffet table was fully covered with all sorts of food, along with wine, beer and other beverages. When Peter saw the alcohol, he took Gordon aside.

"I don't usually mind being around people drinking," he said, "but intense emotion mixed with alcohol still gives me the jitters. If it's OK with you, I'm going to take a pass on this."

Gordon nodded. "I'll stay just long enough to get a bite to eat and talk with the daughter. Maybe 45 minutes to an hour."

"I'll wait for you at the Happy Scoop."

Gordon let the locals have first access to Olema Marsh's family. It was half an hour before the line dwindled to a few people. He shook hands with Olema's brother, Hugh, who had driven down from Reno. He introduced himself to her other daughter, Linda Farrell, and said a few general words of condolence. Then he got to Marilyn Rossi.

"I'm so glad you could come," she said.

"Nothing would have kept me away." He looked around. He'd been the last in line, and Hugh and Linda were moving away. He lowered his voice. "I'm going to keep working on what she asked me to look into in Barnstaple. I feel it's the least I can do, and I think it's what she would have wanted."

"I think so, too." She looked around. "I came across something last night. Can we step outside and talk?"

THE SOAP OPERA ENDED, and Millicent Samuels turned off the TV set. She'd already eaten a light lunch (she didn't seem hungry these days), and a long, lonely afternoon lay ahead. She missed Walter. Even though they hadn't talked all that much in recent years, having him around the house made her feel comfortable.

She felt the anxiety coming on and knew she had to do something. She decided to walk to the corner store three blocks away and buy a quart of milk. She didn't really need the milk, but she needed the walk and needed to get out of the lonely house.

Despite walking slowly and exchanging some banter with Rasheed, the store owner's son, she was back in just over half an hour. The walk had helped, but the long afternoon still loomed in front of her. She looked at the new computer, a blueberry iMac her son had given her for Christmas. She was still a novice on it, but she was learning and had begun to find out it was fun looking things up on the internet. She made a small pot of Constant Comment tea, poured herself a cup, and slid into the chair in front of the screen.

"What should I look up?" she thought, as she turned it on.

She thought about her walk through the familiar Long Beach neighborhood and how going and coming she had passed the small stucco house that still hadn't sold in five years. She occasionally thought about the neighbor who had lived there and decided to type her name into the search engine, just to get started.

What came up was not at all what she was expecting.

The website had a strange name, but she couldn't take her eyes off the featured article. She read it twice, and by the time she was finished, her stomach was in a knot, her palms were damp, and her hands had developed a tremor. Her untouched tea was getting cold.

Agitated, she got up and walked around the house. Finally, she went to the drawer in the kitchen where she kept brochures, business cards and other such materials. She found the business card she was looking for at the bottom of the pile at the back of the drawer.

As she picked up the phone, she realized her mouth was completely dry. She filled a large glass with water, drank it all, and moved to the phone again. She tried to think what she would say, but nothing came to her, and after several minutes she decided just to call. It was answered on the second ring.

"Homicide bureau, Detective Judd," said a husky female voice on the other end.

"Oh. You're still there."

"I'm afraid so. May I ask who's calling?"

"I'm sorry. You probably don't remember me. My name is Millie Samuels. I was one of the neighbors you interviewed when Francine Hawes was murdered five years ago."

"Actually I do remember you, as I remember that case. It was one of our failures, and it still bothers me." She paused, and then, trying too hard to sound casual, continued, "Have *you* remembered something?"

"No."

"I wouldn't expect so, after all this time."

"But I might have found something."

Millie could hear Detective Judd moving in her chair on the other end.

"Have you ever heard of a man named Carl La Fong?" Millie said.

"No. That's a pretty unusual name. I'm sure I would have remembered it. Who is he?"

"I don't know, but he has a website." She pulled up short. Her mouth felt as if she had never drunk the water, and her throat had tightened up. She didn't think she could get a word out but forced herself.

"There's something on it about Francine Hawes," Millie said. "It's very disturbing, and I'm hoping you can tell me it's not true."

MARILYN ROSSI AND GORDON stepped outside and walked across the church lawn to a bench in the shade of three pines at the edge of the grounds. The temperature had climbed into the high 80s, and the shade was welcome. They sat down and he waited for her to speak. It took a minute.

"I don't know," she said. "It really affected me." She lapsed into silence again.

"You said inside that you came across something last night. Does that mean you found something you weren't expecting to find or found something in a place that suggested it was being concealed?"

"Both, I think." She sighed. "I've been sorting through the things in the house, and last night I was in the kitchen. There's a shelf of cookbooks, and I was going through them to see if there was anything my sister or I might want when I came across this."

She reached into her large purse and pulled out a book that Gordon recognized as a common brand of notebook.

"I had no idea she was keeping a journal," Marilyn said, "though when I thought about it, I realized it made sense. I wasn't sure if I should read it, then I remembered something she said to me a few years ago. 'You can read anything of mine you like after I'm gone. My life is an open book, and if going through my papers helps you remember me, that would be lovely.' So I did."

Gordon nodded.

"I thought I'd start when she was in Bodega Bay last month and read to the final entry. What jumped out was how concerned she was about the accidents in town and how much hope she was putting on you to figure it out. She thought you were the second coming of Sherlock Holmes and Hercule Poirot."

"That's a bit extravagant," Gordon said. "And it seems to me she had a bit of Miss Marple in her own makeup."

"I guess she did. But this whole situation was troubling her more than she let on to me. And in the last few entries she made, she was getting even more agitated." She opened the book and turned to a page. "I'd like you to read the end of the last entry. It was written the night before she ..." She handed him the book. The entry was dated June 1, which would have been the night before Olema Marsh had her fatal 'accident.'

The feeling of anxiety is almost more than I can bear, and I am counting not just the hours but the minutes and seconds until Mr. Gordon arrives. The suspicion I am forming can't be shared with anyone in town — can't even be committed to this journal. If I am wrong — and I fervently hope I am — no one must know I ever thought such a thing. I must confide in an outsider, and Mr. Gordon will be the one. Only three more days to get through before I can get this off my chest.

"Wow," Gordon said, setting the book on his lap. "I don't suppose there was anything before this to suggest what she was thinking?"

"Not a thing, and I've read it over three times now. But the fact she was so worried has me worried, too. Do you think I should take this to the sheriff?"

Gordon knew the answer but took a few seconds to phrase his reply.

"Not yet," he said. "The sheriff already knows your mother was suspicious, and he's discounted that. It would be good to have something more concrete to take to him. Would you be willing to give me a few days to see if I can turn anything up?"

She hesitated for a minute, then nodded.

"My mother trusted you," she said. "I should, too. See what you can find out. And feel free to keep that," she gestured to the journal, "if you think it will help."

"As long as you're all right with it."

"I'm all right as long as you return it."

"Give me a day or two to go through it, and I'll give you a call."

She nodded. "Is there anything else I can do?"

"No, I don't think so. Wait! I just remembered something." He paused again. "This is an unusual request, and it may be a bit touchy ..."

"Just say it. If something happened to my mother, I want to get to the bottom of it."

"All right, then. Dr. Delaney and I were talking last night about this investigation, and he said he thought it would be helpful if he could see the coroner's report on your mother's death. Peter's a first-rate medical man and a great believer in second opinions."

"What does it take to get the report?"

"A family member should be able to get it just by asking, and maybe paying a copying fee for putting it together. Would you be willing to do that? I'll pay for the copying, if there's a charge."

"We were going to Sierra Pines — my sister and I — tomorrow. That's where the medical examiner's office is. Mother's still there, and we have to sign to release the body, and there's a funeral home there that does cremations. That's what she wanted."

"You should be able to ask for a copy of the report and get it in a few hours."

"I'll do that. But we're going over late morning, and probably won't be back until the evening."

"We can come by and pick it up on Friday. It's not likely the coroner missed anything, but it might suggest something to Peter."

"I can't tell you how relieved I am that you're looking into this."

"There's no guarantee I'll find something. In fact, the odds lean the other way."

"But you're carrying out mother's last wish, even though she didn't know at the time that's what it was. Whatever you do or don't turn up, that matters. It matters a lot."

"I'll do what I can," Gordon said.

She looked at her watch.

"And I need to get back to being the hostess." She stood up. "Are you going back in?"

"Not holding this," Gordon replied, gesturing with the journal. "Give the rest of the family my regards."

She nodded and started back across the lawn.

"CAN I ASK YOU a question, Elizabeth?"

"Yes, you may, Leah."

"You played basketball in college, didn't you?"

"Uh-huh. I went to the University of Iowa on a full athletic scholarship. Just like Gordon at Cal."

"Gordon must have been pretty good. One of my professors was at Cal back then and he remembers him."

"That's his reputation, all right."

"How good do you think you were?"

"Good enough to start junior and senior year."

"So pretty good. And that's what my question's about. Do you and Gordon ever play basketball together?"

Elizabeth kept her eyes on the road and took several seconds to answer.

"No. We never have, and I doubt we ever will."

"How come? If you have something like that in common, why don't you enjoy it with each other?"

"I don't think Gordon enjoys it in that way. He's a competitor, and his ability is part of his identity. I'm not sure he could handle being shown up, especially by me."

"You think that would happen?"

"I'm younger and quicker than he is. I don't think he'd want to take the chance."

Stella laughed. "It would serve him right," she said.

"Why do you say that?" Leah asked.

"Stella," Elizabeth said, "why don't you call Peter and tell him we're about 20 minutes from Barnstaple."

HAPPY SCOOP WAS ONLY two blocks from the church, so Gordon walked there, Olema Marsh's journal in his right hand. Peter was seated at a table under a large umbrella in the side courtyard.

"What have we here?" Peter said, gesturing toward the notebook.

"We have here the final journal of Mrs. Marsh, right down to the last entry, the night before she died. She was treading lightly when she wrote it, but it would appear she was beginning to suspect someone. We got here a couple of days too late to find out who."

"Too bad. We're not exactly finding out a lot on our own. Anything else in it?"

"I haven't had a chance to look, but I will."

"How'd you get it?"

"Marilyn Rossi found it in the house."

"That goes against the idea of Mrs. Marsh being killed. Surely the journal is the first thing the killer would have taken away."

"Actually, it was pretty well hidden. In plain sight, really. It was tucked in with the cookbooks on a shelf in the kitchen."

"First place I'd have looked for it, but let's count our blessings."

"This helps in more ways than one. When the daughter read it, she swung over to our side a bit more. It gave me a chance to ask if she could get a copy of the medical report for us. She said yes right away. You should have a copy of that report on Friday."

"If they did a good job on the autopsy, it should at least rule out a thing or two."

Peter's phone rang.

"It's Stella," he said, and answered. He listened for a few seconds then held the phone off to the side and addressed Gordon. "They're about 20 minutes away now."

"Tell them to meet us here. Ice cream's on me."

"Last of the big spenders." Peter relayed the message, got a confirmation, and hung up.

"So are we going to get any fishing in once the women arrive?"

"We should be able to," Gordon said. "Elizabeth will be painting."

"Where?"

"There's a ghost town about 20 miles from here, up a bad road. It's called Buckley. She wants to check that out. If it's not what she hoped for, she'll drive around and see what else catches her eye. Leah will be with her, earning her keep for the trip."

"What about Stella?"

"She'll have three choices. She can go with Elizabeth and Leah. She can come with us if we go out fishing. Or she can chill at the resort. It's not a bad place to relax."

"Actually, New York is more her idea of a place to relax. But it's only for a week, right?"

"Most people can handle just about anything for a week."

They talked for a quarter hour until Elizabeth's Subaru passed the ice cream stand, slowed and pulled to the curb. Gordon and Peter went to meet them, and there were hugs and greetings all around.

"This was a good idea," Elizabeth said. "The thermometer at the bank said it's 87 degrees."

"Almost no humidity, though," Gordon said.

They went to the window and ordered. Elizabeth, Leah, Gordon and Peter asked for frostys of various sizes. Stella asked if they served nonfat ice cream, got a what-planet-are-you-from look from the kid behind the window, and ordered the smallest frosty they had. The table Gordon and Peter had been sitting at was just large enough to hold the five of them, and Gordon adjusted the umbrella so that the women were in the shade.

"So how's the investigation going?" Stella asked when they sat down.

"We're compiling a lot of information," Gordon said.

"In other words, you haven't got squat."

"Early days, Stella. Early days."

His phone rang, and the number was from the local area code.

"Gordon!" came Marilyn Rossi's voice from the other end. "Thank God."

"I'm surprised it's you," he said. "Calling from a local number."

"I had to borrow Kathryn Henry's phone, and she still had your card in her purse. Listen, do you have that journal?"

"Right on the table in front of me."

"Well, guard it with your life. Someone stole my purse from the parish hall, and I think it may have been the journal they were after."

AFTER REASSURING Marilyn Rossi that the journal would be safe in his care, Gordon handed it to Elizabeth and asked her to keep it in her purse, out of sight. They discussed dinner arrangements and decided to cook dinner at the cabin. Elizabeth and Stella offered to do the grocery shopping at the DeLuxe Supermarket and sent Leah off to Broderick's with Gordon and Peter.

Leah had one suitcase, a battered, old medium-size hand-me-down of the grip variety, which they put in the cabin Gordon and Elizabeth were occupying. It was slightly larger than Peter and Stella's cabin, with a bedroom and a fold-down couch for Leah in the main living area. With no chores to tend to, Leah took a copy of Dickens' *Martin Chuzzlewit* from the suitcase

("Assigned reading for my Victorian Literature class this summer," she explained) and claimed one of the chairs on the front porch.

"I'm starting to wish I hadn't given the journal to Elizabeth," Gordon said. "I'd kind of like to see what's in the rest of it."

"It'll be here soon enough," Peter said. "They can't stay in that market all afternoon. Do we have time for a bit of fishing?"

"A bit early yet, I think. But go ahead if you want. I'll stay here and act *in loco parentis* for Leah."

Peter went to his cabin, picked up his fly rod and waved as he walked by again on the way to the lake. Gordon waved back. Leah was focused on the book. Gordon made himself a cup of tea and went to one of the windows while he drank it.

After a few minutes, three fit and wiry young men, college students most likely, walked by. One of them looked up at the porch, held his eyes on Leah for a moment, then kept going. After they had gone another 60 feet, the young man who looked stopped and came back to the cabin. He put his foot on one of the three steps leading up to the porch.

"Hi," he said. "My name is Brian."

Leah lowered the book to her lap and looked at him. "Leah."

"Have you been here long?"

"No," she said. "I just got here a half hour ago."

"I thought so. I'm sure I would have noticed you before." He gestured to her book. "You must be going to school if you're reading that."

"Uh-huh."

"Mind if I ask where?"

"San Francisco State."

"Sweet. I'm at Santa Clara."

"That's nice."

"So, Leah, we have a volleyball game on the lawn every night. We could always use a few more players. Would you like to join us?"

"I don't know."

"It's a lot of fun, and nobody takes it too seriously. You should give it a try."

"Well, all right." She looked at the door, but Gordon was out of sight inside. "If nothing else is going on."

"If you can't make it tonight, you can come tomorrow."

"All right. What time?"

"We start around 6:45 and play until it gets too dark to keep going. If you're having a late dinner, you can join us partway through."

Leah nodded. "Thanks."

"Good. Then we'll see you there. Tonight. Or tomorrow. Or the night after."

She smiled. "You're persistent."

"Just want you to know you're welcome. See you tonight, I hope."

And with a wave, he was off. Inside the cabin, Gordon smiled.

ELIZABETH AND STELLA pulled into Broderick's 45 minutes later, with two bags of groceries in the trunk of the Subaru. Gordon carried the bags into the cabin, and Elizabeth set to unpacking them and putting the perishables into the refrigerator.

"Peter's on the lake shore somewhere, trying his luck with the fish," Gordon said to Stella. "I have the second key to your cabin. I'll walk you over."

Her suitcase was large enough and heavy enough that carrying it made him wonder if he was growing older. He opened the door to the cabin and set the suitcase on top of the bed so it could more easily be opened and unpacked. Stella looked around the cabin.

"It's not the Ritz Carlton, but it'll do."

"They're trying for rustic, I think," Gordon said.

"And succeeding. But it was good to smell the pine trees on the way over. It's been a long time since I could actually smell a tree."

Gordon left her to unpack and went back to his cabin. Leah had stood up to greet Elizabeth and Stella when they arrived and was back in her book, seeming to make good progress. Gordon walked past her, closed the door to the cabin, and said, "Well?"

"It was a hell of a negotiation getting the provisions," Elizabeth said. "You have me to thank for the fact there will be chicken in the stir-fry tonight. She was going for tofu."

"Thank you."

"They didn't have any. All she could talk about was how the store seemed to be nothing but canned food."

"They're supplying campers this time of year. And I expect during the winter, people have to be stocked up in case they get snowed in."

"I suppose so. Anyway, she was annoyed that the vegetables in the produce section weren't organic."

"In a mountain town this size, you count your blessings they're fresh."

"You and I know that, Gordon. She doesn't. I hope she doesn't start moping around because this isn't San Francisco."

"Well, on the positive side, she did say she enjoyed the smell of the pine trees."

"Maybe there's hope. Anyway, we should eat all right tonight. How's Leah liking it?"

"She seems totally absorbed in her book. Oh, and she already has a date for tonight."

"What?"

"Relax. Some young man invited her to join in the volleyball game on the lawn tonight."

"Are you sure that's all right?"

Gordon shrugged. "They've been playing every night since Peter and I got here, and the sheriff hasn't been called in yet. And it's only a hundred yards or so away. I wouldn't worry."

"Her parents would."

"They're not here. Say, can I get Olema Marsh's journal?"

Elizabeth took it from her purse and handed it over.

"If you don't need me to help with dinner, I'd like to look this over now. Then I'd like you to read it after dinner."

"While you're washing the dishes?"

"Exactly what I was thinking. Then we can compare notes."

THEY ATE DINNER on the picnic table in front of Gordon and Elizabeth's cabin. Elizabeth, Stella and Leah had put together a meal of stir-fry chicken and vegetables, rice and salad. Stella went heavy on the salad and light on the stir-fry; everyone else did the opposite. They managed to keep a good conversation going throughout, and Gordon — knowing about Elizabeth's tension with Stella — reckoned the first group dinner to be a reasonable success.

After the meal, Peter and Stella took a walk along the trail that curved partway around the lake, Leah went off to her volleyball game, and Gordon cleaned up while Elizabeth read Olema Marsh's journal. Gordon had picked up something during his afternoon reading of it and wanted to discuss it with Elizabeth.

By seven o'clock the temperature had dropped from the 80s into the 70s, with a slight breeze coming over from the other side of the lake. Gordon made tea, and they took their cups to a solitary picnic table near the lake, not too far from the volleyball game.

"I'm wondering if you picked up on the same thing I did," Gordon said.

"You mean May 26th?"

"Was that Friday, almost two weeks ago?"

"I think so. You first."

"Well, up to then, she said, whenever she mentioned the accidents, that she was concerned about the situation, but it seemed she had no idea what was going on. When I talked to her in Bodega Bay, she certainly didn't. But that day, the Friday, it seemed she was starting to twig to what was going on."

"I think the way she put it in the journal," Elizabeth said, "was 'Something happened today that made me rethink the so-called accidents.' That's all she said, but the feeling started coming out more over the next few days until that last entry, the night before she died, where she was beginning to be afraid of what she was thinking."

"Damn it," Gordon said. "Why didn't she say what the something was that happened to make her rethink it? Her coyness couldn't have come at a worse time in terms of our investigation. It reminds me of a case I had before I met you, where we wasted all sorts of time because someone confided everything in her life to her journal — except the key fact we needed."

"You have to remember she was afraid of what she was thinking. But there is one way we might get at it. If she kept a calendar."

"I know she did. Her daughter said I was on it." He looked at his watch. "It's only a bit after eight. Let me try her."

He called and caught Marilyn Rossi at her mother's house.

"I'm glad you called," she said. "I was going to tell you they found the purse."

"Oh, really?"

"In some shrubbery outside the church. The money was missing, but it was only about 40 dollars. The important thing is that the wallet and credit cards were still there."

"Good to hear," Gordon said.

"So it was probably just a kid trying to get some cash."

Gordon wasn't so sure of that, but he didn't argue the point. He got straight to his reason for calling.

"I was wondering if you could help me out. I recall your mother had an appointment calendar."

"She certainly did."

"Could I trouble you to dig it up and see what was on the calendar for Friday May 26th?"

"Just a minute."

It took her two. "I have it right here," she said. "The 26th, you said?"

"That's right."

"The only thing on it is an appointment with Dr. McCullough at 10 o'clock. I think he's her dentist in Sierra Pines."

"That's all?"

"Afraid so."

"How about the two days beforehand?"

"Empty. Is it important?"

"I don't know. I'm just checking against her journal entry. Could I ask you to keep that calendar in a safe place in case I have to consult it again?"

She agreed, and they ended the conversation. Gordon shared the news with Elizabeth.

"That was a good idea," he said, "but no go."

"So whatever happened that day must have been something that came up in the course of her normal daily activities."

"It would seem so. And good luck figuring that out. But at least Marilyn Rossi's purse turned up. She figures it was taken by a kid."

"Do you believe that?"

"I'm not sure I do. If someone was after her mother's journal, and it was someone smart enough to kill four people without making the sheriff suspicious, this is exactly what they'd do. Make it look like a quick-grab cash theft and get the purse back to her before she makes too much of a stink about it."

Gordon leaned back in his chair.

"Anyway," he said, "it looks as if the trip is getting off to a good start. That was a nice, convivial dinner we had."

"It still leaves us with six more meals to plan, and I'm telling you, Stella is obsessed about her diet. She's worried about getting old and fat."

"She seems to look all right to Peter," Gordon said. "That and feeling good about herself should be all that matters. However, there's a fallback position for dealing with Stella's diet."

"What's that?"

"We can always bump up the restaurant budget for the trip. So she can order for herself."

Thursday June 8

THE FIRST TIME Elizabeth and Leah drove by the turnoff to the ghost town of Buckley, they missed it altogether and kept going for several miles before realizing the mistake. On the way back, Leah spotted the sign (not a large one) on the right side of the road, and Elizabeth made the turn.

The road to Buckley was easy to miss, in part because it went straight into a canyon, out of sight of the highway. A mile up, it opened onto a meadow, framed by wildflowers, where at least a thousand sheep were grazing. A solitary sheepherder with a border collie at his side was tending to them. On the far side of the meadow, against a hill that would block out the afternoon sun, stood a small travel trailer, apparently home to the sheepherder and the dog.

Five miles from the highway, the road went from badly paved to reasonably good gravel and hugged the side of a mountain as it climbed upward, dropping off to a series of ravines and small meadows below. In three more miles, it became a dirt road, and not a terribly good one. Elizabeth had to swerve and slow down for numerous bumps and potholes. They had gone high enough by now that the snow-capped Sierra loomed over the foothills behind them. On this road, there were only a couple of small pockets of snow in sheltered parts of the slope, and the mountains were covered in brush with a few lone pines randomly adding variety to the landscape.

Finally the road went over a rise and descended into a slight depression between two slopes rising a thousand feet above. In that depression was what was left of the mining town of Buckley. Its population had gone from thousands near the end of the 19th century to zero, but the old wood buildings, empty for years, had remained standing longer than would have seemed possible. The state of California placed a historic marker at the edge of the former town, and Boundary County made it accessible by providing a dirt parking area large enough to hold 20 cars and a pair of portable toilets for the few tourists and the occasional local willing to brave the road up.

There was one car in the parking area when they arrived, and as they were unloading Elizabeth's painting supplies, a family (husband, wife and two daughters) speaking German came up to the other vehicle, waved, got in and drove off. Elizabeth and Leah were on their own, 12 miles of bad road from the main highway and 11 miles from the sheepherder and his collie.

"How did anyone ever find this place?" Leah finally said. "I mean to build a town and look for gold. How would you even think to come up here?"

"The early settlers did," Elizabeth said. "They were a curious lot."

"They must have been. Don't you find it kind of spooky, being all alone up here?"

"A bit. But I have a gun in my purse."

"You pack heat?"

"Only when I want the security. Gordon doesn't like it, but he's never had to be a woman alone in a place like this." She paused. "I've never come close to using it."

Neither of them said anything for a minute, then Leah asked:

"What do you want me to do, Elizabeth?"

Elizabeth was looking over the landscape with her painter's eye and didn't answer right away.

"I'm going to like this town," she finally said. "Why don't you start by helping me carry my things down to the church," she pointed to a building in the distance. "I'll make a few sketches there, and while I do, why don't you look around and see what you think is interesting. Then later, you can show me."

"Sure."

"But be careful, dear. There are abandoned mine shafts here, and the buildings don't look any too steady."

"I'll be careful."

"THERE ARE SEVERAL promising places on the far shore," Gordon said. "And there's no road over there, so this is probably the best way to fish them."

Peter nodded. They had rented a boat for half a day, beginning first thing in the morning, and were cruising slowly across Lower Gemini Lake. It was too early yet for the speedboaters and water skiers to be out, and putting a hand in the water, feeling its iciness, Gordon thought they probably wouldn't be out until afternoon, when the air temperature (if not the water) was warmer.

He was making for a sheer cliff on the other side, intrigued by the bushes growing out of the rock face at irregular intervals. When they got there, he stopped the boat and dropped the anchor about 75 feet from the edge of the water. The sun was behind them, shining on the cliff face and throwing its reflection on the water.

"It may be a bit early yet," Gordon said, "but there could be a fish or two waiting for an insect to drop off the bushes. Worth a few casts with a dry fly."

"What are you using?"

"I'm going to try a grasshopper imitation."

"Grasshopper? Why would a grasshopper be falling out of those bushes?"

"Why would the fish know it wouldn't? It's worth the experiment."

Gordon tied on a Dave's Hopper, and Peter put a Yellow Humpy, a buggy-looking dry fly that imitates no insect in particular but has a proven record of appealing to trout. They were both ready at the same time. Gordon cast to a spot five feet from the edge of the cliff, under a shrub ten feet above the water line. A few seconds later, Peter cast slightly to the right of another shrub.

Two seconds after Gordon's hopper hit the surface of the water, it was smacked by a 14-inch Rainbow Trout.

"I guess the hopper works," he said.

Peter was looking where Gordon had cast when he heard a loud splash on the lake surface. He instinctively raised his rod sharply and felt a fish pulling on the other end.

"So does mine," he said.

STELLA HAD PASSED on joining Leah and Elizabeth on the excursion to Buckley and on joining Gordon and Peter in the boat. She said she wanted to take it easy for a day, and that was true. She'd been working overtime the last two weeks, was exhausted, and was not her best self. And she knew herself well enough to know that. Peter had let her sleep while he and Gordon went out early, and Elizabeth and Leah were gone by the time she woke up.

She had a bowl of oatmeal with one percent milk (they didn't have nonfat) at Broderick's Café, then settled down on the porch of her cabin to read *He Shall Thunder in the Sky*, the new mystery by Elizabeth Peters, set in early 20th-century Egypt. She liked the protagonist, Amelia Peabody, and marveled at the way she and her husband combined work and marriage. She couldn't quite get comfortable on the chair on the deck, and after a few minutes got up with the book and began to walk around.

In the course of her stroll, she wandered toward the lake and found a shaded area with a hammock strung between two trees. How long had it been since she had relaxed in a hammock? She looked around and seeing no one, got herself into it. It was midmorning by now, getting warm enough to be pleasant, and she leaned back against the hammock pillow and opened the book, sighing with contentment.

Five minutes later, she was asleep. It was fatigue, not the book.

WHILE LEAH WAS OFF exploring, Elizabeth set up her folding chair in front of the church and took out her sketchbook. A modest sign identified it as the Presbyterian church — one of five surviving churches that had once served Buckley. It was a wooden building, unpainted, with a bell tower but no bell, and it sat on what appeared to have been the town's main street.

The morning sun at her back illuminated the side of the church, bringing out all the details in the weathered wood. Behind the church, a sagebrush-covered rise rose to a vividly blue sky without a cloud in sight. Farther to the left on the same rise was the town's cemetery, fenced and isolated, a true Boot Hill. At this elevation, the air was perfectly clear, accentuating the stark harshness of the sunlight. She tried to think of how she might render that light on canvas and came to no immediate conclusion.

After sketching the church from the side, she moved in front of it and did a quick drawing from that view. She quickly decided the composition from that angle was less interesting than the side view, but in the course of doing her sketch, she noticed that the steps leading to the front door of the church appeared fairly well preserved and sturdy. Tucking the sketchbook under her arm, she decided to test them.

After climbing all five of them, she reached a landing outside the front door. Surely it would be locked, she thought, as protection against vandals, if nothing else. But, yielding to curiosity, she gave the door handle a gentle tug, and it opened outward.

She stepped inside and looked around. There were ten rows of pews flanking a center aisle and what clearly had been the altar at one point, now stripped of ornament. Probably, she thought, it had been deconsecrated years ago, when it stopped being a going concern. But the bare wooden simplicity of the interior sparked her imagination, and she immediately knew she'd be painting it.

A collection box with envelopes and a slot for money stood against the wall to the right of the door, with a hand-lettered sign above saying donations for the upkeep of the church would be welcomed. After taking out five dollars, she placed her purse on the floor under the box and dropped the bill into the slot. Now she could sketch with a clear conscience. She walked down the center aisle to the fourth row of pews and slid in on the left side. Sunlight coming in through the church door lit part of the bench, but she was sitting in shadow. Opening the sketchbook, she quickly began making a pencil drawing of the front of the church, focusing on its proportions and trying to imagine what it once might have looked like. She was so totally engrossed in the task that it took her a few seconds to realize that a shadow had fallen across the pews to her left. Looking at the shadow more carefully, she realized it was cast by a man wearing a hat.

She instinctively reached out her right hand to grab her purse with the gun inside. It wasn't there. It was still under the collection box by the front door, where the man was standing.

AT MIDMORNING, Gordon pulled the boat into a small cove, where tall pine trees provided shade against the warming sun. He took out a thermos of coffee and poured cups for himself and Peter. After the strong opening, the fishing had tapered off considerably.

"Any plans for this afternoon?" Peter asked.

"I was thinking of heading into town and paying a visit to the editor of the local newspaper. And there was something I wanted to check along the way, but I need an accomplice for that. Would you and Stella care to join me?"

"I'm in. We can ask her when we get back. She was saying she really wanted to take it easy today."

"Whatever she wants. Then I was thinking that after dinner, we could all get together in our cabin and have a group discussion of this case so far. We haven't been making much progress ourselves, so maybe other perspectives will help. What do they say — five heads are better than two?"

"Probably four heads, but I take the point," Peter said.

"Why four?"

"Well, unless my powers of observation are seriously declining, I'm guessing Leah's going to be off to that volleyball game the instant she's excused from dinner."

"I BEG YOUR PARDON, ma'am. I didn't mean to startle you. I should have guessed from the easel outside that someone might be in here."

The voice was a calm, high baritone, and it lessened Elizabeth's anxiety a notch. She lowered her tightened shoulders a half-inch and turned around. A man was standing in the doorway. Backlit by the bright sun outside, he was nothing but a completely black silhouette.

"You left your purse by the door," he continued. "Would you like me to bring it to you?"

"Thank you. Yes. I'm sorry I'm so flustered. I really thought I was alone here." She paused for a moment and added, "My assistant's out looking over the rest of the town."

"It's quite a relic, isn't it?" He stepped inside and bent over to pick up her purse. She wondered if he could see the gun inside it. As her eyes began to adjust, she could see that her visitor was a man of about 50, wearing black jeans, a black long-sleeved shirt with a gray pencil stripe, and a black felt hat with a broad brim. Had he been wearing a six-shooter, he would have looked like a cowboy from a '50s western.

"I like to come here from time to time when I'm feeling at loose ends. There's something in this place that speaks to me. It feels like home."

"Do you mean Buckley or this church?" Elizabeth said.

"The whole town, though I do like this church." He looked around as he walked toward her. She guessed that his height was close to her five-ten. "Hard to believe that a hundred years ago, this church was probably full of people every Sunday, praying for salvation in a town full of wickedness."

"This was a wicked town?"

"Aren't they all? Have you been to the county historical museum in Barnstaple?"

Elizabeth shook her head.

"You should pay a visit. They have a nice exhibit about Buckley. On one of the information cards, it says that in 1896, the town had a population of 7,300, with eight churches." He paused and smiled. "And 13 brothels."

"How would they know — about the brothels, I mean?"

"I suspect everyone knew, and somebody wrote it down. That's usually how history gets passed on."

He handed her the purse. She couldn't resist taking a quick glance to see if the gun was still inside. It was.

"My name's Joe, by the way." He put out his right hand.

She shook it. "Elizabeth," she said.

"Pleased to make your acquaintance, Elizabeth."

"So are you from around here, Joe?"

He took his time answering, as if she'd asked a trick question.

"You could say that. Your paintings. Are they available anywhere locally?"

"I'm afraid not. Last night, when I got here, was the first time I ever set foot in this part of California."

"It's one of the more beautiful parts. Nice people, too. I asked about your paintings because I'd like to have a good one of Buckley. I don't doubt yours will be good."

"You can contact Shaughnessy Gallery in San Francisco. They handle a lot of my work."

"Shaughnessy Gallery. That's easy enough to remember." He paused and sighed. "Well, I'm interrupting you in your work."

"Oh, it's no bother, really."

"Kind of you to say, Elizabeth, but the easel and the sketchbook tell me you didn't come here to talk. It was a pleasure getting to know you."

He walked to the front door with a relaxed, loose-limbed gait and was outside and out of sight in less than a minute. It took Elizabeth a few minutes more to get her breathing back to normal, and not because of the altitude.

Joe had seemed polite and harmless enough, and given that he'd had plenty of opportunity to do her harm if he wanted, he probably was no danger. But having him materialize behind her had been unnerving. Thinking it over, it occurred to her that he hadn't told her his last name and was evasive about where he was from.

He hadn't gotten her last name either, and his speech was courtly, almost dated.

And there was something else bothering her, but it took a few minutes for her to think of it.

When she'd started up the steps to enter the church, she'd looked toward the parking lot, and her Subaru was the only car there. She walked through the front door of the church to the stoop and turned to look at the parking lot.

The Subaru was still the only car there.

STELLA'S EYES FLUTTERED OPEN. She had been sleeping so deeply she was utterly disoriented. Lying on her back and looking up from the hammock, she could see the branches of the pine trees and a couple of patches of blue sky. She closed her eyes again and listened. Children were playing somewhere not too far away, their happy shrieks and shouts filling the air. The sound of an outboard motor went from a roar to a purr as the boat it was on slowed down approaching the marina. A solitary bird chirped out a couple of notes, then was heard no more. A gust of wind came up and rattled through the branches above. A falling pine needle landed on her nose, and she heard a pine cone hit the ground nearby.

Time to get up.

She lifted her left arm to look at her watch, and the arm felt like lead. It was nearly noon, and she must have been sleeping for nearly two hours. Sleeping deeply.

She willed herself to sit up in the hammock and looked woozily around. It was coming back to her. She was at Broderick's Gemini Lakes Resort, with Peter and the Gordons and the kid, Leah. She tried to shake the cobwebs from her brain.

After a few minutes, she got up and walked back toward the cabin. She realized the nap in the hammock must have been the soundest sleep she'd had in ages, and that she felt more refreshed than she had in weeks. As she got back to the cabin she and Peter were sharing, she was thinking she felt like doing something this afternoon.

LEAH WAS WALKING down Buckley's main street, looking at the buildings on her right, when she heard a voice from her left.

"You must be Elizabeth's assistant," a man said.

She stopped and looked in the direction of the voice. A man, dressed entirely in black, with a black hat, was leaning against one of the old buildings. The building was throwing out a few feet of shadow, and he blended into it.

"I'm afraid I gave her a bit of a start," the man continued. "She was inside the church." He paused. "My name is Joe."

"Do you have a last name, Joe?"

"Price. Joe Price. And you are ..."

"Leah."

"Pleased to meet you, Leah. And do *you* have a last name?"

"Leah will do for now."

She thought she saw the man smile, but the contrast between the shadow of the building and the bright light behind it was disorienting enough that she couldn't tell for sure.

"I intend no harm," the man said, "but I suppose these days a lady can't be too careful. Tell me, is Elizabeth a good painter?"

"I think so, and so do a lot of other people. Why?"

"If she's doing paintings of Buckley, I might be interested in buying one."

"They're pretty expensive."

"That's another indication she's good. I don't know. I feel a part of Buckley, and when I saw Elizabeth and her easel, it occurred to me that it would be comforting to have a picture of it at home."

"Where's home, Joe?"

"Ah, that's a good question. But wherever it is, there will be a wall to hang a painting on, I suppose. Does Buckley do anything for you?"

"I've only been here a couple of hours." Leah paused. "But there does seem to be something a bit magical about it. That so much of it is still around after all this time. It's kind of a miracle."

"It's on the dry side of the Sierra, and very much exposed. The sun dries things out quickly. That's probably why the wood hasn't completely rotted. But you get a bit of the feeling, do you?"

"I think Elizabeth does, too. It's the kind of place she likes to paint — western landscape, with signs of the human hand."

Joe looked to his right, where a rusted piece of machinery stood between two buildings.

"The signs of the human hand are here all right, even if the humans aren't anymore. That is, except for the few who make the trip up these days. I think in a way, that's what moves me. Walking through here, I can imagine how once upon a time, it was full of people, working, living, playing, dying. All of them preoccupied with their own problems. And now they and their problems are long gone. It's a humbling reminder of how little our lives matter."

"You don't really believe that, do you, Joe?" Leah said. "That our lives don't matter?"

"They matter while we're living them, which isn't all that long. As you can see by looking around. But I'm probably keeping you from your work. It was good meeting you, Leah."

"Likewise."

She turned and began walking toward the church. She saw another car pull into the parking lot and stop about 20 feet from Elizabeth's. They were the only two cars in the lot, and it occurred to her there should be a third. She turned around, calling out as she did:

"Joe!"

He was nowhere to be seen.

ON THE WAY INTO Barnstaple, Gordon turned up Quail Run Lane, heading toward the Rowan house.

"Where are we going?" Stella asked.

"A place Peter and I visited yesterday," Gordon said. "I want to try a little experiment."

At the top of the road, just before the subdivision, there was a gravel turnout big enough for two vehicles. He pulled into it.

"Peter, I want you to walk up to the Rowan place and listen while I shut the car door. I want to see if you can hear it from there."

"I won't be able to see you." The turnout was slightly below the level of the street where the houses were.

"Stella can stand up there and give you a signal."

"What do you want me to do?" she asked.

"Stand up there at street level, and when I say, 'Now,' raise your hand. Then bring it down when I close the door."

"Is that some sort of Boy Scout secret code?"

"I was no Boy Scout. Can you do it?"

She nodded. Peter walked to the end of the loop, near the Rowan house, and Stella assumed her position.

"He's ready," she said.

"Now." She raised her hand. Gordon closed the door as quietly as he could, and she lowered her arm.

"He's shaking his head," she said. "He didn't hear it."

"One more time," Gordon said. He opened the door all the way and said, "Now." He slammed it as hard as he could, and she lowered her arm.

"He's walking back," she said.

"I think I heard it the second time," Peter said as he arrived, "but it was pretty faint. If I hadn't been listening, I wouldn't have noticed, and it's hard to imagine the sound would have carried into the house."

"Then I was right," Gordon said.

"What's this all about?" Stella asked.

"We'll explain on the way into town."

"Cloak-and-dagger stuff," she said. "All right." They got into the Cherokee. "Next time, you should ask Leah to help you out. I'll bet she'd get a real kick out of it."

THE BARNSTAPLE MINER was owned, published and edited by Maxwell Rutherford, known in the community as Max. When Gordon walked into the office that Thursday afternoon, Max was sitting at his desk smoking a cigarette. There was no one else in the office, and Max could smoke there because it was on the ground floor of the house he owned on a side street across from the courthouse. Gordon introduced himself and asked to speak with the editor. Max put out his cigarette, which had burned down to within five millimeters of the filter, and said he was speaking to him.

"Can we talk off the record?" Gordon asked. "It might lead to a story later, and you can have it first."

"Have a seat. I have to cover the water district meeting tonight. Anything that takes my mind off that is welcome." He motioned Gordon to sit down in a worn armchair facing his desk, which looked like Army surplus from World War II.

"Can we count on being alone?" Gordon said.

Max looked at his watch. "For another hour at least. Ethel's out delivering this week's papers. Ethel does advertising and circulation; I handle news and business. Just the two of us now."

Gordon nodded and briefly explained how Olema Marsh had contacted him the previous month and asked him to look into the rash of accidental deaths in town. "Could I start by asking if all these accidents looked suspicious to you?"

"Of course they did. Do I look dumb or something? They looked suspicious to the sheriff, too, though he won't say it for publication. Problem is, there doesn't seem to be any evidence to show that they were anything but accidents. Mind if I smoke?"

"Your house."

"If you're from San Francisco, you probably think this is a backwoods county. And in some ways it is." He paused to light a cigarette, took a deep drag on it, coughed, and continued. "But thanks to the ski resort in Sierra Pines, we have some pretty good medical people here. And the Highway Patrol called in a special investigator from Sacramento to look into Dave Rowan's crash."

"I didn't see anything about it in your paper."

"I didn't learn about it until a month later. The investigator didn't find anything to suggest Dave's pickup had been tampered with, though it was in such bad shape, he couldn't rule it out altogether. By then it was old news."

He took another drag on his cigarette and blew the smoke out slowly, looking at the ceiling as he did.

"I'll tell you one thing," he continued. "I bought this paper 32 years ago, so by now I have a pretty good idea of what counts as news here. Any one of those four accidents would have been a once-in-five-years story. Two accidents like that in one year would be a helluva coincidence. Four in four months? I'd say damn near impossible."

Max finished his cigarette and lit another without asking.

"Now I have no idea what's going on here, and I'm pretty sure the sheriff doesn't, either. I know him well enough to know when he's sitting on something, and all he's sitting on now is the john once a day." He took another drag on the cigarette and stared at the ceiling for half a minute after exhaling.

"So what's *your* angle?"

"I don't have one yet," Gordon said, "but I have a couple of lines I'd like to pursue. I'm here today on a bit of a fishing expedition."

"This is good country for fishing."

"I'm intrigued by the Valentine's dance. Two of the accidents happened almost within a month of it, and I'm wondering …"

"Do you realize that almost the whole town was there?"

"I expected that. But Diana Rowan told me her husband was bothered by a conversation he had at the dance. I know it's the slimmest of threads, but …"

"It's not much," Max said, "but I guess it's more than what anyone else has."

"I don't suppose you noticed anything that night?"

Max shook his head. "I was too busy working. But I tell you what. I shot three rolls of film that night, 36 shots a roll. That's over a hundred photos. You're welcome to look at the contact sheets, and it won't take but a minute for me to lay my hands on them."

"Thanks. I'd appreciate that. I'm particularly interested in seeing who Luther Whitman, Dave Rowan, Lucy Starr and Mrs. Marsh were talking to that night."

"You're out of luck with Lucy. She had the flu that night, and Jim stayed home with her. But I know there are shots of the other three that didn't make the paper. Hold on a minute."

He walked down a hallway and returned with three contact sheets made from the negatives of black and white film he'd been using. Gordon said a silent thank you. He knew that most professionals now used digital cameras and regularly deleted the pictures they didn't need. Max set the sheets on the other desk in the room, along with a magnifying loupe to help see them better.

"You can use Ethel's desk," he said. "If you want help with IDs, say the word."

Gordon sat at the desk and looked at every photo on the contact sheets. Then he did it again. After 45 minutes, he was done, and none the wiser. There were several photos of each of the people he was interested in, with at least one other person in each photo. He recognized a few of the other people, but nothing seemed amiss. Or was it simply that he didn't know what he was looking for?

Finally, he stood up and brought the contact sheets and loupe to Max.

"Well?"

"Nothing I could see," Gordon said. "It was a long shot, anyway."

"I'll take a look at these after dinner and have Ethel do the same. Maybe we'll see something. If we do, I'll let you know."

Gordon gave him a card. "Thanks. You should at least be able to leave a message on my cell."

"I appreciate your coming by. If this is as bad as it feels, I hope you or someone can get to the bottom of it." He stopped to light another cigarette. "If you have any more news or just want to ask a question, stop by. We put the paper down on Wednesday and that's a pretty busy day, but just about any other time I can make a half hour to talk with you."

GORDON BARBECUED CHICKEN for dinner that night, and Elizabeth made rice and steamed asparagus she'd brought from San Francisco. It was another beautiful evening, and they ate on the picnic table outside the cabin. People passed by from time to time, but no one was stationed close enough to overhear long stretches of conversation, so they agreed it was all right to hold an outdoor group discussion about the case.

For the benefit of Stella and Leah, Gordon went over everything, beginning with his lunch with Olema Marsh in Bodega Bay last month. He gave a precise and accurate rendering of what he and Peter had learned since their arrival on Sunday.

"So what it amounts to," he concluded, "is that we have suspicion and probability on the side of a killer being at work in this town. But what we don't have is facts, evidence, or any unifying theory that would connect all these crimes, if we're right in thinking that's what they are. Does anybody have any thoughts or observations? No idea too wild to throw out there."

No one spoke for a moment. Gordon looked at all of them.

"Elizabeth," he said. "You look like you're deep in thought. What's on your mind?"

"If you must know," she said, "I was thinking you missed your calling by not going into teaching."

"It doesn't pay."

"Tell me about it. Well, I know this isn't terribly brilliant, but it seems as if the first order of business would be to figure out what the connection between the victims was."

"I second that," Stella said. "As long as it's random accidents, or looks like it, nobody's going to take it seriously or figure out who's behind it."

"The women are right, as usual," Peter said. "From what I've seen so far, I'm pretty well convinced that something bad is afoot. It's not just the number of mysterious accidents that bothers me, but the fact that every one of them went against the character of the victim. And there's another thing about the totality of the four accidents that I find highly suggestive."

He paused for effect.

"Go on," Gordon said.

"I don't want to antagonize the women at the table, but if there was a creative intelligence behind these so-called accidents, I think we're looking at a man. And I'll tell you why.

"It's possible that a woman could have hit Olema Marsh on the head and drowned her in the tub. And it's possible that a woman could have sneaked up Quail Run Lane and tampered with David Rowan's car that Sunday night in March. But that would be unusual. It's hard to imagine, though, a woman going up that church tower with Luther Whitman and chucking him out of it. Likewise it's hard to imagine a woman being confident of her ability to throw Lucy Starr into the river.

"What's more, these were incredibly bold crimes, if crimes they were. In every one of them, there was a serious risk of being caught. If one of the neighbors had looked out the window at the right time or taken the dog out for a walk in Rowan's neighborhood — game over. If someone had been passing by when Luther Whitman hit the ground or when Lucy Starr was waylaid, or if the mailman had come by while the killer was at Olema

Marsh's house — same thing. You're frowning, Elizabeth. Do you disagree?"

She shook her head. "I'm for equality of the sexes, but common sense has to trump ideology. It's probably a man, but all I'd say is that until we're sure, let's leave the window open just a crack to the possibility of a woman."

"Fair enough," Peter said. "But in the absence of other evidence, I'm looking for a man, and furthermore, one with brass balls. Maybe even someone with a Special Forces background."

"Don't women serve in the military?" Leah asked.

Elizabeth and Stella laughed.

"She's got you there, Peter," Stella said. "You'd better make that crack in the window a bit bigger."

"Point taken," Peter said. "And if it was a woman, that's a likely explanation."

"The military angle might be something for us to keep an ear to the ground about," Gordon said, given what Dave Rowan told his wife about Vietnam. "And when you mentioned Olema Marsh, I remembered her daughter was getting the autopsy report today. Will you have a chance to look at it tomorrow?"

"I'll make the time."

"I'll call her after dinner. Maybe we can get it in the morning and you can look it over while I accompany Elizabeth and Leah to Buckley. I've never seen a real ghost town, and I'd like to."

"Wow!" Stella said. "So I guess I have a date tomorrow morning to sit in the cabin with Peter while he reads an autopsy report. Lucky me."

"You know, Peter," Gordon said, "if you want to make it up to her, you could take Stella to Barnstaple tonight."

"What's there to do in Barnstaple?" she asked.

"I understand from the newspaper editor that the water board is meeting. That should be entertaining."

"No thank you," Peter said.

"It wouldn't be the worst date he's taken me on," Stella said.

"Aren't we getting off topic?" Elizabeth said. "I thought we were talking about the case."

"We are," Gordon said. "We just took a little detour. Does anybody else have any thoughts about it?"

No one spoke for a minute, then Leah raised her hand. Gordon nodded at her.

"Maybe this is so obvious that everybody else already thought about it, and that's why it hasn't been mentioned. But I was thinking ..."

"Yes," Gordon said calmly.

"Well, from what you were saying, it seems that everybody who was killed in one of those accidents has lived in this town for quite a while, right?" Gordon nodded. "So if they were living here for years with no problem, and then all of a sudden this bad stuff started happening, something must have changed to cause that. If we knew what the change was, there'd be something to go on."

"Good point," Peter said. "Gordon and I were looking at the papers before the accidents with that in mind, but maybe we weren't looking far enough back."

"Thank you, Leah," Gordon said. "We definitely have to pursue that. I'm not sure how, but we have to."

He looked around at the group.

"Anyone else have something to say about the case?" When no one responded after 15 to 20 seconds, he continued, "Then we'll wrap up the discussion. Thank you all for your help. Five heads are better than two."

"And since you brought up Buckley a bit earlier," Elizabeth said, "I have to tell you what happened to Leah and me there today."

ONCE SHE WAS SURE she had everyone's attention, Elizabeth continued.

"We got there around midmorning, and I found myself right away entranced by the old church there," she said.

"There's another one a couple of blocks away," Leah said.

"Right. But I didn't know that at the time. I sent Leah off to do some scouting and started to make some sketches of the exterior. Then I went inside and sat in one of the pews, with the light from the door hitting the benches to my left. All of a sudden, there was a shadow there."

"Oh, God," Stella said. "That must have …"

"It did. I was freaked out. But I'd taken my pistol up there, only it was in my purse, which I'd put on the floor by the door when I dropped a bill in the donation box."

"That's the trouble with guns," Gordon said. "You never have one on you when you really need it."

"So I looked back," Elizabeth continued, ignoring him, "and there was a silhouette of a man in the doorway. All black, with the sun behind him. Later, when he started coming toward me, I could see he was dressed entirely in black — pants, shirt, hat."

"The shirt had a faint stripe," Leah said.

"Anyway, it turned out to be a man named Joe, and he seemed pretty nice, after all. He brought the purse to me, gun and all, and we chatted for a couple of minutes, then he left. But then comes the strange part. A couple of minutes later, I went to the door and looked up toward the parking lot. My car was the only one there. So how did he get up to Buckley?"

"He probably had already driven off," Peter said.

"Not so. Leah saw him about a half hour later. Tell us about it."

"I was walking down the street," Leah said, "when I heard a voice on my left. He was standing in the shadow of a building, and the sunlight was so bright it was hard to see him there, all dressed in black. He asked if I was Elizabeth's assistant."

"Did he actually use her name?" Gordon asked.

Leah nodded. "We talked for a few minutes, and then I headed back toward the church where Elizabeth was. I thought of something and turned to look for him. He was gone. I went back to the building he'd been leaning against and called his name and looked and called up a couple of side streets, but nothing. It was as if he'd just vanished into thin air."

"And when Leah got to the church a couple of minutes later, my car was still the only one in the lot."

"A couple of tourists from New Mexico drove up just then," Leah said. "I asked them a few minutes later if they'd passed another car on their way in, and they said no. I thought it was all pretty spooky, but he seems to be a harmless enough ghost."

"And all you know about him," Gordon said, "is that his name is Joe."

"Joe Price," Leah said.

"How did you find out his last name?" Elizabeth said.

"I asked."

"An interesting and entertaining story," Peter said, "but there are two logical explanations for the absence of a car, and in any case, he was no ghost."

"All right, Mr. Scientific Mind," Elizabeth said. "How did he get to a place miles from anywhere without a car?"

Peter held up his left hand and raised the index finger.

"Number one," he said, "someone could have dropped him off there earlier and was coming back to get him later. Maybe he was even planning to sleep in a ghost town overnight."

"No camping allowed," Elizabeth said.

"Which just bolsters the theory. He may have disappeared so quickly and not responded to Leah's calls because he'd found a place to hunker down for the night and didn't want you to know about it. And then there's the second explanation. He could have been riding a horse, which he had tethered out of sight."

"You sure know how to ruin a good story," Leah said.

"And as long as you're pontificating," Elizabeth said, "how can you be sure he wasn't a ghost?"

"Easy," Peter replied. "Ghosts don't cast shadows."

HALF AN HOUR LATER, the dishes had been cleaned and put away, Leah was off to the volleyball game, and Peter and Stella had repaired to their cabin. Gordon remembered he had to call Marilyn Rossi about the autopsy report.

She answered straightaway.

"I'm glad you called," she said. "We got a copy of the report without any fuss, but I can't bring myself to look at it, and it's creeping me out having it here. How soon can you come and get it?"

"How about first thing tomorrow morning?"

"What's first thing for you?"

"Say 8:30 to 9, after we have breakfast."

"Great. I'll see you then."

Gordon and Elizabeth decided to go for a walk in the direction of the lake. They passed the volleyball game and continued to one of the piers. An hour of light remained, but no one was fishing from the pier though they could see several boats out on the lake. There was a two-seat bench on one side of the pier and they availed themselves of it.

They sat and looked silently at the lake for a quarter of an hour. Gordon counted four or five fish rising to insects out in the lake, but it wasn't a consistent rise, and the fish were out of casting range from where they were.

"So aside from the tall dark stranger," Gordon said, "how did it go with Leah today?"

"He wasn't that tall, and it went fine. I sent her out to scout the town, looking for things that were visually interesting. She did surprisingly well. For an untrained eye, she saw an awful lot and saved me some time."

"She's a deep one, all right."

"She can give you the grand tour tomorrow if you still want to come up."

"More than ever now. I'm hoping to meet Joe."

"Don't hold your breath."

"Why not?"

"I have a feeling — and it's just a feeling — that Joe only shows himself to women."

"You know him better than I do. So it sounds like you might get a painting or two out of that old ghost town."

"Better than that, I think." She paused. "I got an email this morning from the Shaughnessy Gallery. They want to know by the 15th whether I can do a show in December. Two days ago, I wasn't so sure."

"And now?"

"I wasn't sure because I felt I needed another half-dozen paintings to do a proper exhibition. After today, I think I can do it. In fact, I can get six paintings easy, just out of Buckley."

"So you're good." She nodded. "Now I really have to see Buckley tomorrow. It sounds as if the place really speaks to you."

"It does," Elizabeth said. "Some places just have the magic, and when they do, you know it right away."

They looked out over the lake in silence for a minute, and Elizabeth continued.

"Funny you should use those words."

"What words?"

"That Buckley speaks to me."

"Doesn't it?"

"Oh, yes. Very much so. But that's not what's interesting. Those were the words Joe used today to describe how he feels about Buckley. It apparently speaks to him, too."

Friday June 9

FOR BREAKFAST, Peter and Gordon checked out the Hi-Mont Café just off the main street, a block from the courthouse. It was not as well decorated as the Barnstaple Inn, the menu was not as creative, and the wait staff tended toward women of a certain age in comfortable clothes rather than college students in starched white shirts. But the coffee was hot, the prices were fair, and the grub was good. On this fine June morning, that was enough.

After their order was taken, Gordon, holding his coffee cup in both hands, leaned against the back of their booth.

"So what are you looking for in the document you're reading today?"

"Ah, the document." Peter took a sip of coffee. "Something that doesn't fit, I suppose."

"And what might that be?"

"I don't know, but I feel fairly confident I'll know it when I see it."

"What if you don't?"

"Then I don't. I never said I was perfect — just the best."

"If you do find something, why would the coroner have missed it?"

"Well, assuming he — or possibly she — is capable, the most likely reason would be that they weren't looking for evidence of foul play and shrugged off some seemingly small detail that ought to have raised suspicion. And probably would have if they'd gone into it being suspicious."

"I guess that's why you're supposed to get a second opinion before you make a major medical decision."

"That's the logic behind it, but it doesn't always work that way."

"What do you mean?"

"There's a built-in problem with second opinions. If two medical men or women with impeccable education and credentials disagree, who's the ignorant layman supposed to believe? Answer me that."

"I never thought of it that way."

"A lot of times it just leads to overthinking things. And now, with the internet, people can go online and look up all kinds of stuff they have no basis for evaluating. And they're as likely to believe the junk as the good medicine."

"So what do you suggest?"

"If it's me, I'd say go with the first doctor's opinion if it's someone you can trust. But I have an edge that you don't."

"Which is?"

"I'll ask that doctor better questions than you would. Guaranteed."

"It's always a pleasure talking medicine with you, Peter. I come away from it with a feeling that my only hope for living to a decent age is never to get sick in the first place."

"That's about right, but easier said than done. Oh, and Gordon, if you ever need another surgery, I have a bit of advice."

Gordon tilted his head.

"Don't ever ask what the mortality rate is for complications following so-called routine surgery." Peter took another sip of his coffee before continuing.

"Trust me, you don't want to know."

MARILYN ROSSI LOOKED as if she'd been waiting for Gordon and Peter. She was dressed like a woman who was going somewhere, which she was.

"I'm sorry," she said. "I just got the call half an hour ago. They said mother's ashes would be ready soon."

Gordon and Peter looked at each other.

"She's being cremated this morning instead of this afternoon." She looked at her watch, and so did they. The time was 9:14.

"We won't keep you then," Gordon said. "Uh, do you mind if I ask ...?"

"What we're doing with her?"

He nodded.

"We're taking her to a place called Anderson Meadows. It's about a mile and a half up a trail from Upper Gemini Lake. It was one of her favorite places, and that's where she asked us to scatter the ashes." She paused. "I don't know if it's legal, but I don't care. She put it in her will, and I'm going to do what she wants."

"I doubt there'll be any trouble about it," Gordon said.

"I really don't need any more stress. I'll have to ask a couple of her friends to come, but most of them probably can't make the hike anymore. Lucy Starr could have, but she went first."

"If there's anything I can do ...," Gordon said.

"You're invited, too, if you're still here. I should know in a day or two when it'll be."

"That's very kind of you."

"I don't want to shoo you away, but I need to get to Sierra Pines." She reached into the large purse that was hanging by a strap from her shoulder and took out a manila envelope. "Here it is. When do you think you'll know something?"

"Probably not right away," Peter said. "The odds are that the report won't raise any questions, and we're just doing due diligence. If it does raise questions, it could take a while to answer them."

"One way or another, we'll let you know what we can," Gordon said.

"That's all I can ask. Do you need anything else?"

"Not now," Gordon said. "You'd better be off."

She pulled the front door to the house shut behind her and walked briskly to the car in the driveway. Thirty seconds later, she had gone around the corner, leaving Gordon and Peter standing in the front yard.

"Hell and damnation," Peter finally said.

"What?"

"I never thought to ask what they were doing with the body, and now it's too late."

With his left hand, he held up the manila envelope containing the autopsy report, and with his right hand, he gave it a good whack.

"If I see something screwy in this report, there's not much that can be done about it. Now that she's cremated, nobody can take a second look at the body."

111

ELIZABETH AND LEAH had already left for Buckley by the time Gordon and Peter returned to Broderick's. Before Gordon left to follow them, there was a fishing consultation, the outcome of which was that he and Peter would try to get in a few hours on Barnstaple Reservoir in the afternoon. Peter agreed to call the marina and reserve a boat for a half day.

Gordon had been to Buckley once before, when he was nine years old. His parents had taken him and his two sisters there during a summer family vacation. Buckley had bored him then, but now, at the age of 41, he looked forward to seeing it with fresh eyes.

It was a quiet, peaceful drive, during which he tried, with no success, to make something of the information to date on the Barnstaple "accidents." On the road up to Buckley he saw two cars coming down and none going his way. When he reached the top of the rise before the road dipped down to what was left of the town, he stopped and took a panoramic look. Elizabeth's Subaru was in the parking area, along with one other car. He couldn't see any people, but at this angle they could easily have been out of sight behind buildings.

He sat in the roadway at the top of the rise for five minutes, and no one came along to bother him. He put the Cherokee in gear and headed down. As he drove into the parking area, he saw Elizabeth below, outside an old church, sitting at her easel. A few seconds later, Leah came out of the door to the church and joined her. He stepped out of his car and felt a cool breeze hitting him from behind, from the west. The rise kept him from seeing the mountains in that direction, but he wondered if a thunderstorm might be coming. He walked down the dirt pathway to Elizabeth.

"How's it going?" he asked.

"It's going," she said. "I don't want to jinx this with any predictions, but I think I'm going to get some good paintings out of this place."

Gordon looked around. "I wouldn't be surprised," he said. Buckley, he thought, should be fertile artistic ground for her.

Elizabeth turned to Leah.

"Did I ever tell you how Gordon and I met?"

"No," Leah said, "but he did."

"I'd be interested in hearing his story."

"He said he bought one of your paintings."

"The best one," Gordon said. "When she had a show in San Francisco two years ago, I loaned it to the exhibition. Several people offered to buy it from me."

"If it's the one in your apartment, I can see why," Leah said. "It's really good."

"Thank you," Elizabeth said. She turned to Gordon. "So did you pick up the report?"

"We did. Peter should be reading it now."

Elizabeth nodded. "If there's anything there, he'll find it. He can't be faulted as a medical man."

"Maybe for bedside manner. There was a complication, however." Elizabeth cocked her head, and he continued, "Olema Marsh was cremated this morning."

"Humph," Elizabeth said.

"Yeah. So if he does see something that might merit another look, forget it. If she'd been buried, they at least could have exhumed the body."

"This conversation is getting weird," Leah said. "Do you always think like this, Gordon?"

"Only when he's on a case, dear," Elizabeth said.

"I'm afraid it has to be done," Gordon said. "Crime isn't pleasant."

A gust of cool wind kicked up, blowing dust and a couple of stray tumbleweeds down Buckley's main street.

"We didn't have this breeze yesterday," Elizabeth said.

"It sometimes means a storm's moving in. I didn't check the forecast this morning, but it feels like it."

"If you're right," Elizabeth said, "I hope it holds off for a while. This painting is starting to take shape."

Gordon cleared his throat.

"Before I headed up here, we were talking about having dinner at the Barnstaple Inn tonight."

"Is that the big white building?" Leah asked.

Gordon nodded.

"Sounds good to me," Elizabeth said. "I could use a break from cooking."

"When I get back to Broderick's, I'll make a reservation for six o'clock." He looked over at Leah. "Actually, maybe 5:30. That'll get us back about when the volleyball game starts."

"Thank you," Leah said.

"And now, I'm going to take a look around and then head back."

"Let Leah show you around. She explored the town pretty well yesterday."

"I'd like that," Leah said.

"Then consider it done. It's not often a man gets such an enchanting tour guide."

"You can take your time. I'm all set up now, and if there's a storm moving in, I want to be able to paint furiously and without interruption."

STELLA CAME INTO the cabin and closed the door. Peter was sitting at the table, leaning backward in his chair. In his left hand, he held a copy of the autopsy report, and in his right hand, a cheap ballpoint pen, the cap of which he was nibbling.

"That breeze is getting a bit chilly," she said. "I think I'll read inside."

"Mmm," Peter said.

"Are you finding anything interesting in that report?"

"Mmm."

"Can I get you a cup of coffee?"

"Thanks."

"Wow. A speech."

"Mmm."

There was enough left in the morning's pot for a cup for each of them. She put nonfat milk in hers and took a cup of black coffee to Peter. He picked it up and took a sip without saying anything.

"You're welcome," she said.

She curled up on the couch by the window and returned to her book. They read in silence for ten minutes.

"Hah!" Peter said suddenly, leaning forward. He set the autopsy report on the table and jabbed it with his right finger.

"Hah!" he said again.

"Are you going to tell me about it?"

He turned the report back a page and re-read the section he had just finished. When he finished it again, he nodded.

"Have you found something?" she asked.

"I do believe I have. Too bad the cremation's taken place, though."

"Are you going to tell me?"

"Sure," he said. He put his hands behind his head and leaned back in the chair, staring dreamily at the ceiling before turning back to her again.

"Have you ever heard of George Joseph Smith?" Peter said.

"Who?"

GORDON KEPT CASTING nervous glances to the west as they walked through the town. He could see clouds beginning to peek over the rim of the mountains surrounding Buckley, and they could be rain clouds. If Leah noticed the clouds, she gave no indication. She was absorbed in the task of being Gordon's tour guide.

So contagious was her enthusiasm that Gordon got caught up in it and almost stopped checking the western horizon entirely. Leah had practically memorized the guidebook put out by the county and was pointing out the buildings that used to be the fine homes, saloons, mortuaries, the post office and the town's three hotels. At one edge of town, she pointed to a couple of buildings in the distance, nearly falling down now, and said they were all that was left of what had once been a larger Chinatown.

The town was fascinating, and yet Gordon found that it lowered his spirits at the same time. He was only 41, but Buckley was making him aware of his own mortality, and how little, seemingly, nearly any life seemed to matter a hundred years after the fact. He wondered if serial killers looked at it the same way to justify their crimes. Best not to go there, he thought. Focus on what Leah is showing and don't try to be too profound.

She broke his reverie with a question.

"There's just one thing about the guidebook that doesn't add up," Leah said. "You know a lot about the mountains and their history. Maybe you can help."

"I'll try."

"Well it shows all these businesses you'd expect to find in a town, but there's one type of business that's not listed. And in a mining town with a lot of single men, you'd think there'd be a lot of ..."

He didn't finish the sentence but waited to see what word she would use.

"Brothels," she said. "Are they just trying to sanitize the past?"

"Probably not that so much as just leaving a bit to the imagination. Think about the houses you pointed out on this tour."

"What about them?"

"Most of them had a man's name attached, but three of them had just a woman's name. Not a lot of women owned property on their own back then."

"You think that's the answer?"

"Part of it, anyway. There may have been an honest widow in the bunch, too. I don't know."

Leah was looking at him with the faintest hint of a smile on her face. It was an expression she'd acquired since starting school at S.F. State.

"That was a good catch, Gordon. I won't ask how you knew."

"Elizabeth is going to love this place, if she doesn't already. It's a landscape almost tailor-made for her."

"You're changing the subject, but she was really excited yesterday. There are a lot of places, especially at the edge of town, where the buildings are right in front of a vast open space behind. That's her kind of scene."

Gordon, who knew Elizabeth's paintings well by now, had to agree. He looked toward the east. A quarter mile outside town was a fenced-off area with several ramshackle buildings that seemed to be industrial in nature. He pointed in that direction.

"Is that where the mines were?"

"Most of them. Apparently the buildings are almost falling down and there are a couple of barely covered mine shafts that are pretty dangerous now."

116

"Those mine shafts were pretty dangerous when men were working in them," Gordon said.

"I'm going to go up and take a closer look today or tomorrow."

"You're not going to ..."

"From outside the fence. Chill, Gordon. I don't have a death wish. But the mining area and the cemetery," she pointed toward a hill on the other side of town, "are two places I didn't have a chance to check out yesterday. But I'll bet that before it's over, Elizabeth will use that cemetery in one of her paintings."

"No bet," Gordon said. "Not at any odds."

They began walking back toward the church, where Elizabeth was painting. Gordon was looking at the western sky again, and there were more clouds in it, but they weren't advancing with the full charge by which a Sierra thunderstorm often makes its appearance. Maybe he and Peter would get some fishing in after all.

Halfway to the church, Leah stopped.

"Can I ask you a question, Gordon?"

"Sure."

"You went to Cal on a basketball scholarship, right?" He nodded. "And Elizabeth went to Iowa on a basketball scholarship?" He nodded again. "Do the two of you ever play basketball together?"

Gordon let out a nervous laugh.

"No. We never have and probably never will."

"How come?"

Gordon took his time before answering.

"You probably know by now," he said, "that Elizabeth is a pretty competitive individual. So am I. And there are some situations where it's maybe not a good idea to get into a competitive situation. I never saw Elizabeth play, but I've done a little research since I met her, and everybody says she was really good. I'm sure it's a source of pride with her. But the hard reality is that I'm bigger, stronger and more experienced than she is. It wouldn't be a fair contest, and nothing would be gained by having it. Does that make sense to you?"

"I see," Leah said 10 seconds later.

117

BY THE TIME GORDON and Peter arrived at Barnstaple Reservoir's marina, clouds were covering most of the sky and had blotted out the sun. They're not friendly clouds, Gordon thought, but maybe we'll be lucky and it'll only rain. That could trigger a feeding frenzy with the fish. Thunder and lightning, on the other hand, would mean an end to the fishing and a race back to the marina. Only a fool would stay out in the middle of an open lake in an aluminum boat holding a graphite fly rod.

They quickly loaded their gear into the boat, and Gordon backed it away from the pier. A steady cool breeze was blowing and kicking up small whitecaps on the surface of the water. He followed the shore line northeast, in the direction of the dam, which they could barely see in the distance. A quarter mile from the marina, a small peninsula protruded into the lake, and on the other side of it was a cove. Gordon maneuvered the boat into the cove and dropped the anchor. The peninsula blocked the wind slightly, but they could still feel it cutting through their jackets.

"Fish here?" Peter said.

"Talk here," Gordon answered. "You were grinning like a Cheshire cat when I picked you up, Peter. We're not making a cast until you tell me what you found in the autopsy report."

"This cove looks like a good spot," Peter said, looking around. "Lots of weeds on the bottom. Fish probably move in there when they're ready to feed."

"Peter! The autopsy report — *please.*"

"You know, Gordon, for someone who's so good at fishing, which is a sport of patience, you can be amazingly impatient when it comes to other matters."

Gordon glared at him, and Peter continued.

"All right then. The autopsy report. Does the name George Joseph Smith ring a bell with you?"

"Of course."

"Good for you. Stella drew a blank on it."

"Maybe if you'd said the Brides in the Bath Killer ..."

"Nope. She whiffed on that one, too." Peter shook his head. "For a woman with such a nasty, suspicious mind, she has an amazingly wholesome frame of reference. People are such contradictions. Anyway, I was reading the report, and in the section where it was describing the overall appearance of the deceased, was a seemingly insignificant detail that made me sit up and take notice."

"Don't tell me. The ankles?"

"Right you are. The autopsy report was signed by a doctor named Carmine DeSapio, and he was a very thorough fellow, was Dr. DeSapio. He dutifully noted that there were two small bruises on either side of each ankle. Now of course, those bruises could have been caused by tight, ill-fitting shoe straps."

"Or by fingers."

"Which is what I'm thinking. It's a shame we can't go back and look at the body because there might be enough of an indication to tell us which. But you see the relevance."

"Totally."

"It's not easy to drown someone who's lounging in a bathtub. If you try to grab them and shove them under water, they'll put up a hell of a fight. There'll be water all over the place. And the victim will have bruises and maybe other marks from the struggle. Even the most incompetent coroner would have to be suspicious. But if you did what Smith did ..."

"Grab the victim by the ankles and lift up, plunging their head suddenly under water ..."

"They lose consciousness immediately and die very quickly. They don't even take in much water in the lungs. The investigators in the Smith case tried hiring a female diver to recreate the method of killing, and when they tipped her head into the water by lifting her ankles, she went unconscious so fast, it took half an hour to bring her back and she almost didn't make it."

"Smith was hanged for killing three wives that way, as I recall."

"While married to a fourth at the same time," Peter said. "I take a dim view of that. Serial husbandry is one thing, but I draw the line at bigamy."

"So how much water did Olema Marsh have in her lungs?"

"Not much. Dr. DeSapio explained that away by saying that the shock from hitting her head was a contributing factor. Which, I suppose, it could be if this was indeed an accident."

They sat in silence, looking out over the cove. The wind had picked up, and the whitecaps were becoming more pronounced.

"I thought about calling Dr. DeSapio and seeing if we could have a little phone conversation about those bruises, but I held off. You're the principal in this investigation, Gordon, and I wouldn't want to do anything like that before checking with you first."

"Thanks, Peter. Off the top of my head, that sounds like a good idea, but we're not going to do anything about it now." He shook his head. "I'm surprised a forensic medicine specialist wouldn't pick up on those ankle bruises."

"It's understandable, though. Most coroners will never see an ankle-grab bath dunk in an entire career, and when a case is brought in as an accident and that's what you're looking for, it could easily get by. I spotted it because I was looking for something like it, but still it was only suggestive, not conclusive."

"The problem is," Gordon said, "I don't like what it suggests."

"Neither do I."

"If that's what happened to Olema Marsh, we could be dealing with someone who's really educated about killing and is cold-blooded as hell."

"I'd go a step farther than that," Peter said. "We may be dealing with a monster."

SHORTLY AFTER THREE O'CLOCK, a jet-black Corvette pulled into Barnstaple. It slowed to 25 as soon as it entered the town and went up the length of Main Street to the other side of town before turning around and coming back. The driver signaled for a left turn and pulled into the Lake View Motel. It had no lake view, but the sign in front showed there was a vacancy.

The driver got out of the Corvette, surveyed the exterior of the motel and decided it would do. A few minutes later, the driver, room keys in hand, emerged from the motel office just in time to see a flash of light behind the mountains to the west.

Seconds later, there was a loud thunderclap. It began as a loud explosion, then continued as a diminishing rumble. Another bolt of lightning flashed in the western sky as the Corvette parked in front of room 17.

SOME GOOD FISH had moved into the cove as the storm drew nearer, and Gordon and Peter had caught and released several of them when the first thunderclap came. It felt as if it had occurred directly over them, and Gordon wasted no time getting the motor going and returning the boat to the marina. They were in the Cherokee, heading back to Broderick's, when the rain began to fall in sheets, practically obscuring the view of the road. It didn't ease up until they were back in their cabins.

The rain had stopped when they left the resort with Stella two hours later. Large drops were still rolling off the branches of the trees overhead, the dust had been tamped down by the rain, and the air smelled impossibly fresh. The rain held off until they reached town, then a violent squall hit. Gordon had to park around the corner from the inn, and he, Peter and Stella were almost soaked by the time they had run to it.

Familiar faces were there that night. As they walked in, Gordon saw Maxwell Rutherford, the newspaper editor, being served a martini at the bar. The bartender had been one of the servers at the Hi-Mont Café that morning. Kathryn and Skip Henry said hello on the way out the door after an early dinner. Sheriff Rod Kanehl was nursing a gin-and-tonic at the bar and getting a head start on his next re-election campaign. With the tourists added in, the place was nearly full, loud and energetic.

Elizabeth and Leah hadn't arrived yet, but the table Gordon had reserved was ready. It was a corner table, and the seats backing against the wall afforded an excellent view of the community Chautauqua at the bar. Peter, who no longer drank, insisted on sitting with his back to the bar, across from Stella, and Gordon took the chair to Peter's left.

121

"I'm famished," Stella said, picking up a menu.

"Rough afternoon?" Gordon asked.

"Actually, no. I was mostly reading my book and sleeping. There's something about the air up here. It makes me sleepier and hungrier. Here they are."

Elizabeth and Leah had just come in, and Elizabeth's short dark hair was wet from the rain. She and Leah sat next to Stella, with a view of the bar.

"Did it rain in Buckley?" Gordon said.

"Just a few drops," Leah replied.

"But it looked as if the sky was going to open up any minute," Elizabeth added. "We were about ready to wrap up anyway, so we called it a day. It didn't rain all the way back, but we got hit with this," she indicated the downpour outside, "the minute we hit town. How was the fishing? Did you get wet?"

"The fishing was just getting started when the storm kicked up," Peter said. "We caught a few nice ones, then got back to the marina before the rain started."

"This looks like a happening place," Leah said.

"Already seen several people I know," Gordon said. "That man with the blue corduroy shirt and beat-up hat sitting at the bar with a martini — he's Maxwell Rutherford, editor, publisher, photographer and everything else at *The Barnstaple Miner*. The gent in khakis, blazer, blue shirt, and red tie with gold stripes is Sheriff Rod Kanehl." He took a sip of water. "Who does *not* approve of my independent investigative efforts here."

"You weren't even looking when you described them," Leah said.

"I saw 'em once. That was enough."

"Pay no attention to him, Leah," Elizabeth said. "He likes to show off."

"Who's that woman who just walked in?" Leah asked.

"Obviously, I can't see," Gordon said, "and it would be rude to turn around and stare."

"She looks official," Leah said.

"Let's test your powers of observation," Gordon said. "Describe her to me, and tell me why she looks official."

"She's probably five-nine, five-seven without her heels. The heels are a giveaway. The women I've seen in this town all wear comfortable flats. She's wearing an expensive sweater from Nordstrom."

"How do you know it's expensive and from Nordstrom?"

"I tried it on at the Stonestown Nordstrom a few weeks ago and looked at the price tag. It's navy blue with a tan accent that goes with her very nice tan slacks. The cream-colored blouse, open two buttons at the top, doesn't look cheap, either, at least not from here. Her hair, which is short and dark with blond streaks, is very smartly cut — definitely a good stylist. The earrings are small, understated, and I'm guessing from the rest of her get-up, not cheap. And the way she moves and looks around — you can tell she's used to being in charge."

"You know," Stella said, "I think she might be a cop."

"Evidence?" Peter asked.

"I've seen plenty of cops in the ER, The way they move, the way they look around — you just know. It's tribal behavior."

"Stella may be right," Elizabeth said. "Plus, she just cased the room and went straight over to the guy you identified as the sheriff. They seem to be having a professional discussion."

"*She's* having a professional discussion," Stella said. "*He's* checking her out. Poor schlub. He hasn't got a chance."

"Come on," Gordon said. "Next thing you know, you'll be telling us the woman in the far corner is from Gettysburg, Pennsylvania, because of the straw hat she's wearing."

"I don't know anything about straw hats in Gettysburg, but I say she's a cop," Stella said.

"All right," Elizabeth said. "We need to settle this." She stood up. "I'm going to the bar to get a glass of wine, and I'll strike up a conversation with her as soon as she puts the sheriff in his place. Anybody else want anything?"

"I'll have a glass of white," Stella said. "Sauvignon blanc if they have any. And if she *is* a cop, I think Gordon and Peter should buy the wine."

"Deal," Gordon said. Elizabeth moved toward the bar.

"Do you really think she can find out if that woman's a police officer?" Leah said, after Elizabeth was gone.

Gordon took another swallow of water.

"Oh, she'll find out, all right. And she'll probably invite officer what's-her-name to join us for dinner."

TWELVE MINUTES LATER, Elizabeth returned to the table, two glasses of wine in hand, with the mystery woman at her side. A server followed them with an extra place setting.

"I'd like to introduce you to someone I met at the bar," she said. "This is Detective Lindsay Judd of the Long Beach Police Department. She's here by herself tonight, and I took the liberty of asking her to join us for dinner. I hope you don't mind."

"Not at all," said Gordon, who was already standing. "A pleasure to meet you. I'm Quill Gordon." He introduced the others at the table.

"It was very kind of you to ask me to join you," Lindsay said, sitting down at the newly set place next to Gordon. "When I found out who I'd be dining with, I had to say yes. Elizabeth told me you were the one who unraveled the Dutchtown case a couple of years ago."

"Unraveled might be putting it a bit too strongly," Gordon said. "I started looking into it as a volunteer, and then things happened."

"That's how a lot of investigations turn out."

"I'm surprised you heard about it down south," Gordon continued. "I thought it was a Northern California phenomenon."

"Not at all. The *Los Angeles Times* did a big story about it, and we devoted one of our monthly meetings of the Detective Squad to it. It's actually a very good case study in how an investigation can go south because of what seems like obvious evidence at the beginning."

"I had no idea," Gordon said.

The server stopped by the table to ask whether they were ready to order.

"You probably need a minute," Stella said to Lindsay.

"I'm good. When I saw grilled trout on the specials board, I knew what I was having."

"I'll have that, too," Elizabeth said. "It's a treat we never get at home."

"I thought you said Gordon was a fly fisherman," Lindsay said.

"He is, but he releases everything he catches."

"I'd be out of a job if I did that."

There was a break in the conversation while everyone else ordered.

"So," Lindsay said, looking across at Gordon, "Elizabeth tells me you're looking into something suspicious in this small town."

"There's not much to tell, and you probably don't want to talk shop," he said.

"I'm fine with talking shop when it's something I'm not working on. No pressure. Not for me, anyway. Go ahead."

Gordon summarized the whole case in the next several minutes, beginning with his meeting with Olema Marsh less than a month ago. He ended by deferring to Peter, who gave his interpretation of the autopsy report, which was also news to Elizabeth and Leah.

"So you see," Gordon concluded, "we have a lot of suspicious deaths, several tantalizing clues, but at the end of the day we're nowhere. There's nothing positive enough to go to the sheriff with, and we really have no idea at all what the underlying connection might be in all these accidents. If, in fact, there is one." He paused and looked across the table at Lindsay. "If you have any thoughts, I'd love to hear them."

She took a sip of wine and collected herself before answering.

"It sounds to me as if you've done as much as you can, given your standing. You said you've gotten nowhere, and I'm afraid that's where you're likely to wind up. I'm guessing the sheriff isn't entirely satisfied about these accidents ..."

"I have a good source who says he isn't," Gordon said.

"All right, then. He's probably going to keep going on this to the extent he can, and if there's anything to turn up, well, with his resources and his knowledge of the town and the people in it, he has a better chance of getting somewhere at this point than you do. You might want to conclude you've done what you can and spend a bit more time fishing."

"It may come to that."

"Still, having told you, in effect, to go home, I have to say there's one thing about what you said that troubles me."

She paused and looked out the window. The rain was falling hard again.

"The timing of Olema Marsh's death. I don't like it at all. The fact that she sought you out and brought you up here, then had that 'accident' just before you arrived, is something that should set off red flags. Does the sheriff know she'd just called you in?"

"I tried to explain, but he wasn't very interested," Gordon said.

"Understandable. I assume you've tried tracing Mrs. Marsh's activities the last few days before she died?"

"I don't know how. She lived alone."

"Did she have an appointment calendar?"

"It's already been checked. The dental appointment a few days earlier was the highlight."

"You might want to take another look. I'm afraid that's all I can come up with now. Has anything occurred to anyone else?"

She looked around the table. No one said anything for a minute, then Leah raised her hand.

"This is just a question," Leah said. "I mean, Peter's idea about the bath creeped me out, but if there's anything to it, doesn't it seem pretty obvious that it had to be someone who knew her pretty well? Well enough to know where her house was and that it had a tub?"

"You can't say for sure," Lindsay said after a silence. "But yes. Yes, the evidence would seem to point that way."

IT WAS A CONVIVIAL DINNER, and by the end of it, Lindsay Judd — whether she wanted to or not — knew the general outline of Gordon's past cases. That was through no fault of Gordon's (he would just as soon have stayed off the subject), but rather was owing to Peter, Leah and Elizabeth, who kept bringing them up. By the time they got to dessert, he was more than ready to change the subject.

"So, Detective Judd," he began.

"Lindsay. Please."

"All right. Lindsay. You've been hearing an awful lot about what we're up to, and you've asked a lot of good questions. But you haven't told us much about yourself. What brings you to this far corner of California — business or pleasure?"

"That's a good question."

"Surely, it shouldn't be too hard to answer."

"All right," she said, after a pause. "But I'll have to keep it pretty general."

"Fair enough."

"I'm off the clock right now. I took a couple of days off to check out a lead in a cold case from five years ago. I'm doing it on spec, but if I come up with something — and odds are I won't — I may be able to get retroactive approval for time and expenses."

"And you think there's a connection between your five-year-old case and Barnstaple?" Peter asked.

She shook her head. "No. Barnstaple's just where I'm stopping for the night. Tomorrow, I'm going to a place called Dandelion Terrace, where there's somebody who claims he knows something about it."

"Dandelion Terrace," Gordon said. "That doesn't ring a bell at all."

"It's a suburb of Twin Rivers, in Nevada."

"I've been to Twin Rivers, though not recently. I didn't realize it had suburbs, but then a lot of people in California have been retiring to Nevada lately. Anyway, it's what — 60 to 70 miles north of here on a state highway?"

"Sixty-six. And you know more than I do, because I've never been to Twin Rivers."

"It's a bucolic little place, or at least it used to be. I remember it's in a rich, fertile valley, where the East and West Gemini Rivers meet."

"Sounds lovely. Anyway, my informant — if, indeed, he has any real information, is there. It's the first lead of any kind in three years, so I was willing to take time off to follow it up."

"You're here alone," Elizabeth said. "Don't you have a partner — detective partner, I mean?"

"My partner on the original case was Tony Morales, who's long since moved on to the Orange County Sheriff's Department. I called to let him know about the lead, and he wished me luck, but he's out of it now."

"Can you tell us a bit about it?" Gordon said.

"I really shouldn't be talking about it while I'm investigating. Not the details of it. But I'll tell you this. When you work homicide, you don't solve every case, but some of the unsolved cases bother you more than others. This one's my dream catcher."

Gordon remained silent, and after a minute, she continued.

"By all rights, we should have solved it quick, but we didn't come close. And I had a bad feeling about it from the very beginning. The first two weeks it felt like we were swimming in Jell-O, and it never got better. As far as I'm concerned, there's only one good thing that came of it."

"What's that?" Elizabeth finally said.

"The day we found the body, I smoked my last cigarette."

"WE COULD LOOK IT UP on the internet," Elizabeth said. "There can't have been that many murders in Long Beach five years ago, and the newspaper's online archives must go back that far."

"Maybe later," Gordon said. "Right now I don't want to be distracted from my own investigation. Such as it is."

They were at the table in their cabin at Broderick's. Night had fallen, and they were sipping herbal tea.

"And you have to admit," Elizabeth said, "Stella was right about her being a cop."

"I already admitted it on the way home. And paid for your wine. Good catch. Livened up the dinner conversation, anyway."

"You liked the fact she was asking about your cases."

"I guess I did, but she was just being polite. A detective in a city the size of Long Beach isn't going to be impressed by anything I've done. And to change the subject, did Leah say when she'd be back?"

"I told her she had to be back by 11 so we could leave for Buckley by 8:30 tomorrow."

Gordon looked at his watch. "So an hour or less."

"Don't get any ideas. It could be any time."

A gust of wind came up outside, followed by a brief downpour that lasted less than two minutes. The rain was still dripping off the roof of the cabin when Elizabeth spoke again.

"I guess there wasn't a volleyball game tonight, what with the weather."

"No, but her admirer is still around. She was checking her phone furtively the last half hour of dinner."

"I noticed that, too. The dinner ran kind of long. I hope she's all right. It's chilly out there with the rain and wind."

"I'm sure they'll find a way to stay warm."

"Gordon! Good God! What kind of a father are you going to be?"

"A realistic one, I hope. Leah's old enough and savvy enough to take care of herself. And even if she weren't, I doubt she'd listen much to me."

"Maybe more than you think. Perhaps I should sound her out a bit when we're alone in Buckley tomorrow."

"I thought Stella was going with you tomorrow."

"Stella can take a hint. I'll give her that. What are you doing tomorrow?"

"I don't know. My investigation seems to have stalled. I'm thinking Peter and I can do some fishing and talk it over during the slow spells. Maybe one of us will have an inspiration. Something has to start moving on this thing — and soon."

Saturday June 10

GORDON'S CELL RANG at 5:45 a.m. The sun had been up for seven minutes, but Gordon hadn't. It took him 20 seconds of fumbling to find the trilling phone on the small table next to the bed.

"Gordon, this is Lindsay Judd. I hope I'm not calling too early."

"No," he mumbled. "It's fine."

"I woke you up, didn't I? Sorry about that, but I need to ask a favor, and time's of the essence."

Wondering what she was talking about, he struggled to get partially upright, and in so doing, awakened Elizabeth.

"Something that came up at dinner last night got me thinking."

"Uh-huh."

"It was when Elizabeth asked about my partner."

"And you explained why he wasn't here."

"Right. But when I got back to my room, I realized it would be a good idea to have one. Don't get me wrong — I doubt the guy I'm going to see is anything worse than an obsessive crank, and I'll be checking in with the local sheriff beforehand. Safety's probably not an issue. Still, in an interview, it's a good idea to have two people for situation control and to provide two perspectives on what's said. And it wouldn't hurt if the second one was six-four ..."

"Six-five."

"Whatever. And athletic looking. That could nip a bad thought in the bud."

"Where are you going with this, Lindsay?"

"I'm meeting my tipster in Dandelion Terrace at 10:30 this morning, so I want to leave here by 8:45. How'd you like to be my partner for the day?"

He didn't answer immediately, then said:

"Are you in the habit of asking people you've only known 12 hours to help you on a case?"

"Only if they have good references, and yours are A-1. I called Sheriff Huntley in Alta Mira last night ..."

"I wish I'd known. I'd have asked you to give her my regards."

"Well, she sends hers and she spoke very highly of you. And speaking of regards, she said Diane said to say hi. I won't ask."

"Diane's the district attorney."

"I guess that's your story and you're sticking to it. But we're getting off topic. Are you interested?"

"Sort of. But tell me exactly what you expect and what the terms are."

"Show up at the Lake View Motel at 8:45. I don't suppose you brought a coat and tie with you on a fishing trip?"

"As a matter of fact, I did."

"Wear 'em. It'll make you look more official. We'll leave Barnstaple, drive to Twin Rivers, check in at the sheriff's office, and visit our informant in Dandelion Terrace. I'd be surprised if the interview runs longer than 45 minutes, and then we can discuss it over lunch at the Wortle Hotel."

"The Wortle. Is that still there?"

"Apparently so, and lunch is on me. Then we drive back here, and you can still get in an afternoon of fishing if you like. What do you say?"

Gordon looked at Elizabeth, who was clearly trying to figure out the conversation from the one end of it she could hear.

"Yes, on one condition. On the way to Twin Rivers, you have to brief me on the case you're investigating."

"No problem under the new circumstances. It would be stupid to send you into the interview cold."

"All right, then. I'm in."

"Great, and thank you. I appreciate it. I'm in room 17. Knock three times, and I'll be right out."

"Room 17, Lake View Motel, 8:45 a.m., knock three times."

"See you then."

He turned off the phone, set it on the small table, and sighed. He turned and looked at Elizabeth.

"Well?" she said.

"Looks like I get to wear the coat and tie."

FOLLOWING BREAKFAST at Broderick's Café, Gordon and Peter drove into Barnstaple. Gordon was wearing tan khaki pants, a blue dress shirt with a maroon tie dotted with images of Rainbow Trout, a brown herringbone sport coat and Mephisto loafers. He brought along a small notebook and had two pens in his shirt pocket. He may not have looked like a cop, but he looked as if he meant business.

He pulled the Cherokee into the Lake View Motel and drove down the horseshoe driveway until he came to room 17. He stopped in front of it, engine still running, and looked around.

"Lost something?" Peter asked.

"I don't see her car anywhere."

"How do you know what her car looks like?"

"I don't. But nothing here looks like government issue." He turned off the engine and handed the key to Peter. "What are you doing with the wheels today?"

"Since the ladies are all going to Buckley, I figured I'd do some solitary fishing. Probably try the East Gemini below the dam again."

"Good luck, then. I should be back by two or three. Want to meet me at the Happy Scoop?"

"Sure." He paused. "How come you're going off with the detective on her case, when you're getting nowhere on our case?"

"That's exactly why. Maybe looking at another case helps. And if it doesn't, at least I get a break."

Gordon got out and checked his watch. It was 8:43. He walked to the door of room 17 and gave it three hard raps. It opened almost immediately. Lindsay was wearing expensive jeans, a blue blouse and a leather jacket. She did a quick inventory of Gordon's appearance.

"You said to wear a coat and tie," he said.

"You're too well dressed to be a detective," she said, "but I'm guessing our guy won't know any better. Shall we go?"

She ducked back into the room and emerged with a shoulder bag. Gordon waved to Peter, who drove off.

"Where's your car?" Gordon asked.

"Take two steps backward, and you'll be sitting on the hood."

"The black 'Vette?"

"I'm off the books right now, so I'm driving my car. You have a problem with that?"

"No." He looked at the Corvette. "I've never ridden in one of those before. It should be fun."

He got in awkwardly. It was lower than any vehicle he was used to. Lindsay slid effortlessly into the driver's seat. When they were both in the car and its doors were closed, Peter drove off in the Cherokee.

"I see your friend was waiting for us to get in the car before he left," Lindsay said. "I hope Elizabeth isn't apprehensive about your coming with me."

"Only a little."

"Tell her not to worry. I never had any luck with married men, and I've stopped trying."

Two minutes later, they were on the highway to Twin Rivers. It was a beautiful, sunny day with only a couple of stray clouds in the sky. The previous day's storm had scoured the air and tamped down the dust and dirt on the ground. They passed the Barnstaple Marina, the Beck house, and the dam. Below the dam, they saw Gordon's Cherokee in a turnout, where Peter had left it. Fourteen minutes after leaving the motel, they had crossed the state line and were in Nevada. Neither of them had said a word since leaving town.

"You were going to tell me about your case," Gordon said.

She sighed. "I guess a deal is a deal."

"A PENNY FOR YOUR THOUGHTS, Elizabeth."

"Thanks, Stella."

"You're worrying about him, aren't you?"

"Only a little." She swerved to avoid a pothole on the road to Buckley. Leah pitched sideways in the back seat of the Subaru.

"There's no point to it. It never does any good."

"I know that. Everybody knows that. Still …"

"Listen, honey, you have to be a realist about this. Gordon is tall, rich and mysterious. Of course, women are going to be attracted to him. You were. But he's never struck me as a man who's looking for trouble."

"Trouble seems to find him."

"He can handle it. Now Peter. He created a lot of his own trouble. Unlike Gordon, he's short, financially stressed from five alimony payments, and crabby. I don't have to worry about other women trying to take him away from me." She laughed.

"What *do* you worry about?" Leah asked.

"I worry about why I want him in the first place."

"FIVE YEARS LATER, this is still a tough one for me to talk about," Lindsay said. "It shouldn't have been a hard case to crack, and yet from the get-go I had a bad feeling about it." She deftly negotiated a sharp curve. "I don't know where to start."

"How about the beginning?" Gordon said.

"Smartass. All right, then. Monday morning in May, just over five years ago. Francine Hawes, the deputy city clerk, doesn't show up for work. It's not like her, but everybody figures she had a doctor's appointment or something and forgot to tell anybody. By eleven o'clock they're not so sure anymore and they ask the PD to check her house, since she didn't answer the phone.

"Officer Mary O'Hara drew the assignment and went over. No one answered when she knocked, and she walked around the house but the blinds were drawn. The back door was unlocked, and after knocking again, she went in. Francine Hawes was dead on the couch, with an electrical wire pulled tight around her neck."

"Oh, God."

"I know. It was O'Hara's first murder and she wasn't expecting it at all, which made the shock even worse. She left the house without disturbing the scene any more than she already had and called it in. Morales and I were put in charge, and practically the whole detective squad was sent over to help."

"Was it a burglar?"

"It was no burglar. There was a suspect who had moved front and center from the start. Francine Stevens had bought the house a few years earlier when she'd just turned 40. She wasn't married, didn't have any prospects, had just gotten a promotion at work and inherited some money from her grandmother. She paid cash for the house. She was living there by herself, seemingly happy and content."

"What kind of person was she?" Gordon asked.

"From what we could tease out of her co-workers, she was generally liked and universally respected. Did her job really well. A smart woman, but shy, not many close friends, and fairly plain looking, though she could have done more with what she had. Anyway, her life as a middle-aged single career woman seemed to be going along fine until she made what turned out to be a bad decision."

"Which was?"

"She decided to go on a cruise. In November of 1994, she left on a ten-day cruise from Los Angeles to the Mexican Riviera and back."

"I have a sinking feeling about where this is going," Gordon said.

"She booked a single room, and on the third night out found herself sitting at a table with a single man named David Hawes. He told her his wife had divorced him for another man and he was lonely. She was lonely. Sparks flew. She fell head over heels. The last night of the cruise, he proposed to her on the deck of the ship, under the moon and stars. She said yes without any hesitation. She'd given up all hope and then found Mister Right on a cruise ship. They were married by a superior court judge the last Friday of December. He said it would be better for taxes.

"So naturally, we wanted to talk to David, but he wasn't there, and their car wasn't there. Everybody in the neighborhood remembered him, but nobody had seen him for a few days and nobody could give us a decent description. Distinguished looking middle-aged guy, soft spoken, friendly when you talked to him but didn't start conversations on his own. It wasn't very helpful."

"How about the house?"

"That's where it became even more obvious. The place couldn't have been more immaculate if you'd sent a haz-mat cleanup team through it. No fingerprints — nothing. And no photos, mementos, handwriting samples. He apparently had a California driver's license because a clerk at the nearest Safeway remembered him showing it when he wrote a check for groceries the week before she was killed. But the DMV had no record of him on file."

"So the license was bogus?"

"Had to be. We put out an APB on the car, and two days later an airport security guard spotted it at long-term parking."

"At LAX?"

"Nope. John Wayne in Orange County. Less than 30 miles away. The car was wiped clean, just like the house. There were a couple of hairs in it, but no roots so we couldn't get DNA from them. Anyway, we went into high gear at that point. We got the passenger lists from every plane that flew out of that airport from 10 a.m. Saturday until we found the car. There was no David Hawes on any of them. No David Hawes rented a car at that airport or stayed in a hotel within five miles of the airport. We got the number of a credit card he used at a local store the week before the killing, but it hadn't been used since the Friday before the Monday we found the body.

"In other words, David Hawes drove to John Wayne Airport Saturday morning, parked his car in long-term parking and disappeared into thin air. That was five years ago, and there hasn't been a trace or sighting of him since."

"How do you know he drove there Saturday morning?"

"One of the neighbors saw the car in the driveway when she was walking to the convenience store a couple of blocks away at eight o'clock. When she came back 15 minutes later, it was gone, and nobody saw it any later than that."

"That is one weird case."

"You haven't even heard the good part, Gordon. We of course checked their financial records, and those told the story. After they got married, they put everything into joint accounts. And apparently, David talked Francine into taking out a home equity loan of a hundred twenty-five grand on a house worth two hundred. The Thursday before we found the body, he went to the nearest FedEx office and sent an envelope overnight to a bank in the Cayman Islands. He'd written checks for practically everything they had, payable to the order of a numbered bank account. Nearly 250K. By the time we found the body on Monday and got through the financials on Tuesday, the checks had cleared, and there was no way of retrieving the money."

"And the bank wouldn't cooperate, I assume."

"In the Cayman Islands? Are you kidding me? The only way you'd get information out of a bank there is if the president sent in the Marines."

"You're dealing with a bad actor here."

"That's the understatement of the year, Gordon. This was as cold-blooded, vicious and premeditated as any mob hit I've ever heard of. There's nobody I want to get my hands on worse than David Hawes, or whatever he's calling himself now."

They were silent for a minute.

"It could be a tough case to prove in court," Gordon finally said.

"Actually not. We have an ace in the hole that I doubt David Hawes even knows about."

Gordon didn't reply, and she continued.

"When she was murdered, Francine Hawes was six weeks pregnant. At the age of 46, if you can believe it. That gave us the father's DNA. If we ever find the creep, he's toast."

LINDSAY CAME OUT of the sheriff's office in Twin Rivers and slid into the driver's seat of the Corvette. It was 10:15. To get to the town, they had driven through a red rock canyon and emerged into a lush valley, irrigated by the West and East Gemini Rivers, which come together here. Between the abundant water and the alluvial river soil, the valley was green and fertile, home to grazing cattle, alfalfa, and various row crops. The town was much as Gordon had remembered it, down to the apparently thriving Rexall drug store on Main Street.

"I did a courtesy check-in," Lindsay said, "and picked up some scuttlebutt on the man we're calling on. Duncan Bennett, probably in his mid-fifties, been here a little less than two years."

"Originally from Long Beach?"

"No. Upstate New York, actually. The story is he worked for a good-sized newspaper there, editing one of the sections. He was coasting through life when his wife asked for a divorce and took the house. Not long after that, he tripped over a computer cord in the newspaper office and broke a hip. While he was recovering and collecting worker's comp, the paper did a round of layoffs, and being out of sight and out of mind, he was one of the ones that got it in the neck."

"An American story," Gordon said.

"He had no luck finding another job, then his aunt, who had no kids, died and left him her house in Dandelion Terrace, free and clear. He moved out here and has been living the recluse life on an SSI check and whatever savings he's got."

She turned left on Fifth Street, heading for the highway that bypassed the town on the west side. They drove through a seedy industrial area featuring storage facilities, auto repair shops, a self-serve car wash, and a convenience store advertising fried chicken, liquor and ammo.

"He came to the notice of the law just once — a year ago, when one of the neighbors complained that he frightened her children by screaming at them for playing on his lawn," Lindsay continued. "And that's about the book on him."

"So how did he get on your radar?"

"Apparently he's been holed up with his computer, investigating unsolved crimes through whatever information he can find on the internet. Earlier this week, he posted his first blog, called Carl La Fong Investigations. One of Francine's neighbors saw it and called me, quite upset."

"And you're not going to tell me what he's saying?"

"You'll hear it from him soon enough, and I want to get your first reaction based on that."

By now she was heading north onto the highway. A mile later was a traffic light, and she pulled into the left-turn lane. On the hillside above the road they were turning onto was a large billboard reading "Dandelion Terrace: A Secluded Community," with a large red arrow pointing left under the words.

"A secluded community?" Gordon said. "Sounds posh."

"Not what I was expecting," Lindsay said. "But let's see."

They drove up the side of the hill, and when they went over the rim saw a huge crater, a mile and a half in diameter on the other side. It seemed to have been gouged out of the earth, with piles of sand and rock, rusting machinery and run-down buildings everywhere. There was no sign whatsoever of anything remotely resembling ongoing human activity.

"Good God!" Lindsay said. "What the hell is this?"

"If I'm not mistaken," Gordon said, "it's an open-pit mine. Deserted now, but it must have been something huge at one point." It occurred to him that the place was a more modern Buckley, only without the charm. It was inconceivable that any tourist would want to come here in a hundred years.

The road led down the other side of the hill to the bottom of the pit, then turned south. The black Corvette was the only car on it. As they drove through the pit, with its man-made detritus all around them, there was no sound but the wind. Nothing to suggest that a human being, or even a bird, was around. As they approached the southern edge of the pit, they could see several rows of small houses built into its side, beginning about 50 feet above the floor of the crater. When they reached the first cross street, they saw a sign identifying the subdivision as Dandelion Terrace. Lindsay stopped the car. There was no reason to worry about blocking traffic.

"What on earth is this doing here?" she asked.

"Probably company housing," Gordon said. "The mining company collected rent from its employees and kept them away from the sinful temptations of Twin Rivers."

"What sinful temptations? Never mind. This is First Street, and Bennett lives on Third, number 309. We're a couple of minutes late already."

She drove up two blocks and turned left. After crossing the north-south street, they were on the 300 block. Number 309 was a white house, about 900 square feet, with chipping paint, a flat tarpaper roof, and a beach-blanket-sized lawn consisting mostly of crabgrass. The blinds on the windows were closed, and the house would have looked deserted except for the 1992 Ford Ranger pickup in the carport. They parked in front and looked at it for a minute.

"The last time I went into a house that looked like this," Lindsay said, "it was occupied by a fat, balding guy in a wife-beater, drinking Oly. The bedroom was full of drugs and guns."

She looked at her watch.

"We're three minutes late, and looking at this place isn't going to make it any better. Let's go."

She flung open the door on her side and got out and up in one fluid motion.

ELIZABETH WAS SET UP in front of the church, and Stella was staying with her for the time being, so Leah was given permission to explore, with the usual warning to be careful. She knew exactly where she wanted to go. Since she first saw Buckley two days earlier, she had been fascinated by the old Boot Hill on the hillside above the town to the east. She headed straight toward it.

At the edge of town, a trail about three feet wide headed up the hillside to the cemetery, which was several hundred yards from the nearest town building. It was surrounded by a chain-link fence, but Leah assumed there would be a gate.

There was, but it was padlocked, and several signs attached to the fence warned that the cemetery was a restricted area and closed to the public. Leah fumed. She just wanted to look at the gravestones and she would have been careful and respectful. It wasn't fair.

After a moment of simmering discontent, she looked back toward Buckley. Owing to the angle of the buildings, Elizabeth and Stella were out of sight. The Subaru was the only vehicle in the parking lot, but another car was coming over the hill toward town. It was Saturday, and there would probably be more people here today. If she wanted to see the cemetery, she should probably act now.

The fence was eight feet high, but there was no barbed wire or other deterrent on top of it. The top of the gate was a smooth metal cylinder, an inch and a half in diameter. Climbing over at the gate should be no problem for a healthy teenager, and Leah was inside the fence ten seconds after she decided to go.

She walked slowly along the row of graves closest to town and was surprised by how many of them were women under the age of 40. It occurred to her that many of them had probably died in childbirth, and if that didn't get them, the times were such that an attack of the flu, an infected cut, or a simple fall could be the beginning of the end. She remembered one of her high school teachers saying that the life expectancy for an American born in 1900 was 47. For the people who came to Buckley in the late 1800s, it was probably lower than that.

Staring at the grave of a woman named Molly Burke (1861-1893, Beloved Wife and Mother), Leah got the sense she wasn't alone. She looked around and saw no one. It took her a minute to realize where the feeling had come from. She indeed was not alone; she was in the silent company of the dead. Once she realized that, she calmed down.

Two-thirds of the way up the hill was a monument that dwarfed all the others, and Leah walked toward it. It was a large slab of gray marble, seven feet high and four feet wide, set on a concrete base six feet wide. She stood at the edge of the base and read the inscription:

William Henry Cox
February 10, 1850 - January 23, 1899
Beloved Husband and Father
Humble Servant of God

She stood there wondering who he might have been. Someone important and wealthy, from the evidence of the headstone. A banker? A mine owner? The mayor? And for all his importance and wealth, he never made it to 50, and he missed the beginning of the 20th century.

She was still staring at the date of death when a man stepped out from behind the headstone.

DUNCAN BENNETT WAS WAITING at the front door when they got there. He was five-seven, with a potato-chip belly and a scraggly, unkempt beard that looked as if it had caught, over the years, the remnants of whatever potato chips hadn't made it to his gut. He wore glasses with dark, thick frames over eyes that bugged out and constantly darted around the room, as if in search of hidden spies and conspirators. His hair was grayish-dark, sorely in need of a trim, and seemed to be simultaneously greased down and sticking up all over. On a warm June day that was getting hotter by the minute, he was wearing black Ben Davis overalls with the straps pulled over a red, white and green flannel shirt.

"Nice car," he said, looking at the Corvette. "I assume it doesn't belong to the Long Beach PD."

"Nope," Lindsay said.

"Is it street legal?"

"None of your damn business." Then, recovering, "I'm Detective Lindsay Judd. This is Detective Gordon."

She offered a hand for him to shake, but he didn't see it. He was looking up at Gordon, who was almost a foot taller.

"So, Gordon, you have a first name?"

"Not that I care to use. And you can address me as Detective."

Bennett turned around and walked back into the house without saying a word. After waiting several seconds for an invitation that didn't come, they followed him inside and closed the door. The interior temperature was in the low 60s, thanks to a swamp cooler that blew in from one of the windows. Books, papers, and bound reports covered almost every available surface, but aside from the clutter, the place wasn't as dirty as it might have been. There was no decoration of any sort on the walls, and in a corner as far from the living room window as possible stood a small work table with a large desktop computer screen and keyboard covering nearly its entire surface.

He sat down on a rolling desk chair in front of the computer, then, remembering his manners, stood up and picked up two folding card-table chairs that were leaning against the wall. He handed one to Gordon and one to Lindsay, still folded, and sat down again. They looked at each other and simultaneously reached the conclusion that their host didn't stand on ceremony. Unfolding the chairs, they sat down facing the computer screen.

"I've put together a little PowerPoint presentation for you," Bennett said.

"Before we get started," Lindsay said, "Could I ask you a question? How, exactly, did you come up with the idea for this project of yours?"

Bennett turned to face them.

"When I was a young reporter, 25 years ago, I had a conversation one day with a detective I've never forgotten. He was investigating a murder that seemed totally random, and he told me off the record they'd probably never solve it. Then, he added that there are serial killers out there who move around from place to place, and nobody ever connects their crimes. I never forgot that.

"So when the newspaper made me redundant and I had some time on my hands, I decided, just for the hell of it, to put the internet to work on his theory, basically searching newspaper stories online. And now, if you'll stop asking questions, you're about to see the results."

He turned back to the computer, opened a folder, and opened a file inside it. A grainy, black and white photograph of a plain-looking middle-aged woman appeared on the screen.

"Meet Darlene Davenport, director of a student internship program at Northern Arizona University. She was 42 years old and had been single all her life when she decided to take a cruise in late 1993. On that cruise, she met a man named Donald Holden, fell madly in love, and married him a month after the ship docked. They settled in Flagstaff, Arizona, where she worked — until Tuesday, February 22nd, 1994, the day after a three-day weekend, when she didn't come into the office. Her co-workers finally called the police, who found her at home with her throat cut. There was no sign of her husband, and their car turned up at long-term parking at Phoenix airport a few days later. He didn't catch a plane — at least not under the name of Donald Holden — and not hide nor hair of him has been seen since. Oh, and all their bank accounts were cleaned out, along with a home equity line he'd talked her into taking out."

Gordon heard Lindsay draw in her breath sharply. Bennett kept talking, his voice growing steadily louder and more agitated. He brought up a photo of another middle-aged woman on the computer.

"That's Francine Stevens of Long Beach, California, who became Mrs. David Hawes. You already know the story, so I'll skip over the details of this one. I'm sure even you see the similarities."

He clicked, and another photo of a middle-aged woman came onto the screen.

"Francine Hawes' body was found Monday, May 15th, 1995. Seventeen months later, on October 14th, 1996, Virginia Burgstrom, who you see here, didn't show up for work as a purchasing officer for a Las Vegas casino. She was 47 and had been married once, more than 20 years earlier, but by this time was long-divorced with no children. They called the police in Henderson, Nevada, where she lived with her new husband, Daniel Hines. She met him on a cruise ship. There was no sign of him, but their car turned up in long-term parking at McCarran Airport in Vegas. It's the closest they ever came to catching the guy because even though it was Columbus Day when they found her, it wasn't a holiday for the casino. He must have thought he had an extra day because he got to the airport on Sunday afternoon, according to the parking records. And, of course, no one named Daniel Hines had flown out of the airport. But all the Hines's liquid assets had been cashed out."

He looked at Lindsay and Gordon and flashed a big smile with his dirty yellow teeth.

"Do I have your attention now? Because there's more."

Another image of a plain, middle-aged woman came onto the screen.

"Our man apparently laid low through most of 1997. Then he ran into Eleanor Gluck, who you see here. She was 51 and single when she took a cruise, where she met a man named Douglas Hurd. Love at first sight, their friends all said. The ship's captain married them on the last day of the trip, and they returned to Eugene, Oregon, where she worked as an academic liaison for women's athletics at the University of Oregon. On Monday March 2nd, 1998, a neighbor dropped by the house and found the back door wide open. And Mrs. Hurd drowned in the bathtub. Her husband and the car were gone, and all their money had been withdrawn from where it was deposited. Would you care to guess where the car was found?"

"Portland airport," Gordon said. "Long-term parking."

"You're good," Bennett said. "Most people would have guessed the airport at Eugene."

"Too small," Gordon said. "A greater chance of being recognized there."

"Right. And in any case, no one named Douglas Hurd had flown out of Portland in recent times, and the man again vanished without a trace. In all these cases, by the way, there apparently were no fingerprints, no DNA, no photograph of the perp. He was described as a quiet, unassuming, distinguished-looking middle-aged guy."

Gordon thought he heard a short, low-pitched groan coming from Lindsay.

"But we're not done yet," Bennett said, sitting up and flashing a big, toothy smile. He called up a picture of yet another middle-aged woman.

"On Monday July 5th of last year, police found Patricia Fairchild Hale dead in her townhouse in Santa Rosa, California. She was killed execution-style, with a single shot to the back of her head from a .38 pistol. The hospital where she worked as accounts manager called the police when she didn't show up for work. They never found the gun, and they never found her first and only husband, a man named Dennis Hale. Would you like to guess where he met her?"

"I think we know that," Lindsay said.

"On a cruise, of course. And, of course, all her money had been cleaned out, and of course, the car was found at long-term parking at San Francisco International. Where, believe it or not, a man named Dennis Hale hopped a flight to Chicago Sunday afternoon."

"You mean …?" Gordon asked.

"Not the right Dennis Hale, though. It was a 23-year-old graduate student at Northwestern University. Like Donald Holden, David Hawes, Daniel Hines, and Douglas Hurd, our Dennis Hale vanished without a trace."

Bennett turned and faced Lindsay and Gordon, who were sitting three feet away. He was practically shouting by now, becoming more profane and spraying saliva as he screamed.

"Don't you see? They're all the same guy! They have to be. He uses the same initials every time — D.H. The motherfucker doesn't even have to change the monogramming on his fucking suitcase! It's been almost a year since his last victim, so he's probably planning another cruise right now. If he hasn't already taken it and found his next victim. He's ready to kill again. What are you going to do about it?"

Drained from his presentation, Bennett slumped back in his desk chair. Lindsay and Gordon sat in stunned silence for half a minute. Finally, Gordon took a handkerchief out of his jacket pocket and, as unobtrusively as possible, dabbed at the drop of Bennett's spittle in the corner of his left eye.

"DON'T DO THAT, JOE!" Leah said. "You startled me."

Taken aback, Joe Price put his right hand on the side of the headstone and smiled sheepishly.

"That was thoughtless of me," he said. "My apologies." He scanned the town and saw that no one else was near the cemetery, or even in sight, and continued, "I figured I was alone here and then I heard someone else. I didn't know who it was, and since I was here illegally, I decided to take cover."

"I guess I'm here illegally, too," Leah said. "But I've been wanting to take a closer look at the cemetery ever since the first day here. I couldn't pass it up, and since I'm not going to disturb anything, I thought it would be OK."

"Same here."

"Is this your first time — in the cemetery, I mean?"

147

"Well, if you promise not to tell anyone about it, no. I've come up here several times before. Like you, I find it fascinating. I guess we're birds of a feather."

"Do you know much about it?"

"A little."

Leah gestured at the large headstone. "Who was William Cox?"

"Ah. Now that I can tell you. He was the manager of the largest mine in Buckley. From what they say, a hard man indeed. He overworked and underpaid the men who worked in his mine. I'm sure he got a percentage of the profits, so he had an incentive to be mean."

"He must have been rich."

"I'm sure he was. By Buckley standards, anyway. But in the end, what did it get him? A bigger headstone than the men who worked for him, or just about anybody else in town. You think that matters much to him, wherever he is now?"

"Probably not," Leah said.

"I don't think so, either. But that's what I like about cemeteries, especially the ones that have some history. They remind you how short and fleeting life is. I'd like to believe that gives me a bit of humility and perspective."

"It almost sounds like you're saying life's meaningless."

"Not at all. It means everything while you're living it. So you have to take care of yourself."

"And help others."

"That too. I'm afraid I don't do as much of that as I should."

"Almost nobody does." She pointed at the far corner of the cemetery. "What are the graves over there — the ones with no headstones?"

"Probably where the people without money were buried. I expect there were wooden crosses at the time, but they've long since rotted away."

"Who do you think they were?"

"People who just got here. People without a family. Disreputable people, like the gamblers and prostitutes. Those poor women didn't have much of a life to look forward to. In a lot of cases, they didn't have very long to live."

"That's sad."

"Yes it is. One of the things about coming here is that I realize I've already lived longer than most of the people buried here. And that my time is coming, probably sooner than I think."

He looked at Leah, a look of curious and abstract examination.

"You're probably 18 to 20, right, Leah?"

"Nineteen."

"A good age to be, if you make the most of it. The road ahead of you is wide. It stretches out almost forever, and it can still take you almost anywhere you want to go. At my age — I'll be 52 on the Fourth of July — the road's a lot narrower and shorter. I maybe have time for one more course correction before it's too late."

"It sounds like you have something in mind."

"I've kind of been taking the first steps, but the early going's been rough. I don't know."

"Do you want to talk about it, Joe?"

He laughed. "Yes and no. It's not an easy thing for me to talk about, and I'm not ready just yet. But I have enjoyed talking with you. I don't get much of a chance to talk to young people where I live these days."

"Would that be in Barnstaple?"

He didn't answer immediately.

"I'd rather not say," he finally said. "Why don't we agree to keep it a secret for now?"

"RIGHT AT THIS MOMENT," Lindsay said, "I can't make up my mind whether to hang myself with a bed sheet or just turn in my badge."

They were seated at a table, covered with red cloth, at the back of the dining room at the Wortle Hotel, near the kitchen door. Gordon had pointed out that it was about the worst table in the house, and that the place was empty enough they could have gotten a much better one. She dismissed the suggestion. "I like sitting back here, with my back to the wall," she had said. "I can see everybody who comes in, and almost nobody can see me."

So they had sat at the table in the back, wordlessly reading the menu, and lapsing into silence again after ordering, until she finally broke the silence with her outburst.

"Is it really *that* bad?" Gordon said.

She shook her head. "It is. We were so fixated on the husband as suspect that it never occurred to us he might have done it somewhere else."

"Do you think it occurred to the detectives in the other cases Bennett was telling us about? It didn't seem like anyone else picked up on it, either."

"Doesn't matter. I should have."

"What should you have done differently? Did you check the FBI database?"

"No, and it probably wouldn't have helped. TV and the movies make it sound a lot more complete and connected than it really is. It's great for making connections on really weird shit, like when a killer carves a pentagram on the body or mutilates it in a specific way. In a case like this, where a husband kills his wife and does it in a different way each time, you wouldn't get a match. If I'd checked the California criminal justice records after that killing in Santa Rosa, I might have made a connection, but it still would have been a long shot."

"Then why be so hard on yourself?"

"Because I realize now this was a planned crime from the beginning, and there were enough clues when it happened to point to that. I should have gotten it and I didn't. When we get back to Barnstaple, I'm going to put in calls to the detectives in all the other towns where our serial husband was at work."

"I'd love to help you," Gordon said, "but I'm hoping when we get back, I can be relieved as your partner."

"Sure," she said, and laughed for the first time. "When you told Bennett to call you Detective, I almost lost it. In fact, it was such a good line, I'm not going to arrest you for impersonating a police officer."

The waitress arrived with their order. They had both opted for the House Special — shepherd's pie, with a pickle on the side. They dug in. It was as good as it was unhealthy. After a few minutes, Lindsay stopped eating and shook her head.

"I can't get over how simple it was, what Duncan Bennett did," she said. "It goes to show that an amateur can sometimes succeed by asking a question a professional would be too smart to raise."

"I know," Gordon nodded. "He had his hare-brained idea, only it turned out not to be so hare-brained. He did an internet search for unsolved murders in Arizona, figuring it was a relatively small state, in population anyway, but big enough to have a few cases. He spotted the Darlene Holden story and picked up on the fact that she met her person-of-interest husband on a cruise."

"And then," Lindsay said, "he did a search on murders and cruises and found four other cases, including mine. All on his own, he turned up a serial killer, who, unknown to all of law enforcement, had married and murdered five different women."

"Aren't you jumping to a conclusion?"

"What? You don't think the same guy committed all those murders?"

"Oh, I'm pretty sure of that. But let me ask you a question. In a case like yours, would the detectives necessarily reveal the cruise ship angle to the press?"

"Good question. And I'd say probably not. Depends on how much of a sense of human interest they had or whether it seemed relevant to the case."

"So what I'm saying," Gordon said, taking a sip of iced tea, "is that Bennett only found the cases where the cruise ship connection made the news story. There could very well have been others. He — and we — could be looking at the tip of the iceberg."

AFTER LINDSAY AND GORDON left, Duncan Bennett strutted around the cramped quarters of his house, working off nervous energy. He was elated that the meeting had gone so well and that he had so clearly dominated it. The woman detective had been clearly floored by his findings; her partner had more of a poker face and was harder to read. Eventually, the adrenalin rush wore off, and he realized he was hungry.

He went into the kitchen and made a sandwich of peanut butter and Smucker's grape jelly, taking care to first trim the moldy edges off the bread. The half-carton of milk in the refrigerator had a sell-by date of the previous Tuesday, but it passed the sniff test and he poured a glass.

Then he remembered the email he was waiting for. He took the sandwich and milk to his computer and, to his delight, saw that the answer had come. Munching the sandwich and sipping the milk, he read over the entire thread of the communication. It began with one that had arrived for him by the time he logged on shortly after eight o'clock that morning:

Mr. La Fong (or whatever your name is):

I have just been alerted to your website, with its post about the murder of Francine Hawes in Long Beach CA in 1995. You state she might not have been the only victim of a serial killer and that information on other cases will be forthcoming.

If one of these involved Virginia Hines, who was killed in Henderson NV in October 1996, I need to speak with you immediately. Let me know if this is the case, and if so, where you are and how I can reach you. If you have any information relevant to the Hines murder, I will be on the first plane I can catch in order to interview you.

Detective Frank Warner
Henderson, NV Police Department

When Bennett had first read the email, a surge of pleasure, unlike anything he had ever experienced, ran through his entire body. Detective Warner had been quoted in the news stories about the Hines case, becoming more and more wretched as time wore on with decreasing hope of an arrest.

And now Detective Warner was ready to give up his weekend to come talk with Duncan Bennett. Life was getting good.

Bennett thought it over and sent the following answer before Lindsay and Gordon's visit:

Detective Warner:

I can probably make time to meet with you tomorrow. You won't even need to catch a plane. My name is Duncan

Bennett, and I live just outside Twin Rivers NV, only a few hours' drive from you.

On Sundays, I customarily have brunch at noon at the Wortle Hotel in downtown Twin Rivers, after taking my pickup to the car wash. If you would like to meet me at the hotel, perhaps we can begin the discussion then.

If this is agreeable, confirm the meeting for noon and notify me what you will be wearing or how I can identify you.

Duncan Bennett
Carl La Fong Investigations

Bennett had read and revised the email several times before sending it to make sure it conveyed the proper sense that he, Bennett, was in charge of the meeting. Mentioning the car wash in the second paragraph was, he thought, a particularly nice touch, putting the detective on notice that he rated lower than Bennett's vehicle. All those years of writing for the newspaper had paid off.

And the detective hadn't blinked. Half an hour after Bennett sent his reply, the detective had answered. Getting ready for his meeting with Lindsay and Gordon, Bennett hadn't seen it until just now.

Mr. Bennett:

Thank you for your prompt reply. I will drive up first thing tomorrow morning and meet you at the Wortle at noon. I will be wearing a navy Ralph Lauren polo shirt and a red baseball cap with the logo of the Clark County Sheriff's Posse. Lunch is on me. Until then,

Detective Frank Warner
Henderson, NV Police Department

Bennett cackled when he read that. Three months ago, he had felt like a loser who was taking up space on the planet, and now people were beating a path to his door. And offering a free lunch, no less.

"LET'S ASK THE WAITRESS," Gordon said. "She's probably been around long enough to know."

"You ask. She'll be friendlier with you."

Seconds later, she came to the table.

"Can I get you anything else?"

"Bring the check to me," Lindsay said, "and my friend has a question."

"Right," Gordon said. "We've just come from Dandelion Terrace, and we were wondering how it got its name. It doesn't seem to fit."

The waitress laughed. "You'd never guess in a million years," she said. "It's a local joke."

"Give us the punch line."

"Well, the mine you drive through to get there was owned by the Copperhead Mining Company for years. In the 1950s, they decided to build company housing for the employees. They cut that terrace into the side of the mine rim and built those houses up there. They decided to name the housing development after the chairman of Copperhead Mining."

She paused and grinned.

"I'm afraid I don't get it," Gordon said.

"His name was Daniel D. Lyon, so of course before you know it, all the locals were calling it Dandelion Terrace instead of Daniel D. Lyon Terrace. By the time the mapmakers got around to it, Mr. Lyon had retired, and the company decided not to argue with the people."

"No kidding?"

"No kidding."

"Then I have another question for you. I always thought company housing was rented, but we were visiting a friend up there who owns his house and inherited it from his aunt, who also owned it."

"You must mean Mr. Bennett. He has lunch here every Sunday at noon. The places there *were* rentals, but the company made one exception. If a man died on the job, his widow could buy the house if she could come up with the money. When Clyde Bennett was crushed by a backhoe that rolled over on top of him, his wife, Ruby, had enough from the life insurance and savings to buy the house. After the mine was closed, Copperhead sold the housing to a local real estate company, except for the three houses owned free and clear by widows. The rest of them are all rented — well, at least the ones they can find tenants for."

She put the check on the table and left. Lindsay started to pay in cash, then put the money back in her wallet and took out a credit card.

"I could be getting reimbursed, now that this trip isn't a wild goose chase," she said. "You've been looking broody the last few minutes, Gordon. Anything on your mind?"

"I don't know. Something Bennett said rang a bell in connection with what I'm looking at in Barnstaple. But he was going a mile a minute, and I lost the thread." He shook his head. "If it's anything important, it'll come to me."

ELIZABETH HAD SET ASIDE the painting of the church for the time being and moved to another part of town. The previous day she'd done a sketch where Buckley's main street intersected another street that ran uphill for a block before leveling off at the top of a slight rise. The part of the street that leveled off was invisible owing to the angle, so that it looked as if the street simply vanished into infinity. The part of the side street closest to the main street had two-story commercial buildings on either side, then became a row of one-story homes. On the right side of the road, a rusted-out Chevy pickup from the 1930s was parked next to one of the houses. The town had maintained a small population up to the early 1950s, so that made sense.

Leah had returned from the graveyard and left again with Stella to show her around the town. Elizabeth had been painting by herself for nearly an hour, interrupted only by a visit from a county parks employee and a family of five from Glendale touring the ruins. She was fiercely concentrating on the canvas when a shadow came over her and it.

As still and quiet as it had been, with not even a whisper of wind, she hadn't heard anyone walking up.

She jerked to attention, whirled around sharply, then relaxed.

"Oh, it's you, Joe. I didn't hear you coming up behind me."

"I'm terribly sorry," he said. "I must learn not to tread so lightly. I'm afraid I gave you a start, and did the same to Leah earlier today."

"It's all right. No harm done."

Neither of them spoke for several seconds.

"I was looking for you over by the church," Joe said. "I was hoping to see how your painting was coming along."

"Very well, I think." She paused, and after a silence realized he was probably waiting for her to show it to him. "I'm afraid I can't show it to you now. I'm kind of superstitious about that sort of thing. I don't even show my paintings to Gordon until I think they're done."

He raised his eyebrows slightly and looked at the ring on her left hand.

"And would Gordon be your husband?"

"Yes. Gordon's his last name, but that's what everyone calls him."

"I see. So I suppose I have to wait until your show opens in San Francisco this winter. I should look for an exhibition by Elizabeth Gordon."

"Actually, no. I took Gordon's name for financial and legal documents, but in my painting and teaching I still use my maiden name, Elizabeth Macondray." She spelled it for him.

"There seems to be a lot of that these days," he said. "In any event, it would give me a reason to get to San Francisco at Christmas. I haven't done that in a few years."

"Check with Shaughnessy Gallery first. I'm supposed to give them a definite answer next week, and with what I'm getting out of Buckley, the answer will be yes if they're still interested."

"I'll make a point of doing that."

Elizabeth turned back to the canvas and saw two people coming over the crest of the hill. It took her several seconds to confirm that they were Stella and Leah.

"Here's Leah now," she said, "and our friend Stella. I'd like you to meet her."

They arrived a fraction of a minute later. Elizabeth stood up.

"Stella, I'd like you to meet Joe. He's visited Leah and me here a couple of times already."

She turned around to complete the introduction, but no one was there. And despite the stillness of the day, she hadn't heard so much as a rustle behind her. Her mouth opened involuntarily.

"That's strange," she said, turning back to Leah and Stella. "Did you see Joe, Leah?"

"Sorry," Leah said. "I was looking at the buildings on the left side of the street."

"I was pretty much looking straight down the street once we came over the rise," Stella said. "I didn't see anybody but you."

"WHAT ARE YOU GOING to do next?" Gordon asked, as they got into the Corvette.

"I'll stay in Barnstaple overnight," Lindsay said. "It's nice and quiet, and I can write up a report on this morning, maybe go for a drive and clear my head. And I'll get a head start on calling the detectives in all the other places where our D.H. has been at work. Tomorrow I'll head back to Long Beach."

"You're welcome to join us for dinner. I'll be doing a barbecue up at the resort."

"That's decent of you, but I need to get my work done." At the western edge of Twin Rivers, she turned south on the bypass highway and said, "I appreciated your coming with me this morning. Bennett got under my skin, and you helped center me a bit."

"Glad I could contribute."

At the southern edge of town there was a traffic light where the highway met the end of Main Street. It turned red just before they got there.

"Tell you what," Lindsay said. "We need to have a little fun." She reached into her purse and took out a $20 bill, setting it flat on the top of the dashboard in front of Gordon. "If you can catch it when I go through the green light, it's yours."

"Come on, Lindsay. You already paid for lunch, and in case you didn't know, I went to college on a basketball scholarship. I still have the reflexes."

"Good for you. The light's about to change."

It turned green, and she was through the intersection in the blink of an eye. Before Gordon even had a chance to react, the bill had whizzed past his left ear. A few seconds later, they were on the open highway doing a steady 70.

"Maybe 90 percent of the reflexes," he finally said.

"Don't beat yourself up, Gordon. That's the same twenty I've been using since I bought the car three years ago. Nobody's caught it yet."

LINDSAY DROPPED GORDON off at Happy Scoop shortly after 2:30. Peter was waiting. Gordon got a small frosty and joined him.

"I tried the East Gemini below the dam again," Peter said. "There was a pale morning dun hatch, and I caught seven or eight on a dry fly. Twelve to 16 inches."

"Not bad."

"How about you?"

"Well," Gordon licked his frosty, "our detective friend seems to have gotten herself hooked up with one helluva case."

"In what way?"

"I'll tell you more later, when we're in a more private setting, but the bare bones of it are that she thought this guy we saw today, Duncan Bennett — who, by the way, is a story in himself — could help her with a five-year-old cold case involving a husband in her city who apparently strangled his wife and disappeared into thin air with all her money. Bennett's theory, which I have yet to find a hole in, is that Lindsay's case wasn't the only one. He claims the guy, under various names, married, killed and made off with the liquid assets of five different women."

"A regular Bluebeard," Peter said. "And I thought I was a bad husband."

"You know, Peter, there was something he said that rang a little bell in the back of my head, but I can't remember what it was. He was talking fast and spittle was flying, and I was trying to write notes with the names and places." Gordon shook his head.

"Regarding our case, I got to the local A.A. meeting at one o'clock, and the conversation beforehand was interesting."

"In what way?"

"Well, several of the people were talking about how many accidents the town's been having this year. Olema Marsh dying apparently made the topic fresh again. Two or three of them were expressing some reservations about whether they were all accidents, saying there were just too many."

"Interesting. I wonder if the sheriff is picking up on that?"

"I don't know. But I found it kind of ironic that it was being discussed in the basement of the church where Luther Whitman fell, or was thrown, from the bell tower."

Gordon jerked upright and forward.

"Luther Whitman. That's what was nagging me. Listen, Peter. Our Bluebeard's first murder — or at least the first one that Bennett cottoned to — happened in Flagstaff, Arizona, about six years ago. It was five or six years ago that Luther moved to Barnstaple from Flagstaff. I wonder if he was there when the crime was committed, and maybe had met the husband."

Peter didn't answer right away. Finally, he said, "It's possible, I guess, but right now it seems like that's an awfully long coincidence. I'd file it away for future reference, but that's about all."

Gordon gave his frosty a few deliberate licks.

"I'm going to take half your suggestion, Peter. I'll file it away for now, but I want to pinpoint those dates so I have a better sense of whether it's worth pursuing."

He whipped out his phone and called Luther Whitman's daughter. He got voicemail.

"Hi, Judy," he said, "this is Quill Gordon. Say, this probably isn't important, but I wanted to pinpoint exactly when your father came here from Flagstaff, and depending on the answer, maybe ask if he mentioned something that happened there a few years ago. Could you give me a call at your convenience? Thanks."

"It's probably a good idea to dot the i's and cross the t's," Peter said after Gordon put away his phone. "But unless you can connect your serial wife killer with someone else in Barnstaple, I still say it's the longest of long shots."

STELLA BEAT ELIZABETH to the punch in asking Leah about her young man. She began the inquiry as soon as they were headed down the mountain, with Buckley out of sight.

"So, Leah," she said, "are you going to be playing volleyball with your — what should I call him — your new male friend tonight?"

"It's not just him. There are eight to ten people on each side."

"I'll take that as a yes, then."

"There's no phone reception in Buckley. I haven't even heard if the game is on."

"All right, supposing it is, that'll be four nights in a row you've gone off with — what's his name again?"

"Brian."

"Right, Brian. I've only seen him from a distance a couple of times, and he seems like a nice enough young man, but don't you think it might be time to introduce him to Gordon and Elizabeth?"

"Gordon and Elizabeth are great, but they're not my parents. And I'm a legal adult, in case you hadn't noticed."

"Oh, I've noticed, all right. But you're a young and inexperienced adult. What do you really know about Brian?"

"I know that he treats me and other people with decency and consideration. I know he has a sense of humor and I can talk to him. I know he has plans. He wants to go to law school and be an environmental attorney. He's no phony, Stella. He's real. So can we change the subject?"

Stella shut up for a few minutes, then tried another tack.

"How about the other man in your life? The mystery man, Joe Price, who seems to be stalking you and Elizabeth."

"Oh, please," Leah said. "Joe's old enough to be my father, but I talk to him just to be nice."

"To be nice?"

"I don't know him that well, but the couple of times I talked to him, I got the sense he holds things in and that there's a lot of sadness in his life. It's even made him a bit morbid. Sometimes I get the sense he's half dead."

Elizabeth finally broke into the conversation.

"Actually," she said, "considering how Joe appears out of nowhere and disappears just about as quickly, I kind of wonder if he's not completely dead."

GORDON BARBECUED PORK CHOPS coated in teriyaki sauce for dinner. Elizabeth cut up potatoes, onions and a green pepper and sautéed them in olive oil, while Stella and Leah threw together a salad. It was a fine night, with a slight breeze coming off the lakes, and they ate at the picnic table outside. Gordon took the lead in the discussion, recounting his trip to Twin Rivers with Lindsay and their meeting with Duncan Bennett. He left out the part about the Corvette and the $20 bill.

When he got to the part about Bennett's website being called Carl La Fong Investigations, Elizabeth and Peter went wild, redoing the Carl La Fong scene from the W.C. Fields movie *It's a Gift*, with Elizabeth taking the part of the insurance salesman and Peter playing the Fields role. Gordon immediately realized why the name Carl La Fong had sounded so familiar. Stella was not amused. Leah wanted to know who W.C. Fields was anyway.

Aside from that, they listened attentively and put forth a number of questions.

"How could this guy keep changing identities and stay off the radar in this age of computer tracking?" Stella asked.

"Lindsay — Detective Judd — said there are plenty of people in Los Angeles, San Francisco, or any other big city for that matter, who can produce very high quality fake passports and driver's licenses," Gordon said. "They're not cheap, but with the money he's stealing from his wives, it's probably just part of the cost of doing business."

"It sounds like the women were old enough to know better," Leah said. "How could he get them to rush into marriage and sign over their money so easily?"

"This guy — assuming they're all the same guy — is probably a skilled predator who has a sixth sense about when women are lonely and vulnerable, and by now he's probably got all his moves down just right."

"How sure are you and Detective Judd that all these killing husbands are in fact the same man?" Elizabeth said.

"Let's put it this way. If two men with the initials D.H. met a woman on a cruise ship, married her after a whirlwind courtship, put all her money into joint accounts, transferred it into a Cayman Islands bank account, killed her and disappeared, it would be one of the most staggering coincidences of the century. When it happens five times, I don't see how you can conclude it's anything other than one extremely bad killer at work."

Stella sighed. "I guess it's good to know there's at least one loser out there I haven't dated."

"I wouldn't exactly call him a loser," Peter said. "So far, he's gotten away with the murders and the money every time."

"He'll lose sometime," Elizabeth said. "He'll slip up and make a fatal mistake. It's only a question of when."

When they finished dinner, Peter was elected to wash the dishes in light of the fact he hadn't helped with dinner. He trudged off to the sink cheerfully, or at least what passed for cheerful with Peter.

Leah asked if she could be excused to join the volleyball game. Gordon and Elizabeth nodded assent. She took three steps toward where it was played, then came back.

"I almost forgot," she said. "There's going to be a nondenominational service here tomorrow morning at ten in the amphitheater. I'd kind of like to go, if that doesn't interfere with leaving for Buckley."

"You're in luck," Elizabeth said. "I was thinking of taking a day off from painting tomorrow."

"Would you like to come to the service?"

Elizabeth and Gordon looked at each other.

"If it makes any difference, Brian will be there. It'll give you a chance to meet him and do your *in loco parentis* thing."

"Sure," Gordon said after a beat. "We'd love to."

WHILE PETER WASHED the dishes, Stella and Elizabeth kicked back in chairs on the porch of Stella and Peter's cabin.

"Funny kid," Stella said of Leah. "She's too young to really know a lot, but she sure seems to know her own mind."

"She's curious and seems to be getting a good education," Elizabeth said. "I doubt if she ever heard the phrase *in loco parentis* before she went to college. In place of the parents. One of the first Latin phrases I ever learned."

"Speaking of vocabulary, did you notice she used the word 'phony' this afternoon? I didn't know kids her age still used that word."

"I have a pretty good guess at the explanation for that. She probably had to read *The Catcher in the Rye* for one of her freshman English classes."

BEFORE HEADING OFF on dishwashing patrol, Peter had taken Gordon aside to say they needed to talk. They agreed to meet later at one of the picnic tables by the lake.

Gordon claimed one at the edge of the picnic area, where they would have privacy, not that anyone else was using the other tables. Peter arrived and sat down. They looked out at the lake and listened to the sounds from the volleyball game in the distance.

"This afternoon," Peter finally said, "when you were giving me the Reader's Digest condensed version of your visit with the mad computer genius, I told you there probably wasn't any connection with our investigation, unless we could connect the Bluebeard character to another one of our victims."

Gordon nodded.

"Listening to you talk at dinner, I spotted a second connection. Remember when we went to see Jim Starr, Lucy's husband, and we asked him to show us a picture of her? What did he bring over?"

"I'm thinking," Gordon said. "It was a picture of Lucy and her sister."

"Correct as far as it goes. But where were they?" Gordon shook his head. "They were on a cruise ship. I remembered that, because Lucy couldn't swim and was afraid of water, but she went anyway. I think it was her sister's birthday."

"Ho-lee cow," Gordon said. "I'd forgotten that. But if it was taken in the past few years ... No. It can't be. I mean what are the odds she ended up on a ship where our wife-killer was pitching the woo to one of his other victims?"

"Long, but not impossible, I'd say. And it would explain things, at least. In any case, I think we'd be negligent if we didn't follow up on it."

"Shouldn't be that hard to do. I'm sure Starr can give me a name and phone number for the sister. And I'm sure Lindsay can get a passenger list for whatever cruise Lucy was on. She'd have to be interested in that. If nothing else, we could at least rule it out quickly."

"So are you going to call Starr?"

Gordon looked at his watch. It was just after eight.

"I'll do it tomorrow. I want to think about how to approach him. This is getting scary, Peter."

"That's why I didn't bring it up at the dinner table. Elizabeth has her hands full with the ghostly character at Buckley. She doesn't need to worry yet about you getting too close to a serial killer."

IT WAS ALMOST DARK when Gordon returned to the cabin a bit after 8:30. He had a cup of herbal tea with Elizabeth, and she told him about her meeting with Joe at Buckley that afternoon. She was getting wound up about it.

"The guy's been nothing but a perfect gentleman," she said of Joe, "but he still spooks me. It just isn't real how he appears and disappears just like that. And I still haven't seen his car parked anywhere. How does he get there?"

"Search me," Gordon shrugged.

"I just hope he doesn't haunt my dreams."

Gordon had been standing by the sink. He set his cup in it and walked to the table where Elizabeth was sitting.

"Let me hold you," he said.

She stood up, and he put his arms around her, pulling her to him. After a minute, he kissed her. The kiss escalated and lasted for some time.

"Why don't we ...?" Gordon murmured.

"What if Leah comes in?"

"She won't be back for at least an hour and a half." He kissed her again. "A lot can happen in an hour and a half."

"I can't think when you do that," she said.

"You're not supposed to."

She took a half-step back, looked at him for a few seconds, then slipped her right index finger between his belt and jeans, pulling him toward her again.

"Follow me," she said.

Shortly before midnight, more than three hours later, Leah slipped quietly through the front door. Gordon and Elizabeth were sound asleep.

Sunday June 11

A MINISTER AND YOUTH CHOIR from Carson City, Nevada, had left at sunrise and come by bus for the nondenominational church service at Broderick's amphitheater. It was a perfect summer morning — clear and warming toward a hot day. By the time the service started at 10:00, about a hundred people were on hand. Gordon, wearing yesterday's khakis and a long-sleeved shirt with no tie, was probably the best-dressed man there. Most people wore more casual vacation attire.

The service was upbeat and lively. The choir sang well and often, and the sermon was on the importance of being less selfish and helping others. It was a sentiment Gordon approved of, even though in practice he could stand improvement. The hour and a quarter went by pleasantly, and at the end he was glad he'd gone.

Afterward, he, Peter and Elizabeth (Stella had passed on the service) thanked the minister for coming down to do it, shook his hand, and complimented the sermon. By the time they'd waited in line to do that, Leah was bringing Brian over to formally introduce him.

He was a bit under six feet tall, with short, dark hair, brown eyes and a strong jaw. He shook Gordon's hand firmly and looked him in the eye as he did so — evidence of a good upbringing, if not necessarily proof of good character.

"Good to meet you, Mr. Gordon. Leah's told me a lot about you and Elizabeth."

"A pleasure to meet you, Brian. And you can drop the 'Mister.' Just call me Gordon. Everyone else does."

"All right." He paused for a few seconds. "I understand your father is Judge Gordon in San Francisco."

Gordon nodded.

"I heard him at Santa Clara this past winter quarter. He was one of the speakers in a lecture series put together by the law school."

"I didn't know that, but I'm not surprised."

"He was talking about the practical reality of running a courtroom."

"Everybody says he's pretty good at it," Gordon said. "How was the lecture? Tell me the truth; I won't be offended if you didn't like it."

"Oh, but I did like it. He was clear, concise and confident. If he had any self-doubt about what he does and how he does it, he sure didn't let on."

"That's him, all right."

"What I really related to was his realistic approach. I like people who understand that the world's not perfect but try to do their part in it the best they can."

Gordon smiled slightly. "We may have a point of agreement there."

"Now could I ask you and Elizabeth a question?"

Gordon and Elizabeth looked at each other.

"My family's going on a picnic to Sumner Lake today," Brian said. "We'd like to have Leah come along if it's all right with you."

"What does Leah think about it?" Gordon asked.

"I'm in," she said quickly. "That is, unless Elizabeth has work for me to do."

Elizabeth smiled.

"I'm not painting today, and I don't think Gordon's investigating today. We all have the day off. Go ahead, and have a good time."

AT EXACTLY ELEVEN O'CLOCK, Duncan Bennett stepped out the front door of his house and locked it behind him. In his left hand was a briefcase given to him as a college graduation present 30 years ago. It held a printout of the presentation he'd given Lindsay and Gordon the morning before. He climbed into his pickup and drove down the terrace to the pit.

He passed through the abandoned mining operation without seeing another car on the road. As he was coming down the other side, heading toward Twin Rivers, a medium-sized black pickup pulled out of a turnout and got behind him. He didn't notice.

Bennett turned off the state highway onto the cross street Lindsay and Gordon had taken the day before. Because it was Sunday, every business but the car wash and the chicken-liquor-ammo store was closed, and there was almost no traffic. He turned left into the car wash. No one was using it, and he wouldn't have to wait.

It was a self-serve wash. A driveway looped around to the back of it, where there was a payment kiosk accepting cash or credit cards. After digesting Bennett's five-dollar bill, the machine sent him forward. A green arrow led him into the wash, and a sign flashed bright red lettering, telling him when to stop. He put the pickup in park and set the parking brake.

Going to the car wash was the best part of the week, he often thought. You sat in the car for five minutes while the soap, water and brushes worked over the vehicle, and it felt as if all your worries were being washed away at the same time. The feeling rarely lingered more than a few blocks from the wash, but five good minutes was as much as Bennett usually got these days.

The first round of soap washed over the windshield, diminishing visibility and making Bennett feel cocooned inside the pickup. He leaned back in his seat and took a deep breath. He closed his eyes and opened them again. He saw movement ahead of him, at the exit to the wash. It looked like a human figure, silhouetted against the bright Nevada sun. It came into the car wash toward the pickup.

"He must be crazy," Bennett thought. "It's dangerous in here. He could slip and fall on the slick pavement."

The man walked up alongside the driver's window, which was covered with rivulets of soap. He raised his right hand. A gun fired three shots in as many seconds. The shooter turned and walked out the front of the car wash, just before the soap spray made its second pass over Bennett's pickup, sending soap and water through the three bullet holes in the driver's window.

Three minutes later, the local agent for a nationally advertised insurance company pulled up at the kiosk on the way back from church with his wife and seven-year-old daughter. The daughter loved the car wash almost as much as Bennett did. He paid with a credit card and got back into the car. Seconds later, the red sign inside the car wash turned green, directing Bennett's pickup through the blow-dryer at the exit. But the pickup wasn't going anywhere.

The agent waited 30 seconds, and when the pickup remained motionless, he tapped his horn lightly as a courteous nudge. When the pickup remained motionless, he hit the horn harder, and when that didn't work, he got out to investigate.

He walked up to the driver's-side window, which was now clear after the soap had been rinsed off. When he saw the bullet holes and what was inside, he recoiled in horror and took a sharp step backward. He lost his footing and fell. His head hit the side of the car wash hard, and he was instantly knocked unconscious.

His wife frantically called 911 on his behalf, and it was the paramedics who called the sheriff about Bennett's body when they arrived six minutes later. It was another four minutes before the first patrol car arrived. By that time, the shooter could have been miles away in any direction.

The coroner's report later said that three bullets from a .38-caliber pistol had struck Bennett in the forehead, neck and to the right of his heart, and that any one of the shots could have killed him in short order, if not instantly. Duncan Bennett died before he had a chance to collect his free lunch.

"TELL ME AGAIN why we're doing this," Elizabeth said.

"I want to check something out," Gordon said.

They were on the road to Buckley in Gordon's Cherokee, Peter and Stella having taken Elizabeth's Subaru to Barnstaple. It was nearly one o'clock; the temperature had passed 80 and was climbing.

A few minutes later, Gordon continued. "I've been hearing about your friend Joe secondhand. Time I did my own investigation."

"What are you expecting to find?"

"I'm looking for Joe's parking spot or, failing that, his horse."

They went over the slight rise leading into Buckley. The tourist traffic had increased on Sunday, and there were eight cars in the parking lot. Gordon drove around the perimeter of the town, looking carefully around, and stopped in the parking area.

"Nothing jumps out at me," he said. "Although I suppose there could be a place to park next to or even inside one of those old buildings."

"I wouldn't count on that. It's really quiet up here. When I'm painting, most of the time I could hear a car engine start up in the parking lot. If stealth was the object, there's too much chance of being seen or heard in town."

"You're probably right. Well, it was a thought, anyway. And not an unpleasant drive."

He backed out and started to drive away from Buckley. When the road went over the rise on the way out, he slowed down, then stopped in the middle of the road. He pointed to the right side, where there was a verdant area with cottonwood trees and green bushes rather than the dry desert brush.

"Must be a spring here," he said, "or the water's right under the surface. I wonder ..."

He eased forward slowly, barely creeping along, looking at the vegetation on the right.

"What have we here?" he said, stopping.

"It looks like a little cart track going into that thicket," Elizabeth said. "I never noticed it before."

"Let's see where it goes."

"Gordon! What if we get stuck in there?"

"Then we wait until one of the tourists is leaving, hitch a ride into Barnstaple and call for a tow truck. Come on."

Gordon turned into it and moved forward slowly. The path was narrow enough that grass and bushes scraped the doors of the Cherokee, but it could keep going. Thirty feet in, the path bent to the right, and a bit beyond that, it opened up into a clearing about 30 by 50 feet. After going forward and backward a few times, Gordon had the front of the Cherokee pointing toward the path again, ready to head out.

"I think we just found Joe's reserved parking space," he said.

They got out and walked around. In one corner of the clearing, half a dozen empty beer cans had been tossed out, and there were a few pieces of paper litter about.

"Somebody's been here anyway," Elizabeth said.

"I don't really feel like doing it in this heat," Gordon said, "but I'm guessing it's only a few minutes' walk into Buckley."

"I wonder how he found this place."

"Other people did. Once you're looking for something like this, it's pretty obvious."

"But who would use it?"

"For starters," Gordon said, "every high school student in Barnstaple. After all, I didn't see a drive-in anywhere in town."

LINDSAY WAS 50 MILES south of Barnstaple, doing 70 in a 55 zone, when her cell phone rang at 1:15. Reaching into her purse, she grabbed the phone and answered without slowing down at all.

"Detective Judd," said the voice on the other end, "this is Sergeant Tom Roberts from the sheriff's office in Twin Rivers. Something just happened that you should know about."

"Yes?"

"You checked in yesterday morning to let us know you were interviewing a man named Duncan Bennett in connection with a cold case down south."

"That's right."

"Well, Bennett was just murdered. Less than two hours ago."

Her stomach tightened into a knot.

"What — how did it happen?"

"He was shot to death in a car wash, if you can believe it. Three shots through the driver's-side window."

"Suspects?"

"Nobody saw a thing. Perp got away before anybody could get there."

"Shit. This is bad."

"You're telling me. We were hoping to talk to you and see if you could give us any leads."

There was no one on the road in front of her or behind her. She saw a turnout ahead and skidded into it, throwing up dust and gravel. After a quick look in both directions, she turned north, heading back toward Barnstaple and Twin Rivers.

"I'm on my way. I'll be there in an hour and a half, maybe two hours. Listen, sergeant. There's something that has to be done, and it's very important."

"I'm listening."

"Bennett was looking into the possibility that a cold case of mine was connected to several other murders. He could have been getting too close to someone for comfort and that's why he got shot."

"But how would the serial killer know?"

"Same way I did. Bennett posted a story on his website, Carl La Fong Investigations." She gave him the website address. "What he posted was only a small part of what he knows, but he was teasing readers with the prospect of more information. Everything he has is on his computer at his house in Dandelion Terrace. You need to take possession of that computer ASAP — if it's not too late."

"Will do. I'll get a unit up there right away. See you in a couple of hours."

She drove up the road several miles and pulled out, less dramatically than the last time, at another turnout. She called Gordon, but the call went straight to voicemail. She left a message and started out again.

Fifteen minutes later, her phone rang again. It was Sergeant Roberts.

"I have an update," he said. "Do you want the good news or the bad news first?"

"The good news. I haven't had much this week."

"We got a state police backup unit to Bennett's house. It's locked up, and the neighbor, who's been home the last two hours, said no one's been near it. Looks like we'll be able to get the computer."

"Great."

"The bad news is I just looked at the Carl La Fong website. The only thing up there now is a cartoon showing Snow White and the Seven Dwarfs doing things Disney never imagined. That site was hacked big time."

PETER AND STELLA walked into the Barnstaple Historical Museum. It was in a two-story white clapboard house about 90 years old. The upper floor housed the administrative offices, such as they were, and served as storage for exhibits not being displayed at the moment on the ground floor.

They were greeted by a woman in her late fifties with short, light brown hair and smiling blue eyes.

"Welcome to our museum. I'm Clara Hammer, one of the docents." Peter and Stella introduced themselves, and she continued, "Where are you folks from?"

"San Francisco," Peter said.

"That's not so far. We had a family from Germany the other day. They didn't stay very long. Is there anything in particular you're interested in?"

"No," Stella said. "We just wanted to look around and see what you have."

"Are you staying in this area?"

"At Broderick's," Peter said.

"That's a nice place."

"We've been enjoying it," Stella said.

"Well, look around, and if you have any questions, feel free to ask."

The main room downstairs featured standing exhibits, maps and black and white photographs depicting the broad strokes of the history and development of Boundary County. Another room was devoted entirely to the history of Buckley, with numerous photographs, diagrams of the town's main mines, and a case of pioneer artifacts. The third room downstairs held a traveling exhibition put together by the California Water Resources Agency about where Sierra water comes from and where it goes. Peter was so fascinated by it that Stella finally had to drag him away.

They spent 35 minutes in the three rooms. A couple in their twenties, who appeared urban in origin, made the pass-through of the museum in half the time and had gone by the time Peter and Stella got back to Clara's desk at the front.

"How'd you like it?" she asked.

"Very interesting," Peter said.

"He could have looked at the water room all afternoon," Stella added.

"That would have been a first," Clara said. "Do you have any questions?"

"Two, actually," Peter said. "I noticed in the Buckley room there wasn't any mention of law and order. Do you know if there was a lot of vigilante justice — lynchings and that sort of thing?"

"There was. For a while, the town was called Bloody Buckley. I've argued that we should say something about it in that room, but the Historical Association has so far insisted that we shouldn't put that sort of thing out. It would harm the area's reputation and all that."

"Were there any lynchings where they got the wrong man, or just an innocent one?" Stella asked.

"I'm sure there were. Everybody who was hanged, or just about everybody, claimed to be innocent. And it's not like there were trained detectives or strictly run courts in those days, so mistakes could be made."

"Are there any legends about ghosts of hanging victims haunting the town?"

Clara smiled. "Some people say the ghosts of wrongly hanged men can be heard moaning at twilight sometimes."

"Do you think that's true?" Peter said.

"It's probably the wind blowing through the old buildings, but the moaning ghosts are a better story."

"So now that we've discussed justice," Peter continued, "let's talk about scandal. There was no mention of it in the Buckley room, but people are people. There had to be some. Dish the dirt for us, Clara. What was the biggest scandal in Buckley? Mayor caught in a bordello?"

"That would have been all of them," she said. "You're my kind of inquisitive visitors. And since we're the only people here right now, why don't we do it right? Pull up a couple of chairs, and I'll tell you the story of Joe Price."

GORDON DIDN'T CHECK his phone until he and Elizabeth were back in Barnstaple, shortly after two o'clock. There was one message from Judy Beck and three from Lindsay Judd. Judy Beck was connected to the case Gordon was working on, so he called her first.

"Thanks for calling back," Gordon said. "Is this a good time to talk?"

"Just getting a start on dinner. No hurry."

"You said your father moved here from Flagstaff about five or six years ago. I wonder if you could give me a more exact time."

"No problem. I remember it really well. Dad drove up just before Thanksgiving in 1993. It was our daughter's senior year in high school. We were glad that he'd be here for the holidays."

The timing could work, Gordon thought. Luther Whitman had moved to Barnstaple three months before Darlene Holden was murdered in Flagstaff.

"Did he ever mention a man named Donald Holden?"

"I don't think so. It wasn't one of his good friends."

"How about a woman named Darlene Davenport?"

"Doesn't ring a bell at all. Sorry."

"I know it was a few years ago, but do you remember if your father subscribed to the newspaper in Flagstaff after he moved here?"

"That I do remember. He subscribed for about six months by mail after he came here, then he let it drop. He said there was no sense living in the past."

"One last question, then," Gordon said. "After he moved here, did he ever mention anything about a murder in Flagstaff? It would have been a few months after he came to Barnstaple."

There was a long silence on the other end.

"You know," Judy Beck said, "I do sort of remember that. Early in '94, I think. A woman was murdered, I think by her husband. Dad said he knew her slightly. Surely you're not suggesting ..."

"I'm not suggesting anything," Gordon said. "I'm just collecting information."

"You've got me going, though." She paused. "And maybe that's a good thing. When Dad moved here, there were several boxes of personal things he brought with him from Flagstaff. They're still sitting in his room above the barn. I haven't had the heart to go through them yet, but now I'm thinking I should. Hold on. All right, I have something to write with now. What were those names you were asking about again?"

"Donald Holden, last name spelled like the actor William Holden, and Darlene Davenport, who became Mrs. Holden."

"Got it. I should be able to find a few hours to look through Dad's things the next few days. If I see anything with those two names in it, I'll call you as soon as I can."

"Can I ask you a favor?"

"Sure."

"Could you make that right away, instead of soon as you can?"

IT WAS A LITTLE AFTER 3:00 when Lindsay Judd blew into Twin Rivers. She pulled into the parking lot by the courthouse and eased the Corvette into an empty space reserved for one of the county commissioners. She figured that at this moment she was more important than the commissioner, and she was right.

She entered the courthouse through an open back door and found the sheriff's office. Sergeant Roberts, who had called her, was at the front desk, and she introduced herself. He led her to the back, where Sheriff Herman Fink was in his office with both his detectives, Mike Daley and Jeff Cook. They all looked tense and irritable, which was understandable. They'd just been hit with the biggest crime the county had seen in decades, and no one had the slightest idea what was going on.

Sheriff Fink, a tall, heavy-set man in his late forties with a reddish-purple face, stood to greet her.

"You got here pretty fast," he said.

"I figured no one was going to be pulling over speeders right now. Did you get Bennett's computer?"

"Jeff?" said the sheriff, looking at Detective Cook.

"We got it all right. Do you want the good news or the bad news first?"

"Don't you guys know any other lines? Give me the bad news."

"The bad news is that somebody got a virus into that computer before we got there, and it's essentially worthless. To put it in tech jargon, the hard drive is a crispy fritter."

Lindsay shook her head. "And there's good news after that?"

"Relatively good," Daley said. "Bennett printed out an email about a noon meeting he was supposed to make today at the Wortle Hotel. It was inside a briefcase on the passenger side of the front seat of his pickup. Didn't even get wet when the soap and water came in through the bullet holes in the driver's window."

"Thank God for paper. Are you going to sit there grinning, or are you going to show it to me?"

Fink handed her two sheets of paper.

Lindsay read the email exchange between Detective Warner of the Henderson PD and Bennett and folded the paper, putting it in her purse.

"You talk to Detective Warner yet?"

"We're trying to," Daley said. "No one matching his description showed up at the Wortle today, and the waitresses were asking about Bennett. He's a Sunday regular. Sergeant Roberts is trying to get hold of Detective Warner, but Henderson is being cagey right now."

"Which makes your information all the more crucial," Sheriff Fink said to Lindsay. "Can you give us some explanation as to what's going on here that wound up with one of our citizens gunned down in broad daylight?"

"I'll tell you all I know," she said. "But it's a long story."

There was a sharp rapping on the door, followed by Sergeant Roberts' voice calling out, "I have something on Detective Warner."

Fink shouted for Roberts to come in.

"Henderson PD just called back," Roberts said. "You're not going to believe this. Detective Frank Warner is in Quantico, Virginia, right now, attending an FBI training session. He's never heard of Duncan Bennett, and certainly did not have an appointment to meet with him in Twin Rivers at noon today. Someone else must have sent that email."

No one said anything for 15 seconds.

"Gentlemen," Lindsay said, "we're dealing with someone who is not only really good at murder but computers too. Let me tell you what I know about him."

"THE FIRST THING you need to know," Clara Hammer said to Peter and Stella, "is that Buckley back then was a town of men without women. In the 1890 Census, the population was 7,216. Only 422 of those people were women over the age of 18. Half, if not more, of those women were working in the dance halls, the brothels, or both, which left you with a couple of hundred married women and maybe a handful of grown but single daughters living at home. Being courted by more than 6,000 men.

"One of the few married couples in town were Olaf and Ingrid Nordlund. He'd come out here from Michigan to work in the mines and wrote back home asking his family to arrange a marriage for him. They sent out Ingrid Bengstrom, and she and Olaf were married in September of 1890.

"It would appear that the arrangers didn't make too good a job of it. Ingrid had just turned 18, and Ole, as he was called, was 44. There couldn't have been much for a married woman to do in Buckley back then, and well, you know how isolated the place is. And it appeared that Ole had some problems with alcohol. There were several news stories in the Buckley paper about his being arrested for drunk and disorderly, including at least once after the marriage.

"So you had a young, attractive and unhappy wife living in a town with more than 6,000 single men. It was an incident waiting to happen, and it did. There aren't many details because no one at the time was talking, but apparently she started seeing more and more of an assistant mine superintendent named Joe Price. He was everything Olaf Nordlund wasn't — young, handsome, well spoken. One thing led to another, and he and Ingrid decided to elope. They were waiting for the right chance, and it came in early November of 1892.

"There had just been an election for president, and word had come by telegraph that the election had been won by the Democrat, Grover Cleveland. The miners were mostly Democrats, so every saloon in town was having a blowout party that Saturday night, November 12th. And word had also come by telegraph that the first big snowstorm of the season was expected that night. It was perfect. The husband would be dead drunk and probably not even notice that his wife was missing until he came to late Sunday morning. And the storm would provide some cover for their getaway.

"Joe Price rented a buckboard and horses from one of the livery stables and paid cash when he picked them up at seven o'clock. Ole left for the victory celebration at 7:30, and Joe picked Ingrid up at eight. They headed straight down the mountain toward Barnstaple, where there was a railroad station at the time.

"The storm was worse than anyone expected. It dropped four feet of snow on Buckley before it was over, and the road to Barnstaple was completely out of commission. But Joe and Ingrid had gotten far enough downhill by the time it started snowing that they were just able to get to Barnstaple. We know they made it, because he left the horses and buckboard at a local stable. By the time Ole realized she was missing the next afternoon, there was no way a posse could follow them. They tried to telegraph to Barnstaple, but the lines were down, and they didn't get them repaired until Tuesday afternoon.

"Barnstaple, being a couple of thousand feet lower in elevation, wasn't hit quite as hard, and the train tracks remained open. A Mr. and Mrs. James Smith, who gave their address as Twin Rivers, Nevada, stayed Saturday night at the Barnstaple Inn and bought tickets on the 10:14 to Reno the next morning. Had to be Joe and Ingrid."

"James Smith," Peter said. "Our man Joe had quite the imagination. So what happened next?"

"They got on the train, and that's the last anyone ever heard of them. By the time the news came through from Buckley, they had a three days' head start, and it was a lot easier for people to change their names and disappear in those days. The end of the story will never be known. For whatever it's worth, most folks around here, at least today, hope they lived happily ever after."

"Happily ever after," Stella said. "I'm not sure there is such a thing. It must have been a huge scandal. I mean, running off with a married woman back in a time when women were practically considered property."

"It *was* a big thing," Clara said. "Not quite as bad as stealing a man's horse, but right up there. It was the lead story in Buckley's weekly paper for the next two weeks, but by then it was pretty obvious that they'd gotten away with it, Joe and Ingrid, and the paper moved on to other things."

"So," Peter said, "if Joe and Ingrid got away with it, it's not likely that Joe's ghost would still be haunting Buckley today."

"Interesting that you would mention that," Clara said. "There was a bit more to the story on the Buckley end. When it became obvious that he was never going to be able to get his hands on Joe Price and give him a horsewhipping, Olaf Nordlund went to seed. Well, even more than he was already going to seed. His drinking got worse, to the point where he couldn't hold a job, and in December of 1893 he was found dead in a snowdrift at the edge of town. He apparently started home from one of the saloons drunk as a skunk and got disoriented. But here's the interesting thing."

Clara leaned forward and lowered her voice to a near-whisper. "The last three months before he died, Ole Nordlund took complete leave of his senses. He was staggering around town, begging for booze money, and telling everyone his name was Joe Price. Some of the people who were new to town thought that was actually his name. So, in a sense, he died as Joe Price.

"And the people who believe there are ghosts in Buckley think Olaf or Joe is one of them, and that you can hear his moaning for his stolen wife. On days when the wind's blowing, of course."

BEFORE LEAVING FOR BUCKLEY, Gordon had called Jim Starr at home and asked him for his sister-in-law's name and phone number. It was Viola Johnson, and she lived in a suburb of Sacramento. Gordon asked Starr to call and let her know he would be getting in touch, and Starr agreed to do so.

After talking to Judy Beck, Gordon decided to call Mrs. Johnson before listening to Judd's messages. He dialed the number (he wasn't sure if it was a landline or cell phone) and got a recording after five rings. After the beep, he left a message.

"Mrs. Johnson, my name is Quill Gordon. I believe your brother-in-law, Jim Starr, has alerted you that I might be calling. I'm looking into something on behalf of Olema Marsh, who was one of Lucy's friends, and a question's come up about when you and Lucy took that cruise. Jim wasn't exactly clear on a couple of points, and I was hoping you might be able to help. I'd appreciate it if you could call me back." He left his number.

At that point he was in the Cherokee in the parking lot of DeLuxe Supermarket, where Elizabeth was shopping for dinner. It took him a couple of minutes to get around to checking Lindsay's messages. It had been his experience, going back to his days as a stockbroker, that when people left several insistent messages in a short time, it generally had more to do with their impatience than with the urgency of the matter at hand. Finally, he listened to the messages.

They weren't what he was expecting.

"Gordon," the first one began. "This is Lindsay Judd. I just got a call from the sheriff in Twin Rivers. Duncan Bennett was gunned down in a car wash late this morning, and from the way they described it, it sounds like a professional job. I'm on my way there right now. Call me."

The second one had come in an hour later.

"Dammit, Gordon, please don't tell me you're fishing with your phone off. I may need to get in touch with you. Call as soon as you get this."

The third message had come in about the time Gordon and Elizabeth had rolled back into Barnstaple.

"I'm pulling into Twin Rivers, Gordon. When I talk to the sheriff, I may need to pick your brain for information. Call me when you're in phone range."

He sighed and called her. He was kicked over to voicemail on the second ring.

"It's Gordon," he said. "I'm in phone range. Keep me posted."

Elizabeth arrived with a bag of groceries, put them in the back seat and got in next to Gordon.

"Any news?" she asked.

IT WAS SHORTLY AFTER 5:00. Peter and Stella were back from Barnstaple, but Leah hadn't returned yet, and Elizabeth was waiting until everyone was back before she began fixing dinner.

Gordon filled Peter in on Lindsay's call about Duncan Bennett, which drew a whistle of astonishment. He said they could talk about it later, and asked Peter how he and Stella had spent the afternoon.

"We spent a couple of hours in Barnstaple, walking around the town," Peter said, "and we paid a visit to the historical museum, which was illuminating. Then we took a little drive out to Grass Lake."

"How was it?" Elizabeth asked.

"Grassy," Stella said.

"I wonder where Leah is," Elizabeth said. "She promised she'd be home by now."

Gordon's phone rang. It was Lindsay.

"Gordon," she said, "thank God we finally connected. I just spent two hours briefing the sheriff in Twin Rivers about Duncan Bennett. I need to meet with you and go over everything in your notes on our interview with him."

"It was more of a diatribe than an interview, but sure."

"How's the Mexican restaurant on the side of Barnstaple, as you come in from LA?"

"Tres Amigos? I've never been there."

"Let's try it. I'll meet you there in an hour."

"Just a minute." Gordon lowered his phone. "Lindsay — Detective Judd — wants to get together and talk about the murder in Twin Rivers this afternoon. She suggested dinner at Tres Amigos, and I really think I should go."

Elizabeth didn't look happy. Gordon turned to Peter.

"I think you'd better come with me, Peter. I'd like to have your backup on what we learned in Barnstaple."

"Go ahead," Elizabeth sighed.

Gordon raised the phone again. "Peter and I will meet you for dinner. He's been with me all along on this end."

"Fine. Tres Amigos in an hour."

"Maybe make it a little later. It's a 68-mile drive on a winding mountain road."

"I said an hour," and Lindsay ended the call. Gordon looked at Elizabeth.

"Go ahead," Elizabeth said. "Someone's been killed, and you have to help if you can."

"If it's just you, me and Leah," Stella said, "you can cut the recipe in half and save the rest."

Elizabeth nodded, and her phone rang.

"It's Leah," she said.

"I'm sorry, Elizabeth," Leah said. "We stayed at the lake longer than we expected, and I tried calling you on the way back, but we couldn't get a good signal until we got to Sierra Pines."

"That's all right. You called as soon as you could."

"Listen, Brian's family wanted to have dinner here since it's getting late, and they asked if I could join them."

"Sure," Elizabeth said, after a pause. "We're kind of going our separate ways around here."

"We'll be back before dark."

"Have a good time, then." She set her phone on the table. "Leah just bailed, too. So, Stella, what would you say to the two of us having dinner at Broderick's Café?"

"Could be fun," Stella said. She looked at Peter. "If it's ladies' night, we can speak more freely."

OVER SALAD, Stella told Elizabeth the story of Joe Price and Ingrid Nordlund as she'd heard it that afternoon. When Stella finished, Elizabeth shook her head.

"That's quite a coincidence," Elizabeth said. "Although Joe Price is not so unusual a name."

"Do you really think so?"

"What do you mean?"

"The first thing I thought of, when I heard that story — aside from the fact I hoped they got away and made a life of it — was that your ghost town visitor must have heard it, too. And appropriated Joe's name."

"Huh. I wonder."

"I mean, come on. It has to be part of the local legend. And your Joe has shown up often enough that he can't be flying in from Milwaukee to do it. He's got to live around here, right?"

"I suppose so. Did I tell you that Gordon and I found a hidden place near Buckley where Joe's probably been parking?"

"No, but it backs up my argument. Joe Price isn't his real name, and you have to wonder why he doesn't use the real one."

"Maybe when Gordon and Peter get back tonight, we should talk about that."

"Include Leah. She's seen 'Joe,' too, and it wouldn't surprise me if she had something to contribute."

"If we can get her away from that damn volleyball game."

"She's been with the guy all day. She needs a cooling-off period."

They finished their salads, and dinner arrived. Stella was having a large bowl of vegetable soup. Elizabeth had ordered spaghetti and meatballs, which was Broderick's Sunday special. As they were about to dig in, Elizabeth looked up.

"Stella, a few minutes ago, when you were telling me about Joe Price, you said you hoped he and she got away. It seemed to me there was something under the surface there."

Stella paused with a full soup spoon halfway to her mouth, as if weighing a decision.

"Do you really want to know?" she finally said.

TRES AMIGOS WAS HALF FULL when Lindsay arrived, three minutes later than promised. Gordon and Peter had taken a table in the corner, where they could see the front door. Lindsay walked in, spotted them right away, and barely broke stride on her way to the table. She pulled out the chair opposite Gordon and pointed to it.

"Can you move to this one, Gordon?"

It took him a second to realize she wasn't joking, and he stood up and moved to the chair, while she slid into the one he'd been occupying next to Peter.

"Thanks." She said. "I don't sit with my back to the door at restaurants. Not after what happened to Wild Bill Hickock."

"That was over a century ago," Peter said.

"Which means it's about due to happen again. I'm starving. Let's order, then I'll fill you in."

The server, a teenage boy with a big smile, came by two minutes later. Being three decisive individuals, they were ready to order.

After the boy left, Lindsay filled Gordon and Peter in on the details of the Duncan Bennett killing, and Gordon told Lindsay about his follow-up inquiries, as far as they'd gotten, regarding Luther Whitman and Lucy Starr.

"I was beginning to wonder if there might be a connection between your case and the investigation I'm working locally," he said. "Bennett's being shot makes me wonder even more. I mean, it stands to reason that whoever shot him isn't too far away, right?"

"Not necessarily," Lindsay said. "If the time stamp on the email is correct, whoever was impersonating the detective — let's call him the killer — confirmed the meeting with Bennett a little after 10 yesterday morning. That would have been plenty of time for the killer to catch a late flight from Boston or New York to San Francisco, then take an early plane to Reno this morning and drive down to Twin Rivers."

"Do you really think that's what happened?" Gordon finally said.

"I think it's more likely the killer lives in the western states. That's where he's been working so far."

"From that perspective," Peter said, "wouldn't it make sense for our man to move to another part of the country for a while? Look for women on cruises in the Caribbean rather than the West Coast?"

Lindsay shook her head. "Anything's possible, but our guy has a preference for the west, and until Duncan Bennett put up that website last week, no one at all was onto him. Maybe now he'll move, but my guess is he's still on this side of the continent."

"You said the computer and Bennett's website were hacked," Gordon said. "Any leads on that?"

186

"They're bringing a computer wizard from the state attorney general's office to Twin Rivers tomorrow to see what, if anything, she can salvage. Having seen a few things like this before, my guess is that the best she'll be able to do is tell us the email and hack were done through a server in Estonia or Lithuania and there's no way of tracking it."

"You mentioned long-distance flights," Peter said.

"State police will be checking everybody who flew from SFO or LAX to Reno yesterday or this morning," Lindsay said. "Anybody who bought a ticket Saturday morning or later, they'll talk to. I'm not expecting much, but it has to be done, and maybe we'll get lucky."

"I don't suppose you have a copy of the email exchange?" Gordon asked.

She took a paper from her purse.

"They gave me a printout. Take a look and tell me if you see anything."

Gordon read it twice and handed it across the table to Peter.

"Let's see if the same thing that struck me strikes you," he said.

Peter looked at it once and handed the paper back to Lindsay.

"The car wash," he said.

"Right," Gordon said. "Why would he mention that he was stopping at the car wash before meeting our man for lunch? I can't imagine any reason at all for bringing that in, and it gave the killer a lead on where to do the hit."

The three of them sat in silence for a minute.

"I hadn't picked up on that," Lindsay said, "but of course you're right. It was a totally weird thing for him to put in that email."

"I wish I knew why he did that," Gordon said.

"You can wish all you want," Lindsay said. "But the only man who can answer the question is lying in the morgue. We need to move on."

"IF YOU FEEL LIKE TELLING ME, I'd like to know," Elizabeth said.

Stella didn't immediately reply. She seemed to be carefully considering exactly what she was going to say.

"I guess I identified with Ingrid," she said. "Because of my marriage."

"That bad?"

Stella nodded. "I was a 24-year-old nurse, and he was a 26-year-old intern at the UCSF hospital. He was handsome, confident and ambitious, and I was so swept away I didn't see the danger signs. I know, it's an old story, but it's mine in the particulars. We went together for six months, got engaged, and drove to Reno one weekend to get married. Jack — that was his name — didn't have much time off. I would have liked a real wedding, but he insisted it would take too long. That should have been a tipoff about his control issues."

"Oh, Stella."

"Looking back, I can see the warning signs were there all along, but once we were married, it just got worse. For a long time, it was just verbal abuse, and I took it even though I didn't understand it. Then about 15 months in, he went into a total rage because he'd seen me smiling at a doctor I was working with. I kept telling him there was nothing to it, but he didn't believe me. Finally he hit me, and that was it."

"You left?"

"I had a black eye and needed 12 stitches in the back of my head, where I fell against the edge of a table. I hate to say it, but in a weird sort of way, he knocked some sense into me. Still, he even tried to get me to agree to say I'd fallen down the stairs. In our ground-floor apartment. When we got to the hospital, there was a police officer there on another case, and I told him what had happened."

"Did he make an arrest?"

"He didn't believe me. That was over 20 years ago, and the police and the public weren't as aware of domestic violence as they are now. But I used the hospital phone to call another nurse, and she took me home with her after I was stitched up and X-rayed. I never spent a night with him again, and the divorce went through next year. So you can see why I was rooting for Ingrid and Joe Price."

"Good for you for leaving."

"I took a lot of crap from my parents and some of my friends for doing it. They couldn't understand why I walked away from such a catch." She paused for a sip of water. "But most of them came around when Jack lost his license in New York seven years later. He threw his second wife off a second-story balcony. She was in ICU for three weeks."

"Did he go to jail for that?"

"She wouldn't press charges. That's the last I heard of him, thank God."

"And you haven't married again?"

"Would you, if you had my record? Actually, Peter asked me last year. I told him I didn't think I was ready, but I'm getting a sense that he's thinking about asking again."

"I'm surprised. After five failed marriages, I didn't think he'd be up for another one."

Stella smiled. "You don't know Peter. He actually *likes* being married. It was just his wives who didn't. At least not to him."

Elizabeth took a swallow of wine, in lieu of saying what she was thinking.

"I'll say one thing for Peter," Stella said. "He's not violent, and he'll back off if you stand up to him. It's just that he's impossible."

Elizabeth hit the wineglass again.

"But I'm beginning to wonder if I can live with impossible. I don't have the answer yet."

"Well, good luck," Elizabeth finally said. "If you want to talk about it more ..."

"Thank you."

They ate in silence for several minutes, then Stella looked up.

"Oh, by the way, there's one more angle to this story that you might find interesting."

Elizabeth, her mouth full, nodded.

"When I filed for divorce, Jack went nuts. He harassed me on the phone, showed up where I was working, even tried to break down the door of my new apartment one night. My lawyer said we could try to get a restraining order against him, and I told her to go

189

ahead. She got a judge to sign it, and that did the trick. He left me alone after that, probably because he was afraid if he violated the order, I'd take him to the cleaners financially.

"It was so long ago, and it was such an unpleasant part of my life, that I'd put it out of my mind. Last month, I was going through some old things, deciding what to keep and what to throw out, and I came across my copy of the restraining order.

"The judge who signed it was Gordon's father."

Monday June 12

SOMETIMES IT PAYS to be old school. Several years ago, on a fishing trip with his friend Sam Akers, Gordon's ATM card had malfunctioned and couldn't be used at the only bank in the town where they were staying. From that point on, he had taken to carrying American Express travelers checks as backup on every trip. It wasn't long before he began making a point of cashing a couple whenever he was away from home. Going into the bank wasn't as convenient as using the machine, but it offered a sense of place, a source of gossip and a touch of human contact, however superficial, on trips when he was alone.

So on this bright June morning, he pulled into a parking space on Main Street and was at the door of Boundary County Bank when it opened at 9 a.m. The plan was to cash three $50 checks, rejoin Peter in the Cherokee, and spend the morning fishing the East Gemini River below Barnstaple Reservoir.

The bank operated out of a solid whitewashed brick building on Main Street. The building was erected in 1903, but Boundary County Bank was considerably more recent. Gordon vaguely remembered it had been one of the large statewide banks when he was younger, and its interior was in keeping with the building, right down to the marble counter tops and window bars separating the tellers from the customers. A pleasant and efficient young woman cashed the checks for him and thanked him for visiting Boundary County Bank.

On the way out he noticed two rows of photographs on the wall to the right of the main entrance. A female bank employee was standing in front of the pictures, taking something out of a brown paper wrapper, a black and white photograph that she hung at the far left of the bottom row, making six portraits on the top row and five on the bottom. Gordon paused to take a closer look at the photographs. A heading above them identified the group as the Board of Directors of Boundary County Bank — ten white males and one white woman. The woman in the photo looked familiar, and it took Gordon a few seconds to realize she was Kathryn Henry, in a different hairstyle and a photo obviously taken a few years ago.

He looked down at the photo that had just been put on the wall. It was Skip Henry, and the caption underneath read "Dwight Henry." Gordon smiled. Not all people named Dwight went by their given name, and Skip is a good all-purpose nickname. He had just stepped outside, when he remembered something Olema Marsh had said at Bodega Bay a month earlier, when she was talking about Lucy Starr's accident.

"Just two nights before it happened, we were at our monthly bridge party at Kathryn Livingston's house. Well, I suppose she's Kathryn Henry now that she married again."

And now, for the first time since he arrived in Barnstaple, Gordon knew Skip Henry's true initials — D.H.

Gordon speed-walked to the Cherokee, 75 feet away, opened the driver's-side door and leaned in.

"The fishing's going to have to wait a bit, Peter. We need to pay a visit to the newspaper office."

MAX RUTHERFORD was banging away at a computer keyboard, pausing for a drag on his cigarette every 30 seconds, when Gordon and Peter entered the office. Gordon was pleased to see that no one else was there.

"*Mis*-ter Gordon," Max said, drawing out the first word. "Do you have that big story you were telling me about earlier?"

"Not yet, chief. But I may be getting closer, and I'm hoping I can pick up some gossip that might help."

"Gossip. A beautiful thing, and the lifeblood of my business. A damn shame those pesky libel laws prevent me from using the best of it."

"No one ever said the world was fair," Peter murmured.

"Who do you want the dirt on?" Max asked.

Gordon sat in a chair next to Max's desk without being asked, leaned over, and said in a conspiratorial whisper, "I'm wondering what you can tell me about Kathryn and Skip Henry."

Max stubbed out the cigarette he'd been smoking, lit another, and blew three smoke rings before replying.

"Well, you picked a good one. That kept the whole town going through a long, cold winter, and if I'm not mistaken, tongues are still wagging. Where would you like me to start?"

"How about at the beginning. I understand Kathryn was married before."

Max nodded. "All right. We'll start there. Her first husband was Ben Livingston, who was something of a local legend. Hence, the heavy-duty tongue-wagging. Ben was a local boy who came back here and went to work for Bank of America. He was the Barnstaple branch manager by the age of 29, president of the Rotary Club at 32, and generally an all-around good guy.

"You may remember that in the mid-'80s, Bank of America went through some hard times and there was a question of whether it would survive. They were closing or merging some of their smaller branches, and everybody figured Barnstaple was on the chopping block. Ben decided to take the initiative. He figured if B of A left Barnstaple, the town would still need a bank, and it should be locally owned and operated. He got a lot of the leading people in town to buy into it, worked to get all the government approvals, and opened Boundary County Bank in September of 1988 — a year after Bank of America closed the local office and moved all the accounts to its branch in Sierra Pines."

"A long way to go to cash a check in the winter," Gordon said.

"Exactly. The new bank was a success from day one. Practically everybody in town moved their account to it, and Ben got the county commissioners to put the county's general fund money in it. Six months after opening, it was rock solid. And then Ben had another brainstorm."

He paused to take a couple of puffs.

"He decided to open another branch in Sierra Pines, and he got the two biggest ski resorts there to switch their business from Bank of America to Boundary County. So Sierra Pines was solid six months after it opened. Ben kept opening new branches to the south, and Boundary County Bank now has ten in all. Quite the local success story.

"Kathryn was behind him all the way, and some folks think the new bank was her idea, though she always let Ben take the credit. She stood behind Ben, was active in community affairs, and was as well liked and respected as he was. They were a great couple. Then in August of '98, Ben went in for his physical, told the doctor he was feeling a bit off, and the next thing you know, he was diagnosed with late-stage pancreatic cancer. Wasn't much they could do for him, and he died two months later. He was only 52.

"That left Kathryn a wealthy woman but not a happy one. People say her stock in the bank is worth 15 to 20 million, and I wouldn't be surprised if it was more. She took Ben's seat on the board, but she really missed him. Her kids were grown and moved away, and from what I hear she was feeling lonely and depressed. Some of her friends were worried about her. Then last October, a year after Ben died, she seemed to decide to stop moping and booked a cruise to Hawaii. It was something she and Ben had been planning to do for years but never got around to, and I think she was looking at it as a way of letting go of the past and starting a new life."

"And she fell in love again," Gordon said.

Max stubbed out his cigarette and started a new one.

"She met Skip Henry on the way to Hawaii, and I gather she fell like a ton of bricks. On the way back, he proposed the night before they landed, and they were married in San Francisco in January."

"I'd like to see the wedding announcement in the paper," Gordon said.

"Well, now, that's an interesting thing. There wasn't one. They said they didn't want a lot of publicity about it, but if you ask me, that was probably more his idea than hers. Most of the folks in town met him the first time at the Valentine's dance. Seems to be a nice enough fella, but it *was* sudden, and people will talk."

"Especially when someone marries into that kind of money," Peter said.

"You said it, not me. But I will say this on his behalf, Kathryn got him put on the Boundary County Bank board of directors, and a couple of the other directors have told me that he made a good impression at the first meeting he attended. Mostly listened, but when he did talk, he asked good questions. I hear he's planning to join the Rotary Club next week, so that may give me a chance to get to know him a bit better. Anything I should be on the lookout for?"

Gordon and Peter looked at each other.

"Not that I can tell you now," Gordon said. "I'm still casting around for information. And you've been really helpful, Max. If anything becomes a story here, I'll feed you everything I can."

"Much appreciated."

Gordon stood to leave, but sat down again.

"By the way, I don't suppose you'd know if there's anyone in town who could tell me more about what happened on that cruise?"

"There's one who would, but she can't help you now."

Gordon shot him a quizzical glance.

"Your friend Olema Marsh," Max said. "She was Kathryn Livingston's roommate on that cruise. Didn't she tell you?"

"HELLO, ELIZABETH. It looks as if your painting is coming along quite nicely."

Elizabeth started. She recognized Joe Price's voice but as usual hadn't heard him coming up behind her at all.

"Oh, hi, Joe," she said, as calmly as her nerves allowed. "Fancy meeting you here."

He stood behind her with his thumb and forefinger on his chin, looking at the canvas. She was painting the side street that led uphill from Buckley's main avenue.

"It's not exactly what's there, but it's what's really there, if that makes any sense," Joe said. "I look at that painting, and right away, I can believe people lived and breathed here once upon a time. I can't tell what you're doing or how you're doing it, but I can tell you're doing something right."

Elizabeth smiled. "You sound like Gordon. He doesn't have the formal training to articulate it, but he has a pretty good sense of when a painting works and when it doesn't."

"He's a lucky man if he's married to you. Do you mind if I ask what he does — professionally, I mean?"

Elizabeth made one more stroke with the brush and began wiping it with a cloth.

"He's an investor. And he manages portfolios for several people, mostly professional athletes. He's done well enough at it that it's become just a part-time career now. I'm afraid he's bored sometimes."

"Aren't we all?"

"I don't have time to be bored. Anyway, he has a little sideline from time to time." She daubed the clean brush in a rich blue and mixed it with a touch of yellow to lighten it, then applied it to the sky in the painting. "He does investigations that interest him, for no charge. He's pretty good at it, actually."

"He should have more time to pay attention to you, then. I hope he does."

"Oh, he does."

"Is Leah around?"

The question was asked casually, but Elizabeth could feel the hairs rising on the back of her neck. There was one family walking through the town; otherwise Elizabeth and Leah were alone there, except for Joe. She had sent Leah to an old stable two blocks away to check on the light coming through the windows and when it would hit the floor at a certain spot but decided not to share the information.

"She's exploring the town," she said.

"Well, then, if I keep walking around, I expect I'll run into her eventually. Nothing urgent, you understand. I just wanted to say hello. She's a fine young woman — the kind of woman who might have had the gumption to live here a hundred years ago."

"I never thought of that."

"You said you might be having a show of your paintings in San Francisco this winter. Shaughnessy Gallery, as I recall."

"Just off Union Square."

Joe was fingering his chin again.

"I might try to make that," he said. "It would be a good excuse to get to San Francisco again. I haven't been there in ages."

"What if it's snowing, and you can't drive through the passes?"

"Driving isn't the only way to get to San Francisco," he said. "There's always astral projection."

She would have expected him to laugh or smile when saying that last sentence, but he said it perfectly straight and looked at her intently. Unnerved, she turned to her canvas, silently counted to five, and turned back to answer him.

He was gone, and she hadn't heard a thing.

LINDSAY JUDD AGREED to meet with Gordon and Peter on the condition that they bring her a bran muffin and a large black coffee. By now, a little after 10:00, the morning chill was all but gone. They sat down at a picnic table in the yard of the Lake View Motel — the one farthest from the children's play area.

Gordon told her what he had learned about Skip and Kathryn Henry and their connection with the Barnstaple accident victims. Lindsay nibbled the muffin and drank coffee, asking no questions until he was done.

"You have to admit it suggests a line of inquiry," he concluded.

"Yes. I guess it does. But I wouldn't get your hopes up too much."

"What have you got that's better?"

"I'm not blowing you off, Gordon. I'm just saying it's a long shot. Worth looking into, but a long shot nevertheless."

"Did you have any luck with the people flying into Reno?"

"Nothing yet. That's a long shot, too, by the way. We follow up the long shots and hope one of them pans out."

"If the airport angle isn't turning up anything, doesn't that suggest Bennett's killer lives not too far from Twin Rivers?"

"What's your definition of too far? Someone who left home at one o'clock Saturday afternoon could have driven to Twin Rivers in time to kill Bennett if they left from San Diego, Los Angeles, San Francisco, Sacramento, Portland, Boise, Salt Lake City, Albuquerque, Las Vegas, Tucson, or Phoenix. Not to mention all the midsize and small towns within that radius. So what are the odds the killer came from Barnstaple?"

"She has a point, Gordon," Peter said.

Gordon's cell phone rang. The call was from the Sacramento area code.

"Hold on," he said. He moved away from the table and took the call.

"Mr. Gordon," said a twangy female voice, "this is Viola Johnson, Lucy Starr's sister. I was out of town for the weekend and just got your message and Jim's when we got in late last night. I'm intrigued."

"Well, thank you for calling back so quickly."

"Can you tell me what this is about?"

"All I feel comfortable in saying right now is that I'm looking into something on behalf of Olema Marsh, your sister's friend."

"I can understand it, but I'm still dying to know. All right, how can I help?"

"Thank you. I wanted to pin down a couple of particulars about the cruise you and Lucy took a few years ago. Do you remember it?"

"How could I forget? It was the trip of a lifetime."

"Good. Now it would be really helpful if you could give me the dates of the trip. And if you need to look it up, you can call back."

"I can tell you this much right off. It was for my 70th birthday, which was November 7th, 1997. We left from San Francisco the Saturday after Veterans Day and were gone, oh, nine or ten days."

"Wonderful, wonderful. And where did you go?"

"Several places in Mexico and back."

"This is great. This really helps." He'd ripped the cap off a pen with his teeth and was making notes in a small notebook he'd removed from his shirt pocket. "And I don't suppose you recall offhand the name of the ship and the company that did the cruise?"

Without hesitation, she gave him both. Gordon had seen more of the cruise ship company's TV ads than he'd care to count.

"That just about does it, then. I really appreciate your cooperation."

"I'm glad to help any friend of Lucy's. I hope I'll know what it's about some day."

"Maybe you will. Oh, and one more thing before I go. Is there any chance that on that cruise you noticed a shipboard romance?"

She guffawed.

"Oh yeah. I'd forgotten all about it until you just mentioned it. But yes. There was a woman from Oregon, middle-aged, and a man. Distinguished looking and rather quiet. But I guess he had something on the ball, because she fell head over heels. They sat at our table one night, and we saw them several other times. Lucy and I talked about it a bit."

"I suppose it would be too much to ask if you remembered their names."

"Sorry. I'm not good at names. Better with faces. And we only actually sat with them one time."

"If you saw either one of them again, do you think you'd recognize them?"

"I'm pretty sure I would."

Then, thought Gordon, Lucy might have remembered, too. And it could have been a fatal remembrance.

"I think I heard at the end of the trip that they were going to get married," Viola Johnson said. "Do you know what happened? I hope they lived happily ever after."

Gordon was silent for several seconds before replying.

"I'm afraid it didn't work out," he finally said.

SHORTLY BEFORE ELEVEN O'CLOCK, rural carrier Harvey Williams turned his Postal Service Jeep onto Quail Run Lane. The houses in Pine Cone Heights all had mailboxes down at the curb, and he could drive the loop and have everyone's mail delivered in three or four minutes. One of the letters he delivered that day was addressed to David Rowan, the late owner of Rowan's

Rod and Gun. Rowan's wife, Diana, had no idea the letter was coming and was shopping in Carson City that day. The letter sat untouched in her mailbox for seven hours before she got back.

GORDON WALKED BACK to the picnic table, tore a page out of his notebook, and set it in front of Lindsay Judd.

"What's this?"

"The name of a cruise ship and the dates one of our accident victims was on it," he replied. "The victim's sister, who was with her on the trip, remembers a shipboard romance involving a woman from Oregon. I'll bet you a hundred right now that the woman from Oregon was named Eleanor Gluck and her seducer was named Douglas Hurd."

"The case from Oregon that Bennett told us about?"

"That's my hunch. The dates of the cruise are right in the time range. Can you get someone to lean on the cruise company to cough up the passenger list?"

"I can if I see the reason for it."

"What reason do you need? If our man was on that ship at that time, we now have a witness who can identify him."

"All right, Gordon, listen. I have to think about how this will hold up in court and about how much I need to know before I pull someone in. Are you trying to tell me that this methodical serial killer, who has eluded five different police departments ..."

"That we know of."

"... that this individual somehow ended up in a town this small and two different people recognized him?"

"That's exactly what I'm trying to tell you."

"That's crazy."

"All the more reason to think it could be true."

"I like simple explanations. So, by the way, do juries."

"Would it kill you to check on that passenger list?"

"Of course not, but it's a question of priorities. I'm getting callbacks from detectives in the other towns, and finding out what they have to say is more important right now than your cruise ship."

"There's a woman in this town who may be married to a man who probably killed five previous wives. Isn't her safety important?"

"You're being melodramatic."

"Am I? Or are you so upset because it's my lead and not yours?"

"Jesus Christ," she muttered.

Peter stood up abruptly.

"I'm sorry," he said. "This is starting to sound way too much like my third marriage. I'm going to take a walk."

PETER TURNED RIGHT onto Main Street and strolled the block and a half to Boundary County Bank. He stepped inside, looked around carefully, then got in the teller line. He was at a window in less than two minutes.

"Sorry to bother you about this," he said, taking out his wallet, "but could I trouble you to break a 20 for me? A five and 15 ones if you could."

He slid it into the tray under the window.

"No problem," the teller said, and counted out his bills. "Have a nice day and enjoy Boundary County."

On the way out, he stopped and looked at the directors' photographs on the wall and decided the likeness of Skip Henry was plenty good. A loan officer was working at her computer a short distance away, and he went over to her.

"Excuse me," he said. "I was just admiring those photographs of your directors on the wall over there, and I was wondering if you could tell me who took them. My girlfriend said she'd like a black-and-white portrait of me, and not too many people take them any more."

"That would be Walt Winston in Sierra Pines. He does all our work. He's very good and very reasonable."

"Would you have his phone number?"

She opened a desk drawer. "I think I have a couple of his cards. Here we are. You can have this one."

"Thank you so much," he said.

As he turned into the entrance of the Lake View Motel, Peter could tell — even from a distance — that

Gordon and Lindsay were still going at it. He walked up to the table and took a deep breath.

"Time out!" he bellowed.

They were so startled, they stopped the argument mid-sentence.

"If I could say something," Peter continued, "I think the two of you are going around in circles and not paying enough attention to a critical fact." He looked at each of them. "We now have a photograph of a potential suspect. Why don't we try showing it around and seeing if anyone recognizes him?"

"We don't have a picture," Gordon said. "The bank does. Are you proposing we steal it?"

"No, even you would balk at that. But if the bank has a photograph, it stands to reason that someone took that picture, and by the simple expedient of asking who that was, I managed to get his business card."

He took the card from his shirt pocket and handed it to Lindsay.

"I'm sure if you asked him nicely and said it was police business, he could email it to you in five minutes."

Lindsay stared at the card for ten seconds, then shook her head.

"I'm losing it," she said. "This should have been the first thing I thought of."

GORDON ALSO REALIZED there was something he should have thought of. After he and Peter left Lindsay, he called Helen Overton, the fourth at the bridge party two nights before Lucy Starr was killed.

When he announced himself, she immediately said, "I still haven't remembered about that night."

"Actually," he said, "I wanted to prompt you. Do you happen to recall, by any chance, if Skip Henry showed up at that bridge party?"

"Oh, yes. He stopped in briefly to say hello."

"And was that the first time Lucy Starr had met him?"

She didn't answer right away and finally said, "I think so. I believe Kathryn introduced them. Yes, she did, and that's what I forgot."

Gordon kept quiet and let her talk.

"She introduced them, and Lucy gave him a kind of funny look and said, 'Haven't we met somewhere before?' Skip does sort of look like someone you've seen before. He said he didn't think so. Why? Is it important?"

"Probably not," Gordon lied, "but now I know what you remembered and I don't have to worry about running it down anymore. Thank you very much."

Gordon ended the call and stared straight ahead through the windshield.

Peter, sitting next to him, asked, "Are you all right, Gordon?"

Gordon waved him off and kept thinking.

Haven't we met somewhere before? Five simple words. And by blurting them out at that time and place, Lucy Starr had probably signed her own death warrant.

WHEN LEAH RETURNED to the stable, after a walk to the cemetery and back, she found Joe Price inside, sitting on a bale of hay. She was momentarily taken aback. It wasn't from seeing Joe; she was by now expecting to run into him when she and Elizabeth went to Buckley. It was because she hadn't remembered seeing the hay in the stable before, and there were no horses around to eat it in any event.

"Hello, Leah," Joe said. "I thought you might be here."

"Really? Why?"

"When I talked to Elizabeth a short while ago, she said you were scouting a painting scene for her. And this," his arm swept in a broad gesture, "is the sort of scene Elizabeth would paint."

"What makes you think that?" Leah said after a pause.

"Am I wrong?"

"No, you're right. I was wondering how you knew. Or guessed."

"I don't know what to tell you. I seem to have an instinct for how women feel. Or so they say."

Leah gave him a sharp look.

"You're not *the* Joe Price, are you?"

"I'm sorry, Leah. I don't know what you mean."

"The Joe Price who was famous in Buckley and beyond."

A smile crossed Joe's face.

"That's a new one to me. How famous was this Joe Price you're talking about?"

"Pretty famous. In his day at least."

"Tell me the story, Leah. What could be better than sitting in the stable, swapping stories?"

"I don't see much swapping going on here. You're not offering to tell me one."

"Maybe someday I will. I have some good ones. But you're the one who brought up Joe, so you go first."

"All right." Leah told the gist of the Joe Price story as Stella had recounted it the night before. It was still and quiet inside the stable and getting steadily warmer. Motes of dust floated through the shafts of light where it came through the windows.

"That's quite a story," Joe said when she was finished.

"So you're no relation to that Joe Price?"

"Not so far as I know."

Neither of them spoke for a moment.

"I'm curious to know, Leah, what you make of that story?"

"What do you mean, Joe?"

"I guess I mean, what do you think about what Ingrid and Joe did?"

"I'm not sure. It's a hard question."

"Is it?"

"My parents wouldn't think so. They see the world in black and white. Marriage is sacred and you don't leave. Period."

"I sense a 'but' coming."

"But a hundred years ago, what choices did a woman have if she was stuck in an abusive marriage? It was hard to get a divorce and impossible to have a career."

"There was one job she could have gone into."

"Would that have been better than her marriage?"

"It would have been different. So are you saying it was all right for her to run off with the other Joe Price?"

"That's not what I'm saying. Like I said, it's hard. I think it's wrong for a married woman to elope. But I also think it's wrong for society to look the other way while that woman is at the mercy of a violent husband. She was put into the position of having to accept one wrong or commit another. I hope I never end up in a place like that."

"Aren't you letting Joe Price off the hook?"

"Not at all. I'm just focusing on *her* decision. I guess because I can relate to it."

"That's fair."

"How about you, Joe? You seem to be awfully interested in this story. Did you ever run off with a married woman?"

He froze for several seconds, then slightly turned up the corners of his mouth.

"Not yet."

"So you think it could happen?"

"You never know, Leah. There's a bit of the outlaw in all of us."

"Is there? Even in me?"

"Sure. Do you ever think of running away from home?"

"I'm a legal adult. That doesn't apply."

"How about when you were a minor — did you ever think about it then?"

"Yeah," she finally said. "I thought about it."

Joe laughed. "So here we are, just two outlaws in an abandoned stable. I do enjoy talking to you, Leah. The more I get to know you, the more I begin to feel you were put into my life for a reason."

IT WAS SHORTLY after two o'clock when Gordon and Peter got around to the fishing they had planned for that morning. They drove to the East Gemini River below Barnstaple Reservoir and had three hours of insanely good action, which, as it turned out, marked the end of their angling on this trip.

For the first two hours they worked P.T. and Copper John nymphs through the riffles, three to four feet below the surface and were rewarded with strikes on almost every other cast. At four o'clock, a caddis hatch got under way and the fish began feeding on the surface. They switched to dry flies, which worked as well as the nymphs had. By the time they knocked off at five o'clock, the fish were still feeding and they had each caught and released a dozen or more fish, mostly Rainbow Trout in the 14- to 18-inch range, with a couple of Browns and a foot-long Brook Trout (landed by Peter) in the mix for good measure.

Tired from the fishing, they decided to stand for a dinner at Broderick's Café rather than cooking. They were back at the resort five minutes after Elizabeth and Leah had returned from Buckley. Stella had spent the day reading at the resort and said she hadn't felt so rested and refreshed in years.

The café was nearly full, and the background noise covered their conversation. Gordon and Peter filled the women in on the latest developments in the local case. They listened intently, and afterward Elizabeth talked about the day in Buckley and the latest encounter with Joe Price.

"The guy gives me the shivers," Elizabeth said. "The way he comes and goes so quietly and talks in riddles. I wish I could get a handle on him."

"Did you bring up the Joe Price from a hundred years ago?" Stella asked.

Elizabeth slapped the table in annoyance.

"No, dammit. I was so unnerved by his astral projection comment that I forgot all about it."

"I asked him," Leah said. "He said he'd never heard about that Joe Price, but we had a good conversation about it."

"You seem remarkably calm. Doesn't he frighten you just a little?"

Leah thought about it for a minute.

"Not really," she finally said. "I mean, he is a bit strange, but I don't think he's dangerous. Not to us, anyway."

"What makes you think that?"

"Just a feeling I have about him. Plus, if he wanted to do something bad in Buckley, he's already had plenty of chances."

"Even so," Gordon said, "it would be better if you didn't let him get you alone."

"Easier said than done."

"By the way, Leah," Elizabeth said, "I checked out the stable later in the afternoon, and I didn't see a bale of hay in it. Are you sure you did?"

"Joe was sitting on it."

"I guess it doesn't matter. It's easy enough to add it to the painting if I want."

AFTER DINNER, Leah was off to the volleyball game. Elizabeth and Stella accompanied her as far as the net and continued along the lakeshore path for an after-dinner stroll. Gordon and Peter returned to Gordon's cabin.

The first thing Gordon did was call Lindsay Judd.

"Getting anywhere?" he asked.

"It's a grind," she said. "It always is. I got the picture of Henry from the photographer in Sierra Pines, and I've emailed it to detectives in three of the towns where our mysterious D.H. probably killed a wife. Still working on the other two places, but I may hear something back tomorrow."

"How about the passenger list for the cruise?"

"A detective in Long Beach is working on that. He's supposed to get an answer tomorrow."

"And while all these leads are pursued, Kathryn Henry lives in mortal peril."

"You know, Gordon, I've been thinking about that, and I don't agree with you. This is different. The others he took for a couple of hundred thousand. From what you say, Mrs. Henry is worth 15 to 20 million. She's the goose that lays the golden eggs. He's not going to kill her like the others. Not any time soon."

"I agree with the last sentence. He'll kill her and make it look like an accident so he can inherit. He's been getting a lot of experience staging accidents lately."

"That's more supposition than evidence. But the clincher for me is that photo. He wouldn't be going on the board of directors and getting his picture taken if he wasn't planning on sticking around for a while. If he's our guy, we'll get to him before he does any more harm."

"I hope you're right," Gordon finally said. "Could you email me his photo?"

He heard tapping on a keyboard in the background.

"I just did."

"Thanks. Should we get together for breakfast tomorrow?"

"Not a bad idea."

"How about the Hi-Mont Cafe. Have you been there yet?"

"I've walked by it. It looks like a hole in the wall."

"It is. But a good hole in the wall."

"I'll give it a try on your say-so."

"Shall we say nine o'clock?"

"Make it 9:30. I'm probably going to be up pretty late tonight."

"See you then."

Gordon ended the call and shook his head.

"She was getting the better of you, wasn't she?" Peter said. "You're not used to that, and you don't like it. But I'm forgetting — you've only been married once."

"Leave me alone for a minute, Peter." Gordon took out his laptop and checked his mail. The photo of Skip Henry was there. He opened his notebook, looked up the email address he'd obtained from Viola Johnson, and sent her the photo with a brief message. Just to cover all the bases, he also called to tell her the email had been sent. She didn't answer, and he left a voicemail.

"I guess that's about it for today," he said, putting away the phone. "I can't think of anything else we can do right now."

"Just as well," Peter said. "Those fish wore me out this afternoon."

Several seconds later, Gordon's phone rang. It was a local call, and he answered.

"Mr. Gordon, this is Diana Rowan. We talked last week."

"Of course. Is everything all right?"

"I don't know. That's why I'm calling. You said to get in touch if anything else came up."

Gordon sat up straighter. "Yes."

"I was out all day, and when I got home, about 45 minutes ago, there was a letter in the mail. I'm afraid it's — well, it's really shaken me up."

"Who's it from?"

"I'd rather not talk about it over the phone. Is there any way you can come out here and read it yourself?"

"Is it that bad?"

"Mr. Gordon, I *really* don't feel like being alone right now. Could you ..."

"Peter and I will be there in 20 minutes. Sit tight."

He stood up and put the phone in his pocket.

"That was the widow Rowan. She got a letter today that's given her a bad case of the heebie-jeebies, and she doesn't want to be alone. Are you up for this?"

"You already committed me. Let's go."

THE SUN WAS SETTING as Gordon and Peter drove up Quail Run Lane toward the Rowan residence. Diana Rowan opened the front door before they got to it.

"This was quite a shock," she said, "and I thought of you right away because of what we talked about last week."

She led them to a formal dining table with eight chairs. Before sitting down she picked up an envelope from a countertop between the kitchen and dining area and fidgeted with it as she spoke.

"When I pulled this out of the mailbox an hour ago, I thought it was some routine benefits letter. But it's not routine at all. You should probably read it yourselves."

She pushed it across the table to Gordon. It was a letter from the Philadelphia office of the Department of Veterans Affairs, addressed to Dave, not David, Rowan. Gordon pulled a two-page letter from the envelope and set it on the table between himself and Peter.

June 6, 2000

Dear Dave,

First of all, my apologies for taking so long to get back to you on this. You deserve an explanation. On March 1, I transferred from the Baltimore office to Philadelphia, with a promotion and raise. The opportunity came up suddenly, and I haven't yet gotten around to notifying most of my friends outside the immediate area. What that meant was that your March 2 letter, sent to me at the Baltimore office, kicked around there for nearly a month before inexplicably being sent to St. Louis, where it sat around awaiting further action for another three weeks. Finally, it was sent on to Philadelphia by some method that took ten days, and it didn't land on my desk until May 5. That was a Friday, on which I left the office at noon to sign escrow papers on our new house. So I've only had your letter in hand for a month, and it took a few weeks to run down the information you asked for, which I was more than happy to do.

After all that runaround, the answer to your question is very simple. The VA has no record of an officer named Dwight Henry serving in Vietnam between 1966 and 1969, when we were there. I double-checked our files against the list of West Point graduates and officers who came in through the ROTC program during the time of the war. No one by that name on either of those lists.

That isn't positive proof that your man is an impostor. There were a number of Dwights in the officer group (Eisenhower-era, you know) with different last names, and one of them could have legally changed his name and been out of touch with us. And there's a very remote chance that there was an officer named Dwight Henry who inadvertently got obliterated from our records. But I certainly didn't find anything that would allay your suspicions.

Just to be thorough, I ran a search of enlisted men and noncommissioned officers named Dwight Henry who served in Vietnam during those years. There were three of them, two of whom, according to our records, are still alive. Their addresses appear below the signature. The one in Georgia has been receiving regular treatments at our hospital in Atlanta, most recently in April, so probably not your guy. The file on the Dwight Henry in Chicago has been inactive for several years. If it helps with identification, our records show he's African-American.

I hope this answers your questions, Dave, and I hope this letter finds you and your family doing well. We keep talking about taking another trip to the West Coast, but with the move and the new house, it won't be this year. If you're out

Philadelphia way, you're welcome to stay with us anytime. Please give my regards to Diana, and give me a call if you can when you've digested this letter. I'd love to chat with you and catch up.

> *Best Regards,*
> *Bud Clifton*

The letter was signed simply "Bud," in keeping with its personal nature, although the records search probably qualified as at least semiofficial business. Peter looked up after reading it.

"He writes pretty well for a government man," he said.

"He and Dave were best friends in Vietnam," Diana said. "We stayed with them for two nights in Baltimore just a couple of years ago. A few years before that, they stayed here for three nights and Dave took Bud fishing."

She stopped, clearly emotional. There had been a cloth napkin on the table near her, and she had been winding it up into a tight roll without being aware of what she was doing.

"Dave never told me he'd written a letter to Bud, so this was a complete surprise. Why *wouldn't* he tell me, and what does it mean?"

"I'm afraid I can't answer either question," Gordon finally said. "But I do remember that when we met last week, you said Dave had been talking about Vietnam with somebody at the Valentine's dance in February. Could this (he held up the letter) have been a sequel to that?"

"It has to be. One of the things that would set Dave off was people who put down veterans. Another was people who served exaggerating what they did."

"So this would fit," Peter said.

"It would totally fit. But I don't understand what it's all about, and I feel so bad."

"Bad about what?" Gordon said softly. "Or about whom?"

"Why Kathryn Henry, of course. She's such a nice woman, and I'd hate to think she married a man who'd lie about something like this."

IT WAS NEARLY DARK when they got back to the Cherokee. Gordon and Peter had gotten Diana Rowan to photocopy the letter and had stayed a half hour to soothe her. She seemed to be less agitated when they finally left.

"That had to be tough," Peter said, when they were in the car. "Your husband's been dead for three months and you get a letter from an old friend who hasn't heard the news and is going on like it was life as usual."

"Dave's friend is going to feel bad, too, when he finds out."

"We've all put our foot in it that way."

"I know I have."

"So have I. Multiple times. Part of life, I guess."

Gordon put the key in the ignition.

"I noticed, by the way," Peter said, "that you didn't respond to Diana's second question."

"Second question?" Gordon said, taking his hand off the key.

"She asked why her husband didn't tell her he was writing to his friend in the VA, and she wondered what it meant. The letter we read tonight told us what it meant."

"I'm listening."

"What it means is that we now have a motive for all four of the suspicious accidents you came to Barnstaple to investigate. Luther Whitman may have seen our Bluebeard in Flagstaff, Lucy Starr may have seen him seducing a previous wife on a cruise ship, and Dave Rowan clearly smelled a rat about our suspect's so-called military history."

"And Olema Marsh was probably getting too close to the truth for someone's comfort."

"Exactly. And if Skip Henry is the stinker we're starting to think he is, we even have a suspect."

"A theory and a suspect," Gordon said. "Not a bad week's work. And something to tell Detective Judd about at breakfast tomorrow."

"Let's head back while there's still some light. The road to this place makes me nervous."

Gordon started the engine.

"Aren't you going to check the brake lines before we start down the hill?"

"I believe in living dangerously," Gordon said. "Besides, I had the same idea you did." He patted the steering wheel with his left hand. "I had my eyes on this thing through the window almost the whole time we were in the dining room. Nobody tampered with it."

ELIZABETH WAS WAITING in the cabin when Gordon returned.

"We need to talk," she said.

"All right. You want to hear about what Peter and I just learned?"

"Later. We need to talk about Leah."

Gordon pulled up short.

"Is it getting that serious?" he said.

"I'm afraid so. Leah's getting to be too intimate with him, and I think we need to put some space between them."

Gordon thought about it for a minute.

"Two questions," he finally said. "First, are you sure our intervention is such a good idea? And second, do you think it'll even work? I mean, she's pretty insistent about being an adult."

"Adult or not, we have some responsibility for her when she's with us. And I worry about her when she's with him. A lot."

"Can I ask why, Elizabeth? He seems like a nice enough guy."

"For crying out loud, Gordon. How can you say that? You've never even met him."

"Aren't you forgetting yesterday morning? After the service?"

Elizabeth stopped, and after a few seconds broke out laughing.

"Brian," she gasped. "You thought I was talking about Brian, didn't you?"

"Who else?"

"I'm totally fine with Brian. Leah has him wrapped around her little finger, though I don't think she knows it yet. She can stand up to *him* if she has to. No, I was talking about Joe Price."

"The will-o'-the-wisp of Buckley?"

"That Joe Price. When we started out after dinner tonight, Leah told Stella and me she'd had a good conversation with Joe in one of the old stables in Buckley. And then she said he said something like 'I think you were put into my life for a reason,' and all of a sudden my blood ran cold."

"That does sound a tad kinky," Gordon said.

"Is that *all* you can call it? You've never seen the guy, but I think you trust my character judgment ..."

Gordon nodded.

"... and this guy is plain weird. I think we need to set some boundaries."

"Do you have a plan?" Gordon asked, knowing full well she did.

"As Peter would say, one day at a time. Let's just make sure she doesn't see him tomorrow. Leah can chill with you and Peter tomorrow, instead of coming to Buckley."

"Who's going to help you with your painting and your materials?"

"I talked to Stella about it. She said she'd come with me tomorrow. And for whatever it's worth, she agreed with me that what Joe said to Leah today was more than a tad kinky, as you put it. She thinks he's disturbed."

"I don't know how much weight to give her opinion. Peter says most nurses take a pretty dim view of humanity."

"They take a dim view of Peter, and for good reason. But that's another discussion."

"All right, then, sticking to this one, is it such a good idea for *you* to be going to Buckley if this character is running around up there?"

"Three-step answer. One, he hasn't been there every day. Or at least he hasn't visited us every day. Two, I have my gun ..."

"And remember he got the drop on you the first time you met him."

"It won't happen again. And three, Stella will be there. If you want to know the truth, I think he should be more afraid of Stella than the gun. So what do you say to leaving Joe to us and taking care of Leah for the day?"

"I don't know if 'taking care' is the right term for it, but all right. I've kind of been neglecting her, so it'll be good to have her along for the day. And she seems to like Peter. Go figure."

"So we have a deal?"

"We have a deal." Gordon laughed.

"What's so funny?" Elizabeth said.

"I was just thinking. There's a touch of the absurd in this situation. In order to protect Leah from a guy who, so far, has just been unnervingly strange, but who hasn't harmed her or you when he's had plenty of chances to do so …"

"Cut to the chase."

"To do that, you're going to have Leah spend the day with Peter and me when we may be getting dangerously close to a serial killer with ten victims to his name. And that's just the ones we know about. Has it occurred to you that you might be pushing her out of the frying pan and into the fire?"

"You haven't met Joe Price and I have. I'll feel better with Leah in the fire."

Tuesday June 13

LINDSAY HAD SECURED the booth in the back corner of the Hi-Mont Café and was waiting when Gordon, Peter and Leah arrived. She cast a sideways glance at Leah as they approached.

"Change of plans," Gordon said, reading her mind. "Leah can be discreet." Leah sat next to Lindsay, facing Gordon and Peter.

"Let's order before we get into it," Lindsay said. They studied the menu, and a waitress — the same one who had served Gordon and Peter the week before — arrived quickly and took their orders.

"What have we got?" Gordon asked when the waitress left.

"You first," Lindsay said.

Gordon took a photocopy of the VA letter Diana Rowan had given him the night before from his messenger bag and slid it across the table. Lindsay read it quickly and looked up.

"So he lied about his service record, too?"

"That's what it looks like."

She shook her head. "I almost believe that should be a capital offense. When you think about what our troops do and how little credit they get for it." She pushed the letter across the table to Gordon. "So what does that do for us?"

"It provides the missing motive for one of my accidents. If Skip Henry thought Dave Rowan was getting suspicious about his story, that would put Rowan in danger."

"Do you have motives for the other three accidents?"

"We think Luther Whitman and Lucy Starr knew Henry from another place and time and under another name."

"When you say 'we think,' I take it you don't have any evidence."

"I'm working on it. Speaking of evidence, is somebody running down the passenger list for the cruise Lucy Starr and her sister took?"

"The company promised it to us this morning." She looked at her watch, which read 9:35. "They didn't say when this morning."

"Anything more on your end?"

"We're working on it, too. I'm hoping to have some answers soon."

Lindsay's phone rang. She looked at the number and slid out of the booth.

"This could be one of them. I'll be right back."

Leah watched as she took the phone outside.

"She's pretty intense, isn't she?"

"You don't see too many detectives who are Type B personalities," Peter said.

They sipped coffee until Lindsay came back a few minutes later, with a smile.

"That was Detective Ray Ayala, Santa Rosa PD. He went out with a photo lineup this morning. The first neighbor he showed it to identified Skip Henry as being Dennis Hale."

"Who's Dennis Hale?" Leah asked.

"He's suspected of killing his wife in Santa Rosa and making off with most of her money. That's the name he was using at the time."

"So what are we waiting for?" Gordon said.

"In a word, more," Lindsay said. "This is a delicate situation. If I'm going to move on this guy, I'm going to have to ask the local sheriff for backup. That means convincing him that one of the wealthiest and most respected citizens in his town is a serial killer with up to ten murders to his name. One neighbor in Santa Rosa isn't enough for that."

"What would he be concerned with?" Leah said.

"The politics, mainly, I'm guessing. If we bring our man in and then can't prove anything, the locals are going to be all over the sheriff about how could he do such a thing to poor Skip. And the locals are who he needs to keep his job."

"He should be up for re-election in two years," Gordon said. "Soon enough that he has to watch his step."

"Gordon! Are you actually agreeing with me?"

"Not really, but I see the point. I just hope Kathryn Henry lives long enough for us to get the evidence we need."

"The trickle's already started. With any luck it'll turn into a flood by the end of the day."

The waitress arrived with their plates, set them down, and topped off the coffee cups. Seconds after she left, Gordon's phone rang. He looked at the number, excused himself, and went outside.

"Mrs. Johnson," he said. "Thanks for calling back."

"Sorry I didn't get to you sooner. I was at choir practice last night and didn't get back until 9:30. I didn't know how late you stay up."

"That's all right. Did you look at the picture I emailed?"

"Yes, I did. And I guess your question is, was that the Lothario Lucy and I saw with the lady from Oregon on our cruise?"

"Something like that."

She didn't respond for several seconds, then said:

"Positively the same guy."

Gordon thanked her, ended the call, went back inside, and, smiling, slid into the booth next to Peter.

"Well?"

Gordon took a bite of his sausage and scrambled eggs and chewed it slowly before answering.

"The flood is beginning," he said.

ELIZABETH HAD SET UP her easel and canvas in front of the church in Buckley. Stella, after helping, had gone on a walk around town. Elizabeth was staring at her palette. The shaded side of the building in her painting wasn't quite the right shade of dark, and she was trying to figure out what other color, lightly added, would make it right, when a shadow appeared from behind her.

"Hello, Joe," she said, almost distractedly.

"Good morning, Elizabeth. How are you?"

"Perplexed. The shade in this painting is too black, and I'm trying to figure out what color it needs a touch of."

Joe stepped to her right and looked at the canvas for a minute, checking the palette from time to time.

"How about the dark green?" he finally said.

Elizabeth looked at the painting, the palette and back to the painting again.

"Of course. How stupid of me. That's exactly right."

"I wouldn't call it stupid. You're just too close to it. A lot of times we don't see things when we're too close to them."

"That's the truth."

"Are you going to be here all day, Elizabeth?"

"I think so."

"You might want to reconsider. Thunderheads are forming over the mountains to the west. We're probably going to get a storm this afternoon."

Elizabeth looked in that direction. She could see the tops of thick gray and white clouds in the distance, and she realized that the wind had been picking up a bit over the past quarter hour.

"Thanks, Joe. I'll keep that in mind."

"That's a fine painting, Elizabeth. It'll be even better when you get the shadow right. Is this one of the ones you'll be selling in San Francisco later this year?"

"With any luck."

"Well, well. Maybe I'll make that trip to San Francisco, after all. I'd rather like to have that one. It would remind me of you and Leah."

"My paintings aren't cheap anymore."

"I don't mind paying for value."

"Then you're the kind of man I like to have at my openings."

They both laughed, and it occurred to Elizabeth that it was the first time she had heard Joe laugh.

"Speaking of Leah," Joe said, "I've been looking for her, without success so far. Do you know where she is?"

"Not in Buckley, I'm afraid. I gave her the day off from being my assistant, so she's with Gordon and Peter today."

"Ah, then that explains it." He stared into the distance, as if trying to come to a decision. At length, he reached into his inside coat pocket and took out a business-sized envelope.

"I wanted to give this to her today. Will you be seeing her later?"

"Oh, yes. We'll all be together at dinner."

"That would be splendid. Could I ask you to pass it along?"

"I'd be delighted."

He extended the envelope toward her and pulled it back, realizing she was holding a brush in one hand and her palette in the other.

"Your hands are full," he said. "Shall I put it in your purse?"

"Thank you."

He knelt by the purse, slid in the envelope, and stood up again.

"There you go. Please remember to give it to her today, and be sure to zip up the purse if it starts to rain. You wouldn't want it to get wet."

"I'll be careful."

"I need to go now, so," he bowed slightly, "till we meet again."

He started up the street, and as he did, Stella rounded a corner, heading in his direction. He pulled down his hat brim, lowered his head slightly, and passed her with a curt, "good morning," then cut left between two buildings.

"This place starts to grow on you after a while," Stella said, as she reached Elizabeth. "I'm beginning to see why you like it so much."

Elizabeth made a noncommittal sound.

"Was that your friend Joe I just passed?"

"Uh-huh."

"You know, I just caught a glimpse of him as we passed, and I got the sense he was trying to avoid me, but right away I had a feeling ..."

"What kind of feeling?"

"That I've seen him before. I have no idea where, but he looks familiar. Oh, well, I guess it'll come to me."

"I'm sure it will."

Elizabeth had been looking at the two buildings Joe had ducked between. She hadn't taken her eyes off them, and Joe hadn't come out the other side.

"Is something wrong?" Stella said.

"Something's always wrong. Right now, I'm just not sure what."

THEY LEFT THE CAFÉ after breakfast, agreeing to meet again at Lindsay's motel at one o'clock. That left Gordon, Peter and Leah with a couple of hours to kill and not much to do. Eventually, Gordon came up with the idea of driving Leah around Barnstaple Reservoir and down the East Gemini River, where she hadn't been. It wasn't much of an idea, but Leah — who had been raised to behave well and respect her elders — pretended to be interested and made a nearly plausible job of it.

Even so, it was nearly noon when they were pulling into Barnstaple with an hour to go. No one was hungry enough for lunch, and Gordon was scraping for ideas when his phone rang.

"Gordon, this is Judy Beck."

"How are you?"

"I'm fine, but the reason I'm calling is I've been going through some of the stuff Dad brought here from Flagstaff, and I've come across something I think you should see."

"Can you tell me what it is?"

"I'd rather you saw it for yourself. Can you come over now?"

"I'll be there in 15 minutes."

He made a U-turn in downtown Barnstaple without anyone objecting and started back down the road they'd just come from. The storm clouds from the west were drawing closer, and they heard the first rumble of distant thunder as they drove along the reservoir.

Judy Beck was waiting outside when they arrived.

"I'm glad you got here before the rain started," she said. "Dad's place is upstairs."

They walked up a flight of stairs along the side of the barn and entered the apartment upstairs. It was slightly dusty but otherwise tidy. A large cardboard box sat on the couch in the living area with papers and photo albums lying next to it. Instead of going to the couch, however, she went to a small table by the kitchen and picked up a drugstore envelope of the type generally used for printed snapshots.

"I saw this halfway down in the box," Judy said. "It was picked up the second week in October, just a few weeks before he left Flagstaff. He was probably busy getting ready to move and didn't have time to put the pictures in the album."

She handed the envelope to Gordon. It had Luther Whitman's name on it and underneath, in a different hand and different ink, "Rotary Barbecue, 9/27/93."

"I put the one you want to see in the front," she said.

Gordon opened the envelope and took out the first picture. It showed three people standing by a picnic table in late-afternoon light. The man on the left Gordon recognized from his obituary photo in *The Barnstaple Miner*. It was Luther Whitman. Next to him was an ordinary-looking middle-aged woman with a big smile on her face. To her left, on the far right side of the photograph, was a slightly younger-looking Skip Henry. Gordon turned the photo over and saw that the names of the other two people had been written in pencil on the back: Don Holden and Darlene Holden.

Gordon whistled.

"Is that ..." Judy began.

Gordon nodded.

"It's Skip Henry all right," Peter said. "Not much doubt about it."

"But then why does it say Don Holden on the back? What does it all mean?"

"Nothing good, I'm afraid," Gordon said. "Would it be possible for me to borrow this photo? I'll take good care of it."

She nodded.

"Excuse me," said Leah. "Could I please take a look at it?"

Gordon handed it to her and kept talking to Judy Beck. "I'll see if I can get a copy made and get the original back to you tomorrow."

Leah, looking at the photo, frowned and forgot her manners.

"Gordon," she said. "You say this man on the right is someone named Skip Henry or Don Holden?"

"That's right. Why?"

She handed the photo back to him.

"Well, Elizabeth and I know him as Joe Price."

BACK IN THE CHEROKEE, Gordon was unnerved.

"We need to do something," he said. "Elizabeth and Stella could be alone in Buckley with that guy."

"No phone reception up there?" Peter asked.

"Totally dead," Leah said. "And not many people there, either. Not on a weekday."

"This investigation is starting to break," Gordon said, "and I hate to walk away from it, but I think we need to go to Buckley right now."

No one spoke for 15 seconds.

"You know, Gordon," Leah said, "for whatever it's worth, I don't think Joe is going to hurt Elizabeth or Stella."

"You don't know what this guy's done."

"I guess not, but I don't think he's dangerous to *us*. And I have a record when it comes to sizing up strangers."

"There's another option," Peter said. "You could call the sheriff's department and ask them to take a message to Elizabeth and Stella. That gets the word to them and provides some backup in case of danger."

"Good idea, Peter, but what do I say when I call the sheriff's department?"

"I don't know, but whatever you do, don't tell them the truth."

"Why not?"

"Because they'll probably think you're a lunatic and put you on a 72-hour mental hold."

THEY ROLLED INTO Barnstaple at 1:05. Gordon had called the Boundary County Sheriff's Department and asked them to contact Elizabeth Macondray in Buckley. They were to tell her that Leah had broken a leg and was being taken to the hospital in Sierra Pines. Elizabeth was to call Gordon on his cell as soon as she got to a place where her phone would work. There was an anxious moment when the dispatcher asked why Gordon hadn't requested an ambulance, but he looked over at Peter and ad-libbed that there was a doctor present who was accompanying them to the hospital.

The sun was completely behind the clouds when they pulled into the Lake View Motel. Gordon wondered how much longer the rain could hold off. Lindsay opened the door to room 17 and waved them in. The room was small and dimly lit. Gordon and Lindsay sat at a small table with only two chairs; Peter and Leah sat on the edge of the bed.

"Any news?" Gordon asked.

"We got a hit from the cruise company. They dug out the passenger list from that cruise in late '97. It included the names Lucille Starr, Viola Johnson, Eleanor Gluck and Douglas Hurd."

"Have you heard from the police in Eugene, Oregon?"

"Nothing. I'm hoping soon."

"How about the other places?"

She shook her head. "I heard back from Henderson, Nevada. It's slow going there. The neighborhood where Daniel and Virginia Hines lived is mostly condos and there's been a lot of turnover, so no positive ID. Otherwise it's hurry up and wait. How about you?"

He took Judy Beck's photo from his shirt pocket and handed it to Lindsay. She looked at it, turned it over, and raised her eyebrows when she read the names on the back.

"Nice work," she said. "Who's the other guy?"

"Luther Whitman. One of the so-called accident victims I've been looking into. Do we have enough to move on this now?"

She looked at the photo again.

"We're almost there," she said.

"Almost! Meanwhile Kathryn Henry is in danger, and so are Elizabeth and Stella." He told her the story about Joe Price.

"If a deputy's going up to give them a message, they should be pretty safe."

"What are we waiting for?"

"One more call."

"One more? From who?"

Lindsay's phone went off. She looked at the caller number.

"This may be it. If you promise to be quiet as church mice, I'll let you listen. Hello, Roy? I'm going to put you on speaker. I'm walking around the room." She hit the speaker button and set the phone on the table.

"Tell me what you got," Lindsay said.

"The jackpot. Three hits so far. Millie Samuels, the one who called you last week, picked our man out of the lineup immediately. Not a second's hesitation. Two other neighbors picked him almost as fast."

"God bless Millie Samuels," Lindsay said. "Are the other two IDs solid?"

"In my opinion, yes."

"Time to move, then. I want you to get an arrest warrant."

"Do you think we have enough, Lindsay?"

"Take it to Judge Adler. He'll sign anything."

"Got it. What name do you want on the warrant?"

"David Hawes, you have the spelling on our records ..."

"Yes."

"... a.k.a. Dwight Henry."

"What's that?"

"The name he's using here."

"D.H. both times. Doesn't even have to change the monogramming on his luggage."

"That's already been pointed out. Call me the instant you have anything."

"I'm on it."

He ended the call, and Lindsay turned off her phone.

"Time to pay a call on the sheriff," she said.

THE HIGHWAY PATROL officer who came to the driver's-side window of the rented Toyota Camry was named Sophia Flores. Bad break, the driver thought. He'd have preferred a white male, preferably older, who might be willing to cut him some slack. A Latina woman was more likely to feel under scrutiny and do everything by the book. But he hadn't gotten this far by living in the wreckage of the future. Best to see how it played out first.

He already had his driver's license out and handed it over when she asked.

"Thank you, Mr. Haynes," she said, adding after a pause, "do you know why I pulled you over?"

"Was I going too fast? I try not to."

"No, sir. You were right at the speed limit. But when you hit your brakes a couple of miles back, the right brake light didn't come on."

Damn deer, he thought. Why did it have to cross the road just then?

"I see you're driving a rental car," she said. "We'll have to issue a fix-it ticket so they take care of it."

He exhaled. That was a break. With any luck, he'd be rolling again in a few minutes. He still had plenty of time to get to Ontario International Airport and catch the 7:15 flight to Seattle. It looked as if a storm was moving in, but even slowing for the weather, he should make it easily. And the less time he spent in the airport the better.

"I'm running a check on the vehicle's license plate," she said. "I'll be right back."

She started back to the patrol car, and he began to feel better. He should be able to get through this.

Officer Flores reappeared by his window.

"I'm sorry, sir. I forgot to ask for the rental car papers. To show that you rented the car. Could I have those please?"

"Of course." He paused for effect. "They're in the glove box. Is that all right?"

"Just take them out slowly, sir."

He saw her lower her right hand to her holster, but he wasn't about to try anything crazy now. He popped the glove compartment open, took the rental car agreement out as slowly as he could, and just as slowly brought it back across his body, handing it to her through the window.

"Thank you, sir."

She started back to the patrol car, and he considered his options. The worst that could happen was that she'd run a check on his Idaho driver's license and come up empty. But would she really make a federal case out of that over a faulty brake light on a rental car? He could say it must be a computer snafu, and she'd probably let it go.

Out of nowhere, he realized he was in deep trouble.

The rental agreement he had given her showed the car being rented to the all-purpose California name and Santa Barbara address he used between jobs.

But after renting the car in Sierra Pines a half hour ago, he had switched his driver's license and passport to Darrell Haynes of Caldwell, Idaho, the name under which he had booked the flight to Seattle.

Nobody would be dumb enough not to get suspicious when the driver's license and the rental agreement had completely different names.

There was hardly any time to spare before Officer Flores spotted the discrepancy and most likely called for help. She might be doing so right now. As he saw it, he had only two choices.

He could take the gun out of the glove compartment, where it had been sitting on top of the rental agreement, and shoot Officer Flores.

Or he could make a run for it.

He checked the driver's-side mirror. An 18-wheel truck was heading their way. It looked to be half a mile behind them and would be there in 30 seconds or less. If he could get it between the Camry and the patrol car, he could buy a few minutes.

He looked at his watch and calmly waited as ten seconds ticked off.

Then he turned the key in the ignition, shifted into Drive and pulled out in front of the truck. Even flooring it, he barely gained on it before it could hit him from behind. The truck driver gave him a long dose of horn music.

He didn't care. He remembered that there was a turnoff to a lake two to three miles ahead. If he could keep the truck between himself and the patrol car that long, he might be able to leave the highway there and temporarily evade Officer Flores. This section of road was narrow with no shoulder, and enough cars were coming the other direction that she might not be able to pass the truck right away. It was a chance, and the only one he had.

The speedometer on the Camry showed that he was doing 92 when he reached the first curve in the road ahead.

SHERIFF'S DEPUTY RON BUELL came out of Sam's Diner in Sierra Pines ready to face what the afternoon had to offer. A large bowl of Sam's chili was mostly responsible for the feeling, along with the fact that he had three days off when he finished today's shift.

He checked in with the dispatcher and was told to take an emergency message to two women who were painting in Buckley and out of phone range. He wrote down the details of the message and said he was on his way. He thought to himself that it didn't sound like much of an emergency, but he hadn't been to Buckley in a while, and this didn't seem like a bad assignment. It would take up about half his remaining time on the shift.

Ten miles up the highway toward Buckley, he saw a red Chrysler Sebring convertible on the side of the road. A tall, attractive blonde who appeared to be of college age was standing by the car waving at him. Ron, who was 25 and single, told himself it was his duty to pull over and check it out.

The blonde, who said her name was Sarah, told Ron that she and her friend Victoria, an attractive redhead — not that Ron noticed — were on their way to Barnstaple when they realized the car was driving funny. They pulled over and saw that the right front tire was flat, and they had no way of fixing it. Nor was there any cell phone reception on this part of the road.

At that point, Ron had two choices. He could call for a roadside assistance truck or put on the spare tire himself. Generally, the policy would be to call for the truck, but Sarah and Victoria were going to be in Barnstaple that night, and that's where he would be getting off work in a few hours. Besides, Victoria was flashing him a smile.

He decided it was his duty to change the tire himself. The women in Buckley could wait a bit longer to hear about Leah's broken leg. After all, a broken leg was hardly life-threatening.

THEY WERE in the office of Sheriff Rod Kanehl for 35 minutes, laying out the case against Dwight Henry and his aliases. Lindsay outlined the story in sharp detail, beginning with the first known murder in Flagstaff six years ago and culminating in the car-wash assassination of Duncan Bennett in Twin Rivers two days earlier.

Gordon listened to her seamlessly tying the elements of the story together, and at one point it occurred to him that she had probably been the kid who got an A on her book reports in school. Every time.

When she had finished, Gordon gave a slightly less polished brief, explaining how the four fatal accidents Barnstaple had experienced in the past four months also had a connection to Lindsay's case. Luther Whitman was known to have met Donald Holden in Flagstaff, Arizona. Lucy Starr had been on the cruise ship where Douglas Hurd had met Eleanor Gluck of Eugene, Oregon, his fourth known victim. Dave Rowan had been sufficiently suspicious of Dwight Henry's service record that he wrote to Veterans Affairs and didn't live long enough to get the answer. Finally, Olema Marsh, who was Kathryn Livingston's roommate on the cruise where she met Dwight Henry, had become so suspicious of the other three accidents that she had called Gordon in to investigate. And then she had died herself in an "accident" just before Gordon arrived.

"You have to admit," Gordon concluded, "that in the stories Detective Judd and I have been telling you, everything fits together with the precision of a Swiss watch. If our stories aren't right, the only other explanation is a series of coincidences that Hollywood couldn't invent."

Sheriff Kanehl had sat impassively through the presentations with a pencil in his hand and a notepad on his desk. He hadn't written a word on the notepad and had spent the entire time fidgeting with the pencil. He was staring at a point on the wall behind Gordon and Lindsay when Gordon wrapped up.

For 20 seconds, he said nothing at all, and his only movement was waggling the pencil back and forth between his thumb and forefinger. Finally, he leaned forward over the desk and set the pencil on the pad.

"Actually, even Hollywood couldn't invent the story the two of you have just told," he said.

"You don't believe it?" Gordon asked.

"I didn't say that. It's so impossible it almost has to be true. The question is, what are you asking me to do?"

"For starters," Lindsay said, "I'd like to bring Skip Henry down here for questioning. I'd appreciate backup when I go get him and a place to do the interview afterward."

"Before I commit to that, Detective, I want to be certain you know how serious this is. This is a small town, and if we bring Skip Henry in for questioning at 4:30, it's going to be the number one topic of discussion during Happy Hour at the Barnstaple Inn at 5:30. And if, God forbid, we should be wrong, if we brought in one of the most prominent men in town for nothing, there will be hell to pay."

"I understand that."

"I know you understand that in concept, but do you really *understand* it? If we haul Skip Henry in and you made a mistake, you can drive back to Long Beach tomorrow morning with no one, aside from a couple of your colleagues, any the wiser. Meanwhile, there will be a shit shower taking place here, and I am going to be the one standing naked under the shower head. Do I make myself clear?"

"Very clear."

"So all I'm asking, Detective, is that you put yourself in my shoes and see what kind of cover you can give me."

In the silence that followed, they could hear a rumble of thunder outside, followed by rain beginning to fall. In seconds, it was coming down hard.

Peter, who had been sitting at the back of the room with Leah, piped up:

"Well, sheriff, you could always blame it on the morons in Southern California."

"Nice try, doc, but I don't think that would fly."

Lindsay's phone rang.

"I have to take this," she said, looking at the number. "Excuse me. Hello, Roy? (Pause) You do? (Pause) He did? (Pause) Great."

She set the phone face down on her knee and turned to the sheriff.

"Do you have a card?"

He reached into the top drawer of the desk and took one out.

"Here's the fax number," she said, looking at the card. She read it and added, "How soon can you send it? Five minutes? Make it three. This is urgent."

She turned back to Sheriff Kanehl.

"That was my partner in Long Beach. We have an arrest warrant for David Hawes, a.k.a. Dwight Henry, for the murder of Francine Hawes in Long Beach on or about May 13, 1995. It's being faxed here as we speak. That changes the equation. We're no longer bringing him in for questioning. I'm asking for backup to arrest a murder suspect."

"And you'll have it," Kanehl said. "If you have a warrant, I'm obligated to help."

He stood up.

"Wait here while I see who I can round up. Most of our people are at the south end of the county right now on a high-speed chase, but give me 15 minutes and we'll go to the Henry house with whatever we've got."

He walked across the room to the door, opened it, hesitated, and turned back toward his visitors.

"By the way, Gordon, just so you know, I always smelled a rat with those so-called accidents, but up to now there hasn't been any evidence. No matter what happens with this, we'll be taking another look. That's a promise."

He stepped through the door and closed it behind him.

THE STORM BLEW into Buckley with a fury. Elizabeth and Stella barely had time to scoop up all of Elizabeth's painting materials and get inside the church before the downpour turned into a hailstorm. The hailstones were small, but there were a lot of them, and within a few minutes it looked like a snowy winter day outside.

Inside the church, Stella and Elizabeth shivered. With the coming of the hail, the temperature in Buckley had dropped sharply, and they had been dressed for a warm summer day.

"Creepy place to have to wait out the storm," Stella said, once they had settled in.

"The good news," Elizabeth said, "is that these mountain storms usually hit hard and fast. I expect it'll be over in an hour or two."

They sat quietly for a minute, listening to the hail pound a tattoo on the church rooftop.

"Do you think we're the only ones here? In Buckley?" Stella finally asked.

"I think so."

"But we don't know?"

"I took a quick look at the parking lot as we were running into the church. I didn't see another car there, but then, I wasn't exactly taking it in slowly."

"I wonder if that guy we ran into earlier is still around."

"Joe? Probably not. He gave me an envelope for Leah and left. He seemed to be in a hurry."

"Damn. I know I've seen him somewhere. But my brain can't seem to call it up."

"It'll come to you when you're not thinking about it."

"He creeps me out."

"Me too. I didn't want him hanging around Leah. That's why I pressed Gordon to take her with him today."

"Has he been giving Leah a hard time?"

"Not exactly that. But he's been taking too much of an interest in her for my taste."

They listened to the falling hail for a minute.

"Where's the envelope?" Stella asked.

"It's in my purse."

"Do you think we should look at it?"

"It's addressed to Leah. I'll make a point of being there when she opens it, though. I can't imagine what it would be."

The wind had picked up along with the hail. As it blew through the town, it squeaked its way through small cracks in the tops and sides of the buildings in Buckley. The friction resulted in a creaking, moaning noise somewhere between a wail and a howl. The clouds had blotted out the sun to such an extent that the interior of the church was dim and the corners were dark.

"The woman at the historical society said the locals think that moaning noise is the ghosts of all the people who died unnaturally in Buckley over the years," Stella said.

"I can believe it."

"I don't suppose we're in any danger here."

"Not unless the church collapses on us, and I don't think it's that bad a storm." A few seconds later, she added, "Besides, I still have my gun in the purse."

"Maybe you should take it out."

"Why? When we're all alone?"

"By the time we realize we're not alone, it'll be too late. And I'd feel better seeing it and knowing it's there. Could you humor me, Elizabeth, and take the gun out?"

Elizabeth sighed and leaned over her purse. She put her right hand into it, slid it around the interior and sat up straight.

"It isn't there," she said.

"Maybe you forgot to bring it."

"No. I checked the purse before we left. It was there then."

"Then what ..."

"Joe Price," Elizabeth said. "When he slid Leah's letter into my purse, the son of a bitch must have taken my gun out. Dammit!"

The sound outside, a combination of wind, falling hail, and the moaning noise the wind made as it blew through the cracks of the old, deserted buildings, had risen in intensity. It felt as if they were alone at the end of the earth.

"That woman at the historical society said something else," Stella said. "She said the moaning noises that we're hearing — it's not just the ghosts of the people who died in Buckley. They say Joe Price's ghost haunts the place, too."

"It's not the ghost of Joe Price I'm worried about," Elizabeth said. "It's the real Joe Price. The one who has my gun in his hands now."

IT TOOK 20 MINUTES for Sheriff Kanehl to organize a posse to serve the warrant on Dwight Henry. It wasn't as impressive a posse as he would have liked, but it was the best he could do under the circumstances.

The group that finally went to the Henry residence in the midst of a torrential storm consisted of the sheriff, an out-of-shape records sergeant counting down the days to retirement, the one deputy who had been patrolling the northern end of Boundary County, and a Highway Patrol officer who had been in the area and was sent to provide mutual aid. The locals were joined by Lindsay and Gordon.

Sheriff Kanehl hadn't wanted Gordon along, but Lindsay argued for him, saying he'd been investigating the case and had provided valuable leads. The sheriff grudgingly relented but insisted that Leah and Peter had to be left out of the group. Gordon was happy to agree and handed over the keys of the Cherokee to Peter, who drove Leah back to Broderick's.

They went to the Henry house in three vehicles. The local deputy drove Sheriff Kanehl and the out-of-shape sergeant in his patrol car, which led the procession. Behind it was Lindsay's Corvette, carrying her and Gordon. Bringing up the rear was the Highway Patrol car.

Gordon kept looking at his watch as they drove the couple of miles out of town.

"Anything wrong?" Lindsay asked.

"Just that I haven't heard from Elizabeth. She should have gotten my message and come down the mountain into cell phone range by now."

"Maybe she was in too much of a hurry to call."

"I hope she and Stella don't go all the way to the hospital in Sierra Pines and we're not there."

"Relax, Gordon. If that's the worst thing you ever do to her, she's a lucky woman."

When the procession reached the Henry place, the sheriff's car turned left and drove up the driveway, followed by Lindsay's Corvette. The Highway Patrol car pulled in front of the driveway entrance and parked there, parallel to the highway, so that no other vehicle could get in or out. As directed by the sheriff, the Highway Patrol officer remained with his vehicle to seal off the driveway and be able to assist or call for help if things got out of hand.

The patrol car and Corvette parked in the flat space at the top of the driveway. A dark green 1998 Ford Explorer was parked near the house. The garage door was open, and nothing was parked inside.

"He's gone," Sheriff Kanehl said.

"How do you know?" Gordon asked.

"He drives a 1999 Toyota Tundra, and it's not here." The sheriff paused. "In this county, if your car's not here, you're not here."

"Maybe they went out together."

"Only one way to find out."

Kanehl whispered a command to the younger deputy, who stealthily moved around the left side of the house to keep an eye on the back of it. The four of them waited until he was out of sight.

"Might as well do it," Kanehl muttered.

They advanced toward the front door in tight formation. Just as Kanehl took a step up onto the small porch, the door flew open, Kathryn Henry behind it. One look at her face was enough to tell that something was wrong.

"Thank God you're finally here," she said. "It seems like I called hours ago."

They stood in place, uncomprehending.

"I'm sorry," Kathryn said. "I'm so upset I'm forgetting my manners. Come in."

She led them down a short corridor to a living area, turned around and began addressing them without asking them to sit down.

"I'm going crazy with fear and worry. I went over to Sierra Pines first thing this morning to pick up an extra copy of the picture the bank had taken of Skip. When I got there, the photographer told me some detective from Long Beach had asked for it, too, and said it was for a murder investigation. He couldn't tell me any more, so I called Skip. He said there must be some mistake, and we could talk about it when I got home.

"And then, when I did get home, Skip was gone and so was one of his big suitcases. I've been calling him on his cell phone every ten minutes, and he doesn't answer. Then I call you guys and you take forever to come over."

Kathryn's voice had been rising and her agitation growing as she talked. It had taken on a quality of fear, panic and anger so great that Gordon wanted to cover his ears. Her next sentence came out as an over-the-top primal scream.

"Can someone *please* tell me what the hell is going on here?"

There was an awkward silence for several seconds before Kanehl turned to Lindsay and nodded slightly, as if to say, "Go ahead." She took a step forward, bringing her close enough to touch Kathryn.

"Mrs. Henry, I'm Detective Lindsay Judd, Long Beach Police Department. It was me who talked to the photographer."

She reached out and laid her left hand on Kathryn Henry's right shoulder.

"It might be a good idea for you to sit down. There's something you need to know about your husband."

Wednesday June 14

Handwritten document turned over to Sheriff
Rod Kanehl by Leah Drake

13 June 2000

My Dearest Kathryn,

By the time young Leah has given you this letter, I will be many miles away, and it is unlikely we shall see each other again. If I express myself badly, please forgive me, as I am writing in haste. But the one thing I want you to know, beyond any doubt, is that this has happened owing to circumstances beyond my control, and it is not what I wanted at all.

Kathryn, you are the love of my life, and it had been my fondest hope that we would be able to live out many long, happy and loving years in Barnstaple, which I have quickly come to feel is where I was always meant to be. I would have done anything to stay here, spending the rest of my life in bliss with you, but it apparently wasn't destined to happen. For that, I am both sad and sorry.

In the days following my departure, it is possible you will hear bad things said of me. Some of them may even be true. I am not a saint and have never pretended to be. All I can ask is that you don't judge me by my worst days and my worst behavior but rather that you remember me as the loving husband who, I hope, brought you a measure of joy and comfort for all too short a time.

Farewell, my love, for you are the only woman I have ever truly loved, and I did my best to be true to you in my way. If we never meet again in this world, I can only hope and pray that there is another world to come in which we shall be reunited, together forever as we were meant to be.

Affectionately,
Skip

Thursday June 22

From The Barnstaple Miner

In a stunning announcement, Sheriff Rod Kanehl said at a press conference Tuesday that Dwight "Skip" Henry of Barnstaple, who was killed last week when his rental car crashed into a tree at high speed south of Sierra Pines, was under investigation as a person of interest in five homicides in four states over the past several years.

The tangled story came out as the sheriff tried to explain the circumstances of Mr. Henry's death, which had shocked this community, to which he had recently moved and in which he had already become active in civic and business affairs.

Sheriff Kanehl explained the circumstances of Mr. Henry's death as follows.

In the early afternoon, Mr. Henry had rented a Toyota Camry from an agency in Sierra Pines, leaving his own pickup truck parked on a street a couple of blocks away. He was driving the rental car south on the state highway, near the county line, when it was pulled over by a Highway Patrol officer who noticed that one of the brake lights wasn't working.

Mr. Henry courteously gave the female officer his driver's license and the rental papers for the vehicle, but investigators speculate that within minutes of doing so, he realized he had made a mistake. The driver's license identified him as Darrell Haynes of Caldwell, Idaho, but the rental papers showed the car had been rented to Joseph Price of Santa Barbara, California.

Apparently recognizing the discrepancy, investigators said, Mr. Henry restarted his car and pulled onto the highway just in front of a tractor-trailer rig, putting it between him and the Highway Patrol car. He drove three miles down the highway at speeds believed to exceed 90 mph but lost control of the vehicle at a curve near the beginning of Dead Rabbit Pass.

His car crashed into a large pine tree and virtually disintegrated, with numerous pieces of the vehicle and many of its contents landing on the roadway and nearly causing collateral collisions involving other vehicles. Sheriff Kanehl said Mr. Henry was probably killed instantly, and that the subsequent cleanup and evidence-gathering closed the highway for three hours.

Searching Mr. Henry's belongings, investigators discovered a ticket for Darrell Haynes on a flight from Ontario airport in San Bernardino County to Seattle later in the day as well as a reservation to rent a car at Seattle-Tacoma airport that evening in the name of Delmer Harkins.

A driver's license with Mr. Henry's picture and the name of Delmer Harkins was found among the debris, along with a passport in the Harkins name. As investigators sifted through the material scattered by the crash, they came across numerous driver's licenses and passports bearing Mr. Henry's photo but other names — all except Joseph Price — featuring the initials D.H.

It was at that point that the investigation took a shocking turn. Several of the names on the passports and driver's licenses matched the names of men being sought in connection with the murders of their wives in five cities in four states, beginning in 1994.

Sheriff Kanehl declined to elaborate on the other cases, but a source close to the investigation of Mr. Henry told *The Barnstaple Miner* that in each of those cases, the man had met a single or divorced middle-aged woman on a cruise ship and married her soon afterward, following a torrid shipboard romance.

After establishing residence in her town, the source said, the new husband liquidated most of the newly joined assets, sent the money to a numbered account at a bank in the Cayman Islands, and vanished without a trace shortly before the wife was discovered killed in her home.

The source also said that a police detective from Long Beach, where one of the murders occurred, was in Barnstaple last week investigating and was about to arrest Mr. Henry when word of the fatal crash reached the sheriff.

But according to the source, there's more to the story. The man known as Skip Henry is also being looked at in connection with the fatal shooting of Duncan

Bennett in Twin Rivers, Nevada, Sunday June 11. Mr. Bennett had posted a blog two weeks before about the murderous husband with changing names, pointing out that the various law enforcement agencies involved hadn't made the connection.

And finally, the source told this newspaper, Sheriff Kanehl is planning to reopen the investigation into at least one accidental death in this area earlier in the year, looking into the possibility that the accident victim had recognized Mr. Henry from one of his earlier locations, thus putting Mr. Henry (and the eventual accident victim) in jeopardy.

Asked about that at the press conference, Sheriff Kanehl barked out an irritable "No comment" and quickly moved on to the next questioner.

The revelation of Mr. Henry's multiple identities and possible past lives raises a painful question locally. He had moved to Barnstaple earlier this year after meeting and marrying Kathryn Livingston following a cruise ship romance.

In May, Mr. Henry was installed on the Boundary County Bank board of directors. Mr. Henry had also been proposed as a member of the Barnstaple Rotary Club and was to have been inducted at yesterday's meeting.

An out-of-town reporter tactlessly asked the sheriff at the press conference if Mrs. Henry had been in any danger from her husband.

"We have no reason to believe that," Sheriff Kanehl said. He added that Mr. Henry had written a brief letter to his wife before fleeing Barnstaple. He declined to make the contents of the letter public or to provide a summary of them.

San Jose, California
Saturday, October 21, 2000

THE DOUBLETREE HOTEL near the international airport was crawling with cops. It was the second day of the annual convention of the California Association of Robbery and Homicide Detectives, and Lindsay Judd was skipping the noon presentation on "How to Read an Autopsy Report" to have lunch in the hotel coffee shop with Gordon, Elizabeth and Peter. More than four months had passed since that day in Barnstaple, but she was still harboring a resentment.

"If stupidity was a criminal offense ...," she began.

"I'd vote for that," Peter said.

"If it was, that photographer in Sierra Pines would be doing life in Pelican Bay. When I asked him to email me the portrait of Skip Henry, I told him in no uncertain terms that he shouldn't tell anyone he was doing that. So what does Joe Camera do? He tells Skip's wife. His *wife* — can you believe that?"

"I believe it because it happened," Gordon said. "Are you sure you don't want a glass of wine?"

"I'm fine, thanks," Lindsay said, looking anything but. "I mean, I told him not to tell *anybody*. And you know what his excuse was? He thought he wasn't supposed to tell Skip Henry because it was a surprise, but that it was OK to tell his wife because she was in on it. Honestly, some people have shit where their brains are supposed to be."

"And Kathryn Henry freaked out, called Skip right away from Sierra Pines and tipped him off," Elizabeth said.

"And he damn near got away," Lindsay said. "It was sheer luck that he rented a car with a bum brake light and a Highway Patrol officer spotted it." She sighed and took a swallow of coffee. "Well, they do tell you in police academy that the vehicle code is the law enforcement officer's best friend."

"With all due credit to luck," Gordon said, "you came up on your own time to look into Duncan Bennett's theory, and you were putting pressure on Skip Henry, or whatever we're calling him. That's the first time anybody had been on his trail at all, and without that pressure, maybe he doesn't make the mistake with the two IDs and bluffs his way out of the traffic stop."

"Maybe. And your investigation into the accidents probably had him worried, too. But I still hate to think how close he came to getting away. Because you know if he did get away, there would have been other victims. Maybe a lot of them. The guy was no dummy."

"Do you have any idea who he really was?" Peter said.

The server arrived at that point, and Lindsay looked up.

"I'll tell you after we order. I didn't have breakfast this morning, and I'm hungry."

"THE BOTTOM LINE," she said after the server had left with their orders, "is that there are a million little things and several big ones in this investigation about which we have no idea and probably never will. That includes who he was. The most likely guess was that his name was Joe Price since that seemed to be his go-to identity, the one he used between marriages. But nothing checks out under that name. It could be bogus, too."

"So the fact that he was using the same name as a notorious pioneer in Buckley was just a coincidence," Elizabeth said.

"Totally. He was using Joe Price and the same credit card with that name since the early 1990s, with a couple of different Southern California addresses. Santa Barbara was the latest, and we also have addresses in Santa Monica and Glendale. There may be others. Until we started looking, I had no idea how many Joe Prices there are just in Southern California."

"And in this day and age, with everything on computers, he stayed under the radar — didn't show up anywhere?" Gordon asked. "How could he do that?"

"It's not easy," Lindsay said, "but it can be done if you're willing to spend money. There are people in Los Angeles County who can generate driver's licenses and passports and Social Security cards that would fool just about anyone who wasn't suspicious and looking at them really hard. All his IDs were high quality. And he obviously had a good computer nerd on board to be able to erase Bennett's hard drive and pose as a Nevada detective. We haven't found the nerd, either."

"Anything with fingerprints or DNA?" Peter asked.

"His prints don't match anything on file, which means he wasn't in the military or the criminal justice system."

"You were able to get fingerprints?" Elizabeth said. "How?"

"A couple of intact fingers were recovered from the accident scene. You probably don't want to know any more about that with lunch arriving soon."

"A couple of intact fingers from a crash at that speed? That's a gift," Peter said.

"It surprises me that nothing showed up from the military," Gordon said. "The way Elizabeth and Leah described how he appeared out of nowhere and disappeared into thin air made me wonder if he had any sort of Special Forces training. To be that good at being stealthy."

"He may have had it somewhere else," Lindsay said.

"You mean he might have been a mercenary?" Peter asked.

"That's one theory. But I can also tell you there are people in this world who have the gift of moving softly and seeming to be invisible. Bing Crosby used to be able to sit out in plain sight, and people would walk by without noticing him. We have a detective sergeant who can shadow people for days and they never notice him. Nobody else in the department even comes close to being that good. And the guy can't even tell you how he does it. He just does."

"Back to my question," Peter said, "how about DNA?"

"It told us one thing for sure. His DNA was a match for Francine Hawes' unborn baby, so our case is officially closed. Otherwise, there's nothing in the criminal DNA registers. I'm telling you, Skip Henry, or D.H. or Joe Price or whatever you want to call him, really knew how to stay out of the whole social network."

"Is there any way you could check his DNA against a broader base to find out who he might be related to and see if you could run him down from there?"

"Good question, Peter. It'd make a great premise for a cop show. But there isn't all that good a basic DNA registry out there to check against. In 10, 20 years there probably will be, but right now it would be a huge undertaking. And with the case officially closed, other crimes to solve, and budgets dwindling by the year, our police chief isn't exactly into putting a lot of time and money into investigating something out of curiosity."

"So we're left with a man from nowhere," Gordon said.

"That's about it."

"Do you have any theories?" Elizabeth said. "Any idea that might explain Joe or Skip — who he might have been and where he might have come from?"

"Actually, I do have a theory, though that's all it is. But it does address some of the key points in his story."

The server returned and began setting down their plates.

"Let me get a little food in me," Lindsay said, "and I'll tell you about it."

"BY THE WAY," Elizabeth said, as they started eating, "did Gordon ever tell you what Leah did with the money?"

Lindsay, her mouth full, shook her head.

"Well, you remember that Joe — Skip — whoever he was gave me an envelope addressed to Leah that last day at Buckley. He put it in my purse when he was stealing my gun. When I finally remembered to give it to her later that night, it turned out that letter to Kathryn Henry was inside in a smaller, sealed envelope. Do you have that letter, by the way?"

Still chewing, Lindsay nodded and slid a file folder across the table to Elizabeth.

"And in addition to the Kathryn letter, there were ten hundred-dollar bills and a note to Leah from Joe, thanking her in advance for delivering the letter and saying he wanted her to use the money for her college education and remember him fondly."

"He seemed to care a lot about his image," Peter said.

"By then," Elizabeth continued, "we knew pretty much the whole story, so Gordon and I insisted she turn the letter over to the sheriff the next day because it could be evidence. She tried to turn in the money, too, but the sheriff said no thanks. He said as far as he could see, the money had been freely given to her and it was hers to do with as she pleased."

"It's a lot of money for a struggling college student," Gordon said, "but she didn't feel she should keep it, given the source.

"So she consulted with us, talked to one of her teachers at S.F. State, and talked to her new boyfriend. And finally, she decided to give it to the Environmental Defense Fund."

"Good for her," Lindsay said, "though I'm not sure I wouldn't have kept it in the same situation."

Elizabeth took the photocopy of the letter to Kathryn out of the file folder and held it up.

"I'm curious as to what the rest of you thought of this," she said.

"I'd like to know your take," Peter said. "You stayed with Kathryn last summer, after all."

"Did you?" Lindsay said.

Elizabeth nodded. "Twice, for a week, when I was up there painting. I went with Leah when she delivered a copy of the letter, and Kathryn and I hit it off. I think she was lonely and reluctant to talk to people in town because of what her husband turned out to be."

"Not to mention the fact that he killed two of her best friends," Peter said.

"Anyway, she asked me to stay with her if I came back to paint. And I did. We talked a lot. She was obviously badly shaken by the whole experience, but you know what? I think that even though she knows who her husband was and what he did, she's still sort of in love with him. She can't help it, and it must be hard on her."

"I can't imagine," Gordon said. "And how could you ever trust your judgment again, after finding out you married a serial killer?"

Lindsay smiled. "Luckily for the human race," she said, "women don't give up on men just because they picked a bad one once. Or two or three or four times. Love's not scientific."

"And thank God for that," Peter said.

"I mean," Elizabeth said, "you get a sense from this letter about how he might have been able to sweep a lonely woman off her feet on a cruise. It's a bit over the top for my taste, but it is romantic and very well expressed." She took a sip of water. "I wish I could teach my students to write that well. But do you think he meant it? Did he really love her?"

"Probably not," Lindsay said. "You look at all the things he did, and there was no feeling or human empathy anywhere. People were just obstacles to what he wanted. So I vote no."

"Let me offer another perspective," Peter said. "Having been married almost as often as our serial killer friend, I think it's possible he really felt something for her. And it could be that he started out planning to kill her like he killed the others but changed his mind. Hand me that letter, Elizabeth. I think the telling line in it was, 'I did my best to be true to you in my way.' I say he may not have loved her the way we understand love, but that doesn't make his own feeling any less real."

Elizabeth looked at Gordon. He made a head gesture toward Peter.

"What he says. How about you, darling?"

Elizabeth took the letter back from Peter and set it on top of the folder.

"I don't know that I believe he loved her, but I'd *like* to believe it. There's a part of me that feels that no matter how bad someone is, no matter what horrible things he did, he might be redeemed by love. Even if it was only an ounce of redemption."

"An ounce of redemption in a bucket of blood," Lindsay said.

Elizabeth looked at her coolly. "It looks like you're done with lunch. Do you want to tell us your theory now?"

THE SERVER HAD CLEARED the table and taken Gordon's credit card by the time Lindsay started. She seemed more energized and laid out her case forcefully.

"The first thing I did when I got back to Long Beach after the dust had settled in Barnstaple was to sit down and ask myself what I missed when I handled the investigation the first time. We locked in on the husband right away, and because of that, it never occurred to us that this might not be an isolated case — that it might be part of a pattern. Now that we know the pattern and a lot of the details, I started out by asking what we know about Joe Price-David Hawes-Skip Henry. When you put all the facts together, there's an idea that suggests itself.

"So what do we know? We know our man had some pretty sophisticated shady contacts. He knew where to get really high-quality IDs. He knew how to get hold of a computer hacker with no scruples. He knew about offshore banking accounts. These aren't things your ordinary law-abiding citizen knows much about. Add to that, the fact he's off the grid and he looks very much like a man with something to hide.

"And he knew how to kill. Look at all the different ways he murdered his victims — shooting, stabbing, bludgeoning, poisoning, strangling, throwing people out of towers and into rivers. When I first saw Francine Hawes in her house in Long Beach with an electrical cord around her neck, I thought of a professional garroting. Since we were looking for her husband almost right away, I thought we'd get the answer when we caught him, but we never did.

"Then don't forget the cold-bloodedness of the man, how he had no qualms about taking the life of anyone who got in his way as if they were just flies interrupting his lunch. Add in the element of stealth and daring, and what do you have?"

They were all staring at her speechless.

"That sounds to me," Lindsay continued, "like the profile of a professional killer. My theory is that he was a highly paid hit man, and that several years ago he decided to stop working for other people and go out on his own. From that point of view, his serial monogamy was part of a well-crafted business plan. And if I'm right about this, I hope I never meet his like again. The Highway Patrol officer and that tree did the world a favor as far as I'm concerned."

"A public service vehicle fatality," Peter said. "But your theory rings true."

"It covers all the bases," Gordon said.

"It makes sense to me," Elizabeth said. "But will we ever know?"

"I wish I could say yes," Lindsay said, "but I can't."

Elizabeth picked up the letter to Kathryn and read it again. When she finished, she shook her head and sighed.

"We'll never know who he was, but we know two things about him. He could speak to a woman's heart, and he wrote in beautiful cursive."

Author's Note

This book is dedicated in the spirit of Ross Macdonald, the pen name of Kenneth Millar (1915-1983). Macdonald's detective novels, featuring private eye Lew Archer, took place in postwar California. In his books, the term "dysfunctional family" would have been a redundancy, and secrets from the past often bubbled up in the present, generally with a lethal effect. His 1964 novel *The Chill* is arguably one of the greatest nightmare-marriage stories in all of crime fiction. His first book, *The Moving Target*, was adapted for a motion picture starring Paul Newman in 1966. Because Newman was appearing in a number of films with H-titles at the time (*The Hustler, Hud, Hombre*) the studio changed the detective's name to Harper and made that the title of the film.

TV shows and movies today often portray police as having all the information in the world at their fingertips, so some readers might wonder at Detective Judd's failure to spot the murder of Francine Hawes as part of a pattern. I ran the question past a recently retired police chief who said that even today, in a case such as hers, most detectives wouldn't ordinarily look for similar cases when the husband was right there as the prime suspect. Furthermore, he said, if the crimes involved different weapons and methods and occurred in different states, the odds of a computer-search hit would be remote.

Olema Marsh's first name is a corruption of a Miwok Indian name meaning "little coyote." It is also the name of a settlement and an adjacent swamp in western Marin County, north of San Francisco. When Gordon is driving to Bodega Bay at the beginning of the book, the route as described takes him through Olema (where Sir Francis Drake Boulevard turns north toward Point Reyes Station) and past Olema Marsh, the wetland, on his way to meet Olema Marsh, the individual, for lunch. Bonus points to readers who picked up on that.

The W.C. Fields Carl La Fong routine is, of course, on YouTube and is well worth a look.

Finally, a word about Detective Judd's stunt with the Corvette and the $20 bill. My late cousin Bill Wallace, who served three decades in the Orange County Sheriff's Department, used to pull that one, and it was such a part of his persona that it was mentioned in his obituary in the *Orange County Register*. And like Lindsay Judd, Cousin Bill always maintained that no one ever caught the bill.

Acknowledgements

Thanks and appreciation are due to several people who helped with this book. The list would include the editor, Debby Rober; Deborah Karas, who realizes my cover ideas; my wife Linda, who edits and comments as the work is in progress; and Terry Medina, who is, as always, helpful with information on police matters. The idea for Duncan Bennett's assassination came to me in a drive-through car wash at a local gas station, but I doubt the owner would appreciate the publicity.

About the Author

MICHAEL WALLACE is a native and lifelong resident of California. He has been the editor of a daily newspaper, a public relations consultant, and president of a Rotary Club. He lives in the Monterey Bay area.

www.ingramcontent.com/pod-product-compliance
Lightning Source LLC
Chambersburg PA
CBHW061954170626
46813CB00006B/2636